CALL OF

THE

NIGHT

PARROT

A novel by

JANELLE VICTOR

A catalogue record for this book is available from the National Library of Australia.

ISBN 978-0-9756328-0-2 (ebook)
ISBN 978-0-9756328-1-9 (paperback)

For my Mum who has always believed in me,
and my Dad who would have been totally confused
about the whole concept and power of an influencer.

"Given that cultural property is one of the principal mechanisms by which we create, maintain, and describe identity, it is unsurprising that parties to international and intranational armed conflicts recognise the strategic value of cultural property. To threaten the cultural property of the opponent is to threaten its identity and it is this poignant link between cultural property and cultural identity that so often imperils the former in the service of the latter."

The Hague Convention 1954

Chapter One

DEAD BIRDIE

EVEN IN DEATH SHE APPEARED CELESTIAL. Her slender frame was cloaked in a striking crimson kimono that draped delicately in the sparkling water. It gave the impression of a luminous halo. Honestly, only she could pull that off. They were all thinking it.

The reaction of the guests although disturbing was predictable. The elegant women clutched designer bags to their chests as if to ward off death itself. The men straightened their ties and smartly signalled for drivers.

Those left behind seemed entranced, the whole scene surreal. Her body gently suspended, her eyes open to the night sky. The siren's song that had once charmed many was silenced, though perhaps now was even more menacing. For she was taking with her a secret – the possible key to recovering hundreds of cultural treasures from the Second World War.

Sonja moaned in irritation, 'Cancel the Ikebana Collection.' This death was to be such an inconvenience for her and thousands of other women. The kimono cape now weighing down the lifeless woman was the signature garment for an upcoming fashion collection.

'Even for you Sonja that is out of line. I actually think Solange might be dead.' Her assistant spoke back to her like a despondent teenager embarrassed by the behaviour of a parent. She stared in disbelief at the older woman.

Sonja held up her hand, indicating the conversation was over. Strumming her chin with long bejewelled fingers she considered the old adage that there was no such thing as bad publicity.

Orpheus was first to react which was most unusual as he was the least likely out of the crowd to perform any heroics. Aware of the fortune he had spent getting his hair styled for the event and mindful his clothes were on loan from an Italian designer with a name so difficult to pronounce that he dedicated the afternoon to practicing the articulation; jumping into a chlorinated swimming pool at night was not his first preference. Pressured to perform, he dived into the freezing water splashing it in a wide arc and surfaced almost immediately shouting profanities about how cold the water was before diving again to scoop up the floating body of his colleague Solange. In a panic he fumbled while trying to secure a hold on her, grabbing at the voluminous fabric of the cape and eventually deciding the best method would be a headlock as he attempted to re-surface. The unexpected weight of his clothing and tightly laced shoes made treading water clumsy, alarmed he considered letting go of Solange as he didn't think his lungs would hold out for much longer.

Eventually Orpheus edged his way to the steps as the fabric of the cape began enveloping him. Coughing and gasping for air, the attention was now all on him. Shivering and more than a little repulsed, he stared at the lifeless slumped body, the skin on her face already starting to take on a grey tinge revealing a sinister bruise on her cheek. He flinched at the long black hair that had wrapped itself around his forearm and slapped it away like the poisoned tentacle of a bluebottle. Once detached from his catch he unceremoniously pushed the body away and scrambled backwards clearly terrified at what had just occurred. However, in the fog of shock his thoughts turned to his smart watch and phone as he contemplated that if they weren't the latest waterproof models their only chance of recovery was a bag of dry white rice.

When replaying the video footage, the authorities remarked how it was a miracle that Orpheus did not become the next fatality. He had taken in so much water after his theatrical rescue that he then spent the next twenty minutes comically dry retching into the manicured hedges. This wasn't the only thing the state-of-the-art monitoring system picked up; it had also captured Sonja's callous comment. They had all heard it in disbelief, over and over on the replay.

The whole retrieval actually took less than thirty seconds – despite the dramatic embellishments that Orpheus would later flourish the rescue attempt with. It seemed half the crowd had now disappeared, and the other half were filming him as he coughed and vomited. He noticed the aloof and demanding French woman Bernadette on her phone barking orders in her native tongue, something about airports while staring right at him.

'Is everyone just pissing off or has as anyone called for help?' he hissed. 'For God's sake she is dead. What is wrong with you people?' The response was inaudible, people were just staring at him. He had expected to be crowded by well-wishers, congratulated for his bravery, and patted on the back. He had also anticipated that someone qualified in first aid would push him aside to attempt resuscitation, but the scene was very different. Solange was still lying across the pool steps, the underwater lights creating an eerie silhouette around her. No one would go near the body, like covering up a dirty little secret everyone was more focussed on their own well-being. They had all come to the embassy with the intention to be seen, to get their photo in the social pages and to hopefully get invited to future events with the red-carpet guest list of diplomats and socialites.

Something like that just doesn't happen at a place like this. And that is exactly what the Ambassador was saying to his security detail. Lockdown had already commenced at the Embassy.

Chapter Two

SHEPHERDING

THREE YEARS EARLIER, Bernadette stood in her penthouse apartment watching for her guests to arrive. Often the most successful people do more listening than talking. This was certainly Bernadette's style. She could feel a change in the air, and it was time to set some traps.

The nervous energy in the small group was obvious as they gathered at the entrance. At the briefing prior to their arrival, Janine had barked at the photographer and lighting assistant to be on their best behaviour. She knew their reputation for being a little flamboyant and sassy. Today she did not need any more attitude, the hairdresser and makeup artist were already delivering that in spades.

Like a secret whispered between friends Janine had been thrilled she had been selected to conduct the interview, a handshake and nod from a family friend ensured she got the scoop. Despite the staged pretence of the interview complete with scripted responses she wasn't perturbed. It seemed the more elusive and influential the subject, the more controlling of their image they were – especially the older women she noted. The success of this interview would be a highlight of her career… other than getting an exclusive on the other First Lady of France.

Deciding what to wear had kept Janine distracted in the days leading up to the interview and in the end, she decided it would be best to keep it simple; black waxed tight pants and a silk blouse - the uniform of most French women. The finishing touch and so very chic were the highest patent leather stilettos in her wardrobe. She had fussed over her hair and nails for almost an hour. The desired result looked like she had made no effort at all.

Reminiscent of the trepidation of heading to see the school principal, Janine shot a look at the troop, prompting them to stub out their cigarettes on the sidewalk. She mustered them and gave a final warning before pressing the button on the intercom. Even this, a series of brass domes set into a scrolled wrought iron frame with ink-black numbers beside them was a statement of Parisian elegance that entranced her. Even the buzzer for goodness sake. She couldn't wait to see the apartment.

A decade earlier Madame Bernadette Bodelle had commissioned France's best architects and artisans to create a penthouse apartment in the 7th arrondissement. To be exact it was actually the two top floor apartments remodelled into one. It was a place of solace. The entire top floor was hers like a spire for a sentry to keep watch over her beloved Paris. This location was selected not only for the stunning view of her neighbour, the Eiffel Tower and her evening sparkling show, but for Bernadette more importantly, the locality for her life's passion. The Musée d'Orsay and Musée Rodin were amongst her favourites, where the cultural icon herself was warmly greeted and just simply slipped in the side door like family. She always shook her head in awe at how the tourists seemed to obey the barricades in place, forcing them to snake along slowly toward the main entrance in all weather conditions for hours on end. The spell was already cast on them before they had even entered.

The location of the penthouse was also selected for the position on the Rive Gauche, the left bank of the river Seine - a scenic enchantment and home to many foreign diplomatic embassies plus several delightful boutique hotels. Simply perfect for entertaining visitors or arranging renowned pastry chefs to create the delights she would serve to guests at her many soirées. A French hostess just doesn't make her own desserts.

Without any of them knowing, Bernadette had been observing the group from the moment they arrived near the building. The cameras were discreetly built into the facade. All passers-by were filmed during their daily activities, whether it be simply chatting on the phone or craning their necks in an effort to photograph the outside of her postcard worthy apartment. She watched the theatrics of the group and could see their leader Janine Roche, the journalist with whom she had granted the interview. She was scolding the others like a primary school teacher and her charades clearly indicated she was directing their behaviour while all the time preening her hair to keep it looking wind-swept.

Bernadette simply pressed the release button from inside her apartment and the front door clicked open. She always enjoyed the look on people's faces when she did that as they were always leaning in towards the intercom, nervously expecting to speak. The group entered cautiously. She watched them from the next set of cameras. Their behaviour changed and they all seemed to walk a little differently as if they were aware they were being scrutinised and observed.

Marvelling at the interior of the elevator as they entered, it was elegant yet unusually eccentric. Distracted by their own reflections and the detailed features of the lift, they panicked momentarily as they started to ascend. They hadn't selected a floor, but they didn't need to, as Bernadette had programmed the elevator to take them to the highest of the eight floors. When the lift slowed it chimed ever so elegantly and they felt they may have been transported through time. The door opened at its own pace, there was no rushing to be done here. It seemed to signal the mood, take your time, breathe it all in, you have arrived. They stepped out and immediately stopped to marvel at what lay before them and to take in the fragrance of vanilla, lime, and pear.

The first thing that struck Janine was the polished parquetry flooring and she looked down at her choice of footwear. Those heels would make this floor look like a hailstorm had hit it. Then her eyes met another pair of shiny stilettos, bright cherry red and clearly worth more than the car she dreamed she would one day own. Trying to take it all in she just seemed to stare at Bernadette while the tentacles of apprehension started to wrap around her. The others formed a neat line and shuffled in behind Janine as if for protection.

Bernadette had a thirty second rule when she met people, and before they even spoke, she had classed each by how she would deal with them to achieve her desired outcome. In a way she had become a mirror to everyone else's vanity, and she was able to work any meeting to ensure she achieved her aims. Bernadette held out her hand and greeted each of them personally in a most elegant way. They felt like they were meeting royalty. Well, they were. The sovereign of French culture and design – the Madame Bernadette Bodelle. This woman had ensured the protection and longevity of true French heritage and style, her reputation preceded her.

Despite her own dominating footwear statement, she glanced at their shoes and that one look was the instruction to remove them. Without a word Janine conveyed the same message to her team and they awkwardly began to fumble about. Now a stiletto heel shorter, Janine felt even more intimidated, exactly as Bernadette intended. The hairdresser and make-up artist were both feeling this was a sweet gig. No effort required, this woman had style and she was sorted. Nothing further for them to do but marvel at this house and this woman. Hopefully she would supply food and drinks.

Bernadette kept them gathered in their neat line and spoke to them. 'Welcome to my home it is indeed a pleasure to host you today. I am honoured you would like to feature me for this article and now please join me for a tour and then we will have refreshments in the salon.' Such an official greeting. Like children on a school tour, they moved about in a herd, as Bernadette effortlessly led them through the apartment, gliding in her heels. They really didn't know where to look as there was so much to take in. The fine furnishings, the colours, the art, and of course that view!

In the salon, a prominent chair caught their eyes. It was an ornately carved antique Louis XV armchair upholstered in duck egg blue, clearly for the lady of the house. The others were to sit on the plump feather filled cream sofas. She had worked her magic again; she would have the upper hand and have control over this interview. The makeup artist had to stop herself from curtsying when she approached Bernadette and pretended to apply pressed powder. The hairdresser didn't dare move from her seat but gave an approving nod to Bernadette and a discreet thumbs up, whispering across the room. 'We're cool... all good!' Of course, as predicted and to their delight, the canapes and hors d'oeuvres were tastefully laid out on an adjoining table.

Janine sat at the edge of her seat and spoke in a confident voice – she had been rehearsing. 'Once again Madame Bodelle, thank you for your time and generosity in granting us this interview. It really is an honour.'

Bernadette was a chameleon, however not in the least bit malleable. She was the "finder of secrets". Elusive, enigmatic, and tantalisingly mysterious. She wasn't one for selfless publicity, the fact she had allowed this interview at all was extraordinary. Poor child, thought Bernadette, but she didn't ease up, and she didn't ever let her guard down. There was always too much at stake in a situation like this. There was an awful lot of information about herself she did not want revealed and a savvy little journalist like this was just the type of person who would have researched and continue to research all she could about her. It was always possible that Bernadette's secret would be revealed, blindsiding her publicly. This was not going to happen. Not ever – there was just too much to lose.

'I just wanted to confirm you agree to me recording the interview using a small device.' Janine leaned forward and placed the digital voice recorder on the coffee table.

Bernadette wanted to recoil, she hated those things and always felt it was a trap. But she smiled and just waved her hand in a nonchalant way.

Janine switched the device on. 'Thank you again Madame Bodelle for your time. Before I go on, I also wanted to clarify that the interview is to be part of a feature article on women of France, those living legends who have dedicated their professional lives to their country.' Janine's eyes looked pleading; it seemed as if she were receiving the keys to a precious vault.

She continued cautiously with a brief disclaimer, 'You also understand the article will be released on the open media market through our agency? So… it may appear in other magazines or online.'

'Yes, indeed that is what I understand this interview to be. I must say I am truly honoured you are here.'

Music to her ears. Janine took a sip of water gulping it a little awkwardly, cleared her throat and continued. 'Madame Bodelle thank you again for granting us this interview. It is an honour to be invited into your beautiful home. Our readers will be enchanted by the decor and your amazing selection of paintings, sculptures, and those incredible wall sized tapestries. Not to mention the view.'

'Janine thank you for your compliments. I will take you on a proper tour of the house later. There are so many beautiful stories about the artworks I would love to share with you.' Bernadette waved her arm like an orchestra conductor and the group couldn't help but pay attention and look around in awe at their surroundings. Bernadette then nodded a silent encouragement for Janine to continue.

'Madame Bodelle, in our interview today I was hoping to focus on the historical buildings you have personally ensured will continue to be part of our heritage. There are many historical buildings in France that more than likely would not be standing today if it were not for you.' She paused for effect, albeit a little too rehearsed. 'How is it you have such power and influence, enough to persuade the government to restore and refurbish these… as you describe them "beautiful orphans"?'

'I can tell you that each of those buildings had a story to tell, they had been abandoned and they just needed assistance, love, and attention. They needed someone to help get them dressed and functioning again. It is inspiring to see the work of many hundreds of talented craftsmen and women have dedicated their passion to ensure these buildings will be here for many generations to come.' She laughed. 'Ahh Janine. I usually get my way. I am very stubborn. I know I have a reputation, so I think people just say it is easier to do as I ask.' The last statement intended as part instruction and part insider joke made them all laugh although a little uncomfortably on cue.

'Yes, I can see how passionate you are and why this has become so important to you.'

'If we don't protect the objects of our heritage and we don't appreciate them… what hope have we got as a society? They are our culture; they tell the story of our ancestors and of our country. They hold such importance in our lives.'

'It has been said the government had cut the budget to the care of heritage buildings and monuments in recent time and yet you were able to get them to re-consider. You must have a powerful ear listening to you there.'

'Yes, there were times when it was a struggle to get people to understand the priorities of budgets being allocated to these buildings. Then when they see each project completed, I see that look in their eye and I know they are changing. The government is listening. I gradually chipped away at them over the years and now I have a healthy budget and a team of staff overseeing numerous projects across the entire country.'

'There are so many dilapidated châteaux dotted across France that have been deserted and left to nature to reclaim them. Is there any chance you will have any influence on preserving some of these sleeping beauties?'

'These projects will never stop. Perhaps age will catch up with me, but I have ensured the legacy will continue through with the solid team I have built up around me. The refurbishment and repairs of these châteaux have certainly been brought to my attention. I have created several websites and Facebook pages to include some of our upcoming projects. Many people from across the globe are even volunteering their time to assist. This is of vital importance the message can be spread this widely with the power of social media.'

'Yes, social media, while it is often frowned upon for all the misuse and malice, certainly can have its benefits. We will include the details of the sites for our reader's benefit. Hopefully that will encourage some new supporters for you.'

'Thank you, Janine it is very kind, and certainly appreciated.'

'Madame Bodelle, it has often been said if you attend an art exhibition launch, the gallery can double the expected revenue. Or double the future salary of the gallery manager… or both!'

She laughed at the intended compliment. 'You flatter me, Janine. I know art. It is my life and I certainly know a good exhibition. As you would be aware, more than half of the time I have been involved in the actual curation and planning for the event. I could tell you the life story of every artist in the exhibition down to the names of their grandchildren. I could tell you the story of their lovers, muse, or the location and why they chose it. I breathe art.'

Paul the photographer had already snapped enough photos that easily ensured he had the one he would use. But there was something about this woman, there was a fire in her he wanted to capture on film. He was intrigued and kept moving about to use different angles and light. He was adept with his manoeuvres, and it wasn't distracting to either of the women. He was definitely in the moment and was totally ignoring the food which was not like him at all!

'So, can you tell me how it is you have become so interested in art? Do you have a favourite work of art?'

'Ahh an individual favourite work of art… now that is a rather difficult task. Perhaps let me answer in this way. If I was to define a moment in my younger life that had a profound effect on my interest in art, it would be the instant I saw an unusual display of huge marble sculptures of saints and religious icons. They towered over me and I was perplexed, as their hands and heads had been removed during the crusades. These vanquished idols caused me to question so many things in life and to understand the true value of art even more.'

Janine glazed over. This wasn't the answer she was expecting, and Bernadette elaborated.

'How is it that a religion which decrees we should "love one another" would dictate the smashing of heads and limbs off statues? Knocking the noses off and carving crosses into the foreheads of deities, heroes, and emperors? I could not reckon with this notion. It was the first time I had experienced such cultural vandalism and it delivered powerful messages. These acts of vandalism robbed us of so much art, history, and culture. The power art can have on our lives and our belief system is immeasurable and the power of those that set out to destroy this way of life so calculated.'

After delivering this manifesto, Bernadette reached out to the silver and mirror topped table beside her and opened a small box decorated in mother of pearl, patterned with highlights of turquoise triangles that rose up like water droplets from the surface. She lifted out her silver and glass vaping pen that contained a purple liquid. Gently lifting the slender device to her lips, she pressed on the small button, and they heard the distinct sound of the device engage and the vapour fed through to the mouthpiece. She inhaled and gently blew the mist down and away from the others. Immediately they could smell a delicious mixture of fresh mint and juniper berry, they were entranced. This woman rocked; she was so in control. Their fingers were itching to get their cigarettes out of their pockets, but they already knew it wasn't an option.

Janine was bewildered. This was not part of the script. Everyone knew Bernadette's favourite piece of art was the Winged Victory of Samothrace. The goddess standing on the prow of a ship overlooking the Sanctuary of the Great Gods on the island of Samothrace. That is what she was supposed to have answered.

Only yesterday in preparation for the interview she had been standing in front of the statue at the Louvre, propped on the Daru staircase marvelling at one of the most celebrated sculptures in the world. Gazing at this masterpiece in marble as many others did even before the birth of Christ. Janine researched all the details of how in 1939, anticipating the outbreak of the Second World War, the great statue was carefully lowered down the stairs on wooden ramps by her dedicated saviours, then sent to the Loire Valley for safe keeping from bombing raids, looting or theft by invading armies. Janine had studied the photographs of the event carefully to show her knowledge and impress Bernadette.

Bernadette's rant continued. 'From that moment, I knew the power of art and the consequences of when it is destroyed. It was a personal mission and I needed to know everything I could learn in my lifetime.' She put the vape pen to her lips and inhaled strongly again, breathing the vapour out as she spoke.

'I also knew the importance of safeguarding our precious history and the significance of the stories that need to be preserved so they can be handed down to future generations. I realised art is many things to different people. Some will see a carved marble statue and see a representation of a person, either real or imaginary. Others will see the enemy of their religion or belief system. Some will see graffiti on a shop front roller door and see vandalism, others will see it is a Banksy and an ingenious message from the artist. Art is a mystery for the initiated. Art is my life.' For the second time she used that sentiment.

This colossal statement was not taken lightly by any of the team as they were all too aware of the sacrifices Bernadette had made in her life to ensure art was her priority. She had decided to dedicate her life to art and therefore did not even enter into any relationship that would have hemmed her in or taken her away from her path. She had no children, no pets and now no parents or living relatives. Art really was her life.

Janine could not stop herself from stealing glances at the house during the speech. This place was magnificent and was truly the grandest house she had ever been in. She discreetly moved her toes through the plush carpet beneath her feet. She had never felt anything so luxurious in her life before. She wondered just how much money this woman was worth.

Sensing the distraction, Bernadette noted it was time to share her house with this young impatient group, and she stood.

She didn't need to ask twice as she offered a tour of the house. 'But first, I don't think I have completely answered one of your earlier questions. My favourite piece of art? It would certainly have to be the Winged Victory of Samothrace standing in all her glory, dwarfing all that gaze upon her.'

Janine smiled as she picked up her recording device acknowledging they were back on track and gravitated towards this inspiring woman to continue the interview. Bernadette looked back at the others and gave them a friendly nod of encouragement. They let out a collective sigh and greedily descended upon the offered refreshments.

As they walked off into the next room, Bernadette took the device out of Janine's hand and flicked it off. It was time to talk off the record and ensure Janine really understood her mission.

In coming weeks, the article went viral. Every design magazine, art newsletter and blogger in the country was using it. And then it went global... and into the hands of just the person Bernadette had planned it for all along.

Chapter Three

STARTING SOMETHING

TO SOME THE SMELL OF FRESHLY GROUND COFFEE was the elixir of life and to others green, jasmine or peppermint tea was their tonic. They all marvelled at how the new food and beverage attendant already knew of their preferences. Her service was exceptional, she had clearly done her homework. Exactly the calibre of employee Luxuriance Resort and Spa proudly promoted in their glossy advertising. Her jet-black hair in a neat ponytail swayed gently as she moved about the room, it was mesmerising. Her name tag was proudly shining out the name Sandi, her uniform immaculate and her smile ever so sweet. However, none of the hotel executive committee were able to pinpoint her, after all there were hundreds of staff on the payroll.

On the first Tuesday of every month Sonja Montgomery gathered her cherished influencers at a luxury destination. It provided inspiration for them to achieve even greater results for her. It was her way of giving back – no expense spared. But then, there was no charge. What luxury hotel hosting Australia's top social media influencers would be mad enough to even consider charging for the publicity they were about to receive? They were a treasured commodity and contra was their unique currency.

This was exactly the rhetoric Henrik Karlsson, the resort General Manager was preaching at the morning executive briefing. This was their second year of operations, and they were in the process of compiling their entry for the annual

Hotels Association Awards. They were entering in the Best Deluxe Accommodation category and Henrik wanted this award so very badly. His annual bonus depended on it.

Palm Beach is known as Australia's secret short-break destination for the beautiful people, with celebrity spotting a well-practiced pastime. However, in the last year competition was firming up with new resorts seeming to open across Australia every other month. He feared the glitter and excitement might just be luring away his shining star guests and their luminary status. Sitting out on its tapered peninsula, Sydney's sea-side retreat location "Palmy" is encased by the glittering waters of Pittwater, Broken Bay and the Pacific Ocean, an oasis to escape the busyness of life. The true "names" arrived by seaplane, departing from the historic WWII Catalina Base in the harbourside eastern suburb of Rose Bay, a community established by old European money generations earlier. This would make the perfect first impression for his next seriously impressionable guests. He had no doubt.

The atmosphere in the management meeting was formal and intense as usual, but today there was a sense of anticipation as most of the executive committee already knew all of the VIP guests on the list intimately. In fact, it could be said they knew more about them, than they did their own offspring. Everything about them: from the names of pampered pets to their favourite recipes, designers, makeup, scent, destinations, travel packing tips, and all the dreamy products they regularly pimped. It was no secret that most of the resort staff would freely exchange the precious hours of their lives liking, commenting, and adding to cart for their beloved bloggers. A few taps on a digital device and the promise of that lifestyle could be theirs, albeit for a brief moment until the buyer's remorse set in or the thrill of the purchase faded. They already knew them very well, but Henrik insisted on conducting the briefing, it was a procedure, and he was a stickler for procedure.

The public relations team had created a dossier on each of the famous influencers. It included a profile photo, their specialist areas of influence, and most definitely their pampering preferences. There was also a second list that was particularly long and read like the ten plagues of Egypt: a catalogue of allergies, known dislikes and a directory of no-goes. That list was designed to strike fear to the heart of those that did not heed the warning. Henrik felt this was comparable to a life-or-death situation. They really were the new world celebrities, the ambassadors of brands, and the voices that would influence, groom, and shape the purchasing decisions of hundreds of thousands.

The maintenance team had been busy as well. The hotel had to be Instagram worthy. Everything had been cleaned and painted. Every lightbulb in the public areas and the suites had been changed to the recommended wattage for the best quality photographic images. The exposure they would receive from a visit like this would be worth more than a glossy front page of any top selling magazine. Hopefully it would not only increase revenue but give Henrik the heavy glass statue he had already planned space for in the display cabinet.

'These people are in the earnest business of frivolous things. They wield great power and influence. Which is perhaps why they are referred to as influencers.' There was something about his Swedish sense of humour that seemed to go straight over everyone's head. He laughed at his own joke, and that in turn brought its own chuckles from the team. He was always doing this.

'On this occasion, it is a very different requirement to impressing a hotel reviewer.' Henrik explained while he adjusted one of his polished cufflinks. They featured navy blue Ralph Lauren polo mallets, something he was sure would not go unnoticed by the agency manager Sonja as it was identical to her company logo. A nice touch he thought.

'Yes, we always aim to impress beyond their expectations, but this will provide a very different kind of review. They are not only rating us by service or cleanliness… they are rating us by our wow factor. Moments of serendipity.' He paused for effect. He was always doing that as well.

'What is so unique about what we offer they will want to share with their readers? We need to provide them with ah-ha moments, intangible experiences they will write about and include in their online posts.' He was speaking to the initiated. They all knew how it worked, half of them had their own blogs, with followers even… albeit only close friends and relatives. But one day, they would tell themselves, one day they would crack it.

The data projector beamed onto the glossy white wall. The face of the formidable Sonja Montgomery stared back at them, and for a moment the team looked to him confused. This wasn't one of their beloved bloggers. Her face was frightful, frozen with botulinum and stuffed with fillers.

'This is Ms Sonja Montgomery, director at The Stables Agency. She has contracted the influencers and manages their rights. She has been described as a practitioner of creative brilliance.' They nodded pensively, raising eyebrows signalling concern as they didn't really understand what the job description of a practitioner of creative brilliance would look like. She however, looked precious and forbidding, there was no doubt this would be one tough customer.

In the photo, Sonja was wearing the same black leather dress she was often photographed in, it had become her trademark. It wasn't age appropriate and did look a little stretched across the bust, the leather shining in the creases. She did not smile at the camera, perhaps because she couldn't. Her blond highlights confirmed there was nothing at all natural about this woman. Her lips resembled two firm lolly bananas covered in a coral lip gloss. The team shuffled uncomfortably in their seats – an instinctive response.

Henrik continued. 'Ms Montgomery will be very demanding, and we are to respect this is her style. She should not need to ask twice. She has extremely high expectations of us during her time at the resort. I am prepared to authorise up to seven thousand dollars of complimentary charges for her stay this weekend. Please alert me when we hit five.' The Public Relations Manager didn't even blink, she knew the currency exchange for that type of publicity, and this was on par with the FX market.

The next photo that appeared was a petite woman with a neck like an elegant bird, her frail collar bones were visible and there was something about her that was so elusive and intriguing. It was the photocopied from her online profile. Her eyes were hidden by large dark aviator sunglasses, and she was dressed in her statement tight black cigarette pants, stripe top and white jacket. Ironically for someone in her industry her fashion choices tended on the minimalist side. Her dark sleek hair hung past her shoulders and there seemed to be a slight audible sigh from everyone in the room as they stared at her image. She was a designer and stylist that everyone loved, so talented, ostensibly shy, and enviably French. The font underneath the photo contained her name, area of speciality and profile name.

Solange Lanquetin – Visual Artist, Designer, and Interior Stylist Influencer

Profile name – French Polish

'This is the first time Madame Lanquetin has visited the resort. I encourage you to look through her social media pages to review the images she puts on her feed. We want to be featured many times in the coming days, so it is essential that if she asks for anything, we comply.' For a Swede, Henrik's French was actually very good and the way he automatically referred to her as Madame made her seem so exotic. Any member of the executive team would have gone out on a limb personally for her, she had already cast a spell on them all.

It was timely that Sandi had passed the General Manager a glass of chilled water at that moment as he looked a little flushed like a schoolboy at a dance. He took a deep sip, cleared his throat, and clicked to the next image.

Ivy Castell stared out of her photo with her large dark almond eyes. They all followed her blog enviably and wished they could travel to all the amazing destinations she dreamily described each week. Some of the places they had never heard of until Ivy had shown them the way. She seemed to find locations that beckoned to your soul and yet catered to real needs with fantastic restaurants and bars, dancing, and live entertainment. They all had a set of Ivy's travel capsule packing cubes; how did they survive without them? In her blog this morning she had mentioned she was coming to Luxuriance Resort and Spa or "Luxe" as she had started to refer to the property and was expecting great things. This team were ready to make those great things happen, they lived for this, and she was their exotic travel guru. Even her influencer name worked for this resort.

Ivy Castell – Travel and Indulgence Influencer

Profile - Luxe Life

Lucy, one of the new mums on the team and Assistant Manager of Housekeeping clapped her hands subconsciously when the photo of Orpheus Butler appeared. She could not control her excitement. He was the stay-at-home dad hero, the "dad-preneur" of the internet, she was forever forwarding his posts to her husband: ways to help get children into a routine as only a dad could do, suggestions for fifteen-minute recipe ideas, and everyone's favourite were all the gadgets he came up with. So many time saving devices - no wonder they all loved him. Even the guys had a grin on their faces as he was so witty. Some of the photos he posted on his feed were absolutely hilarious, many of them had re-enacted the photos with their own children to the delight of family and friends. The video he put up using his voice while moving his son's mouth went viral was gold. Lost in the moment, the team all started mimicking the scene to each other, some reached for their phones to show how their version turned out.

Henrik who was married to his job and only saw children from a safe distance when they were in the care of nannies at the resort hadn't seen the clip and looked at them like they were insane. He had no idea what he was in for.

Orpheus Butler - Dad Lifestyle Blogger

Profile name – Butler Dad

Another sigh, it was Amanda and her glorious envy-inducing long copper locks. They all knew she was celebrating her 45th birthday next week. It had been all over social media, how could they not know? She had included some mention of it in every Facebook post, Tweet, Instagram photo and especially in her blog for the last month. Amanda rarely looked directly into the camera; she had a certain look she was known for. Like a famous model pout, but this was a look where she seemed to look just away from the camera. It doesn't sound like much, but it really worked for her and if she could copyright it she would have. It made her appear a little more intriguing and titillating. Everyone wanted absolutely everything Amanda ever recommended.

Thank goodness that Afterpay - the "buy now/pay later line" of credit was now a thing. So many of her followers must have been in heaven. This was the ultimate in addictive lay-by. She would post her daily update at six o'clock every morning and the most stylish women in Australia would receive an alert to check online. They knew better than to wait until later in the day. A few taps of the screen, payment details already pre-saved for faster handling, and orders would start to be processed. Couriers across Australia would rub their hands together and so would her bank manager. Amanda covered everything from lifestyle stories on topics such as yoga and meditation to food and wine. How she ever kept her figure just doing yoga and meditation was perhaps one of the biggest questions she got asked.

Amanda Starr – Lifestyle, Fashion, Food and Wine

Profile name – Starr Style

Yes, there was other business to discuss at the meeting, but Henrik knew he had lost their attention. It was time to set them free. On the orders to go forth and make magic happen, the executive team were a hum of excitement as they left the room making secret promises to remain true to their professional status and not break rank. Except Lucy, she was getting a selfie with Orpheus no matter the penalty.

The room was quickly brought back to order by the efficient Sandi, she seemed to work in silence and slip around the table without any disruption. Henrik noted she epitomised everything that represented the resort, delivering unobtrusive service of the highest standard. She would definitely be front and centre around this demanding group. He looked up to thank her, but she had already packed up the beverage trolley and left the room. He smiled as this gave him such confidence in the success of the coming days.

Three floors below, the invasion was already commencing in the lobby. Amanda's clothes arrived before she did. Reminiscent of a film star's trip on a luxury cruise liner, the staff had never seen so many clothes arrive for one single guest. Two courier vans pulled up at the porter's desk, where rack upon rack of designer zip up garment bags were rolled through the lobby. Usually, deliveries would be discreetly whisked around the side entrance and scurried into the cavernous passages around the hotel. This was certainly an exception and additional staff were on hand to assist, wheeling them in a long snake through the lobby and towards Amanda's suite. This was quite a spectacle, and the PR team had their photographer on hand snapping away.

A few hours later, Henrik straightened his already straight necktie and brushed away non-existent fluff from his suit. He looked around before he checked his breath in his cupped hand. But it only smelt of fresh peppermint, as it always did. He was ready. These were the moments he lived for. However, an odd feeling was weighing heavily upon him - along with a distinct vision of herding cats.

Chapter Four

CLASH OF EGOS

SHE COULD HEAR THE SHORT CLIPPING SOUND of his hard heels on the marble floor. Every sound echoed in this place. While not exactly a written procedure, it was a directive that all the women were to wear stiletto heels and walk only on the balls of their feet when they were at work. It was to ensure the ambiance and reduce noise pollution. Like a rite of passage, the administrator would make his entrance known. He was everywhere and enjoyed the theatrics of his authority.

While it was his role to oversee the operations of the Embassy, he secretly took great pleasure in remotely observing the work of the secretaries from his computer as he scrutinised their documents while they typed out speeches and event itineraries. They would be informed he was watching their screens by the frozen cursor as he studied the document. His name would appear on their monitor as it halted, Administrator Arnaud reviewing. It was his way of remotely asserting himself. A way of reminding them he was "big brother", and it annoyed the staff to distraction.

If a secretary was in the Ambassador's office simply following her instructions and picking up documents from the in tray, he was there in an instant. Leaning on the door frame in a predatory way with his legs crossed and a finger waving at them like they were caught shop lifting. He would interrogate them, inspect the documents with a flourish and allow them to pass. Nothing got past him.

He was pedantic and forever fussing over the order in which they could park their cars in the staff parking area. He obviously preferred French brands and insisted they were given priority parking spaces, so they could be seen from the street. Some of the staff were forbidden to even drive their beaten-up cars onto the Embassy grounds – well technically it was French soil, his soil and he could do with it what he pleased.

And it wasn't just the cars he was obsessive about. He insisted all the women wear dresses and skirts, for trousers were only for the men. Whenever he would address them about their fashion choices, he would look them up and down blatantly commenting, usually very inappropriately about the fit or the style. Afterwards they would physically shake off his presence like a wet dog after a bath. Clearly an abuse of his diplomatic immunity, Mathieu was not concerned in the least, he planned to continue to exploit the hell out of this privilege.

The only place off limits to him was the ladies' toilets. When he realised the listening devices in there could not compete with the hand dryers, he had the dryers removed and reverted to paper towel. The one thing he could not stop was the sound of the flushing. And he knew gossip was afoot when several of the staff were not at their stations, and he could hear continuous flushing. This infuriated him, and he was forever trying to find a way around it.

Despite having waited over twelve months for this moment, Bernadette looked blasé as she waited until the clipping sound had stopped, indicating the self-imposed warden of the Embassy was by her side.

'Madame Bodelle, I trust the flight was to your satisfaction.' Mathieu felt her prickly manner under his skin already.

She just stared at him and gave a sharp short nod, observing the typical antics of short-man syndrome. Mathieu was used to being around this striking woman and while he did admire her, he also felt more than a little uneasy in her presence. She wasn't exactly the friendliest person, he always felt judged by her. As soon as Bernadette arrived, he sensed an inadequacy creep into his usual flawless demeanour.

He always found it amusing how they all remembered her name, yet she kept her response to a simple address of, "Your Excellency, Monsieur and Madame". She only every referred to him as "Administrator" and he was sure this was not done through any type of respect for his position. He felt belittled by her and yet there was nothing he could really say about it, she had him by the balls on this one. He would find a way to get back at her and he would relish the moment.

Her world revolved around beautiful things, entitled people, protocol and deception. It had always been this way. Thirty-two years in the civil service and she seemed to take precedence over those with medals and sashes. She was treated like a precious living artefact that represented France itself.

How they all adored her he thought with a jealousy that rose up inside of him. He also knew his place. Rumour had it that with a single phone call she had the power to switch out their precious vintage armoire for something a little punchy like a fuchsia velvet settee or if she was really throwing her weight – a gilded-bronze Pinocchio sculpture by Hubert Le Gall. He definitely did not want to be known as the administrator who was forced to commission a giant statue of a cartoon character. She made decisions like this for a lot of reasons, some vindictive, but often because she needed a hero piece that would stand out in the upcoming feature of Parisian Élan for Elle

Magazine. He was not going to be the next victim; he would play it safely and not poke the bear.

It really annoyed him how she had been called all the way from France for something as minor as the refurbishment of the Ambassador's Canberra residence. Honestly it wasn't such a big deal. He was more than aware of the bureaucracy involved in renovating a building of historical significance. However, he did laugh at the fact Australia itself was hardly old enough to have any building that would qualify. The Embassy and residence were originally designed by a French architect and the reception rooms, porcelains, paintings, and tapestries had all been selected for a purpose. They were well known and documented. He did not want this woman poking her nose around in his business. He wanted to keep a cap on his budget and keep things simple. He had this, and he just wished she would leave him to it. If it wasn't for the ridiculous request for a swimming pool by the Ambassador, he was sure he could have had more control over the project.

Despite his many protests to his contact at Le Mobilier National (the source he believed was exactly where he needed to go) confirmed that she pulled rank. They are officially the designated French government department tasked with furnishing official buildings and if only he could go directly to them, he could have had his pick of artwork and then some. He really could not ever see what the fuss was about over the tapestries, they all seemed to just gather dust and were impossible to clean. He felt like he would have an asthma attack when he was in the same room as them. Which now, knowing Madame Bodelle's love of the damn things would mean they would be everywhere.

He couldn't delay any longer. He had to approach the snippy bitch and get this over and done with. Awkward pleasantries were exchanged, and he continued. 'You must be tired from your travels Madame? They say you are a time traveller when you fly to Australia. And in Canberra you are in another time zone all together.' He laughed self-consciously at his own joke and realised his attempt at humour was lost on her.

She stared at him like he was stupid.

He tried to redeem himself. 'I mean after all you are now a day ahead of yourself.'

He watched her for a reaction. Perhaps a response? He registered this woman was emotionally inaccessible and was clearly defining the limits of conduct. Bernadette simply put her vape pen to her mouth and nonchalantly took a decent drag. Because she could. Right there in front of him. An act of domination as predatory as if she were marking her territory by spraying on a lamp post.

Now he was flustered, and way out of his depth. He knew when to stop. Humiliated in front of the staff. He nodded to the maid dressed immaculately in a knee length black dress uniform. The crisp white cotton scalloped half apron cinched tightly at her waist and her jet-black hair was pinned up in a chignon and a lace headpiece. She didn't smile either.

'Sandrine will show you to your room. Our meeting will take place in the drawing room at two o'clock.' With that he faced her and sharply bowed his head forward as he backed out of the room. Kicking himself all the way as he was displaying such spineless behaviour.

Sandrine ever so slightly curtsied to Bernadette, then turned on her heel to guide the auspicious guest to her accommodation. Bernadette followed taking note and making a mental list of items that needed to be pointed out to the handyman and the maids. It was a term she phrased "comfortably blind". The way the cleaners would not notice the slight scuff mark that showed in the afternoon sun or how the wallpaper was ever so slightly about to lift on the corner edge. Just not good enough.

Mathieu watched her through the surveillance monitors, studying these observations. It was no wonder they were all on tenterhooks, she was a witch. He promptly reminded himself again that the whole purpose of her visit was to oversee the renovation of the Ambassador's residence he was the project manager for. He had so many grand plans and he knew he had to play the game her way to get everything he wanted. It was like swallowing medicine that left a bitter aftertaste, he just had to suck it up. She had such high standards they all felt like their evil stepmother was visiting to do a white gloved room inspection.

Even the Ambassador was feeling a little tense, more because he desperately wanted a swimming pool as part of the renovation. He knew she had approved of one recently for New Zealand, so he was feeling fairly confident.

Once in her room, Bernadette sent a short text message. The reply was instant.

'I have her details and I know she is the one. Her background is a perfect match and I believe she is as guilty as hell.'

Chapter Five

BRANDED

LATER HE WOULD WRITE IN HIS PERSONAL DIARY how the day was more exhausting than when he welcomed members of the G20 Summit and their accompanying riot squad. Henrik was looking forward to seeing the back end of this day. He had never experienced so many outrageous demands, even the most unflappable staff were taking flight.

Amanda, sending her two designer dogs without warning in the advance party, perhaps topped the list. What were they again Bernese Mountain Dogs or some type of - oodle? Actually, to him they looked more like small men in bear suits. He googled Amanda's name... an instant result. They were always mistaken for Portuguese Water Dogs which frustrated Amanda no end, but she was able to use the publicity. Yes, that's right. Of course, they look just like the dogs the Obama's have. Of course. He mused with a wry smile. While the pampered pooches of the first family were called Sunny and Bo, Amanda opportunely called hers Sonny and Cher leaching anything she could from their celebrity status. They smelled like green apples and wore fabric bandannas with co-ordinating patterns, the Instagram photos had already been viewed over five thousand times and royalties on the bandannas were ringing in. Thankfully they also came with Pipa, Amanda's multi skilled assistant and dog wrangler.

The fanfare of VIP arrivals by numerous seaplanes guaranteed abundant photo opportunities and top spot on their social media posts. The influencers cheerfully checked into their deluxe suites, snapping away, and unboxing the luxury gifts that had been placed around the room as if it was Christmas morning.

Watching a live unboxing online, the PR team had to explain to Henrik why it seemed so unpolished and clunky. 'It is supposed to look authentic and realistic as if you were opening the box yourself.' The younger of the two explained in a slightly patronising tone as if talking to a five-year-old. She further enlightened him how it was actually a YouTube phenomenon, weirdly hypnotic and would attract thousands of viewers. By the time they finished their social media lesson the hotel boutique had sold out of the gifted monogrammed bathrobes and slippers. The back orders were now getting out of control.

Imagine if they had a tripod and the vision wasn't so shaky? Imagine how many more they could have sold? He shook his head in disbelief that this group who seemed to rule the internet and dominate online shopping didn't think to use a tripod. It just couldn't sink in for a man so used to perfection.

After unboxing, taking numerous selfies and tasting the little treats laid out on the side table (then bringing them up again), Amanda changed into what would be the second of twelve outfits that would all be posted at various stages throughout the day. This was her business chic look for her workwear inspiration blog and she glanced at the finished product as she left her suite very pleased with the result.

At the agreed hour, the influencers all gathered in the beautifully appointed multi-media conference room at the resort. Coffees were being inhaled as Sonja swiftly tapped two buttons on her remote. The lights slowly dimmed, and the data projector shot an image of a quote onto the screen. "They live in a counterfeit world created by their ability to generate fake realities." The article was by a dreaded freelance journalist who was always sniffing at their heels. The editorial had been picked up by the top newsagencies. It addressed concern over the corrupt and narcissistic nature of influencer marketing if left unregulated. They had all seen it. They knew every word by heart.

In the serenity of the luxurious room Sonja's sudden shouting aided by the spectacle of her fiercely tattooed eyebrows made them all jump. 'Can you begin to imagine how rubbish like this written by other journalists makes my blood boil?' She was preaching to the initiated. Orpheus liked that Sonja referred to him as a journalist, he felt it gave his writing vocation a boost of credibility.

'You have the power to make a brand and the power to break it. Select your words and images with caution as they will… and grant my word… they will come back and bite you on the arse.'

The next image was the same quote that had been crossed out, and with the next click the screen went blank. Sonja stood in front of the projector light for more dramatic impact but all it did was make her look macabre. Even though they had all seen her behave like this before it got their attention. Orpheus sat forward in his plush caramel leather chair and thought about how much she really did terrify him. Very old school disciplinarian, if she had a ruler, he was sure she would have slapped it on the table, but she just stood there staring out at them using the silence as her weapon of choice.

'Yes. So true.' He replied in a voice that was a little higher pitched than he would have liked. He was very nervous, he felt like he was about to sit an exam he hadn't studied for, which was quite apt considering he wasn't prepared at all for the meeting. His cheeks were inflamed, and he knew a rash would soon appear on his throat. He had always blushed easily from high emotion; it was a firm indicator of his reaction.

Amanda and Ivy knew better than to comment. Ivy wanted to laugh at Orpheus and his body language, he had a fox-faced menacing way about him, he always looked startled like he was caught in the hen house. He was a very strange man and had weird hands, maybe it was the oversized cuffed shirt he had on today, but his hands seemed to be small and a very odd colour. She thought he must dye his own hair and the colour had stained his hands. Also, what was with the awkward way he had replied? What an idiot she thought he was. He was a study to her.

Solange was standing to the side of the room; she tilted her head to let her hair fall forward to shield her as she thought she might break out into a grin. These theatrics were just impossible to take seriously. She didn't ever really conform to Sonja's strict dominating rules and didn't like to feel hemmed in at the conference table. The others always thought it was odd that Sonja didn't make her sit down. There was definitely something at play here. Like a teacher's pet. Why was Solange so special? Other than the fact she brought in the majority of new clients and with that the most income of all of them. They had to acknowledge that did get you a special seat or in this case non-seat at the table.

'Fake realities.' Sonja continued. 'Tell me Ivy, anything fake about your travels? Any digital manipulations of your photos I need to know about? And Amanda, God help us if anyone thinks you have been up to anything.' She scanned

Amanda looking for evidence of guilt, but there was none… just a well-practiced sideways glance.

Sonja just went on and on about fake realities for the next thirty minutes and then with the snap of a finger she smiled. 'Topic change! Collaborations.' That had their attention. 'We have been approached by a top mattress company who want you all onboard for a new campaign. It's called mattress magic.' She shushed the protest moans. 'I'm sure you will all find a special way to push that line. I know you will. And remember your contracts all include four collaborations a year. This, ladies and gentlemen is a "non-negotiable".' She held her hands up in the air as she charaded inverted commas into the air. It was laughable, and yet no one was.

Sample glossy booklets with poor graphics and woeful images were slapped down in front of them – the marketing team had a lot to answer for. They were calling it a bed-in-a-box, a mattress made from hard foam. It sounded cheap and unappealing. And they were having none of it. The response from the room was immediate, sassy, and uncooperative.

Infuriated, Sonja just walked out. Her doctor had told her to keep the stress levels down and avoid conflict. As she marched toward the ladies' room, she signalled the hotel staff hovering outside to set up refreshments. In the marbled powder room, she opened her handbag, drained her Ventolin, and threw back more medication, today was really going to send her over the edge. These people are so ungrateful. She put her hand over her heart. Should I call my doctor? Sweet Jesus I think I'm having a heart attack… Dramatic images of her on a stretcher, including the spectacle of a helicopter medivac crossed her mind despite easy access to a standard ambulance. She felt the rapid pulse on her neck as she reconsidered her options, … or should I just head to the bar? Her better judgment sent her to her room where she kicked off her shoes and lay on the bed splayed out under the air-conditioning waiting for the fury of another hot flush to pass.

Sandi and another waiter couldn't help but notice the tension of the blond woman who almost knocked them down as she waved a dismissive hand ordering them into the conference room. They discreetly entered unsure of what to expect and were both shocked when they heard the shouting and swearing. Quickly becoming invisible, they placed the refreshment offerings onto the table at the back of the room. They worked in silent unison and a little slower than they perhaps needed to as the conversation was so entertaining, they couldn't resist listening in.

'Aren't mattress shops just a front for money laundering?' They all laughed at Orpheus' joke. He was delighted with himself for getting the response, it made him seem so cool. However, he did believe mattress shops were like those weird Christmas shops, there was never anyone in them so there had to be another reason for them being there. He had heard the money laundering theory from a friend and thought it genuinely had merit.

'Christ how long do we have to put up with her shit? I signed a contract to her for work she would supply me with. I didn't sign my life away to her. She doesn't own me. This will be crap for my profile, I mean how often do people really buy mattresses anyway?' Amanda picked up the brochure and then threw it back down to the table. 'And to tell the truth lately she seems to hinder my chance of getting new work. Promoting mattresses? What next? No wonder she ran out of the room.'

When Amanda spoke like this it really did shock the others in the group, she had worked at her online image, and it didn't give a hint she could speak out like that. When the filter was off... it was off. Her followers would have believed the jobs just landed in her lap and she would not have had a boss as such. They thought she just woke up every morning looking glamorous and the hardest thing she had to do each day was decide what new accessories she would combine with her outfit. And that is exactly how she wanted it and worked hard to keep the dream pulsing through the internet.

'If I hear the word collaborate come out of her mouth one more time, I will slam it shut for her. If that dictator thinks I am going to pair up on some ridiculous concept for us to hustle mattresses she has another thing... what next? Soon she will be suggesting I start selling funeral insurance with one of you.' Ivy re-directed her rant. 'Orpheus, I know you have your pet insurance contract, but it is all yours baby. I don't want to be lumped with crap like that. Mattresses... She is scraping the bottom of the barrel.' They were left in absolutely no doubt as to how Ivy felt about the proposal.

The comment hit a nerve with Orpheus. 'Ivy, I really must insist you stop picking on me, you are very intimidating.' He sounded like he was ten. 'And while I'm at it I want you to stop calling me Mr. Click Bait all the time. You think you are funny but to be honest the humour is a little beneath... the "queen of suitcases"!' His sass continued. 'You know I will show as the top chart holder this afternoon. Have you seen my stats? They love me.' Orpheus should have known better than to pick a fight with Ivy and he really should have checked his stats. There was something about her that absolutely terrified him, and he knew she would find a way to get back at him.

'Orpheus, what planet are you on? I was just giving you a stir about your pet insurance contract plus Mr. Click Bait is pretty appropriate. The way you trick people into clicking into your story is a little beneath our style.'

Before Ivy could finish, he interrupted her. 'Like I said. I have the formula. It works, and I am making a fortune out of it. Simple and clever.'

'I don't mind "queen of suitcases" - it has quite a ring to it.' Ivy hated it, but she knew with someone like Orpheus the more she told him she hated it the more he would use it. A little bit of reverse psychology she learned on the school bus many years ago. She had experienced it many times before, bullies that wanted to get a certain reaction from her. She would refuse to give them that emotion, even though deep inside she felt it, she wouldn't show it had any effect on her. Predictably, they would drop her as she was no longer a challenge, and they couldn't control her. He was clearly seeking fear, humiliation, and power, but she wasn't going to give it to him.

It was time for Solange to talk and when she did, they all went quiet and turned around to her. She uncrossed her arms that were gently caressing her like a safety vest. It was time to enter the fold. She attempted to casually flop down into the chair that was close to the front of the boardroom table. She didn't want confrontation; she was all about unity and keeping it simple. She wasn't concerned about the anger in their words and thought of it more akin to sibling rivalry, something she had wished for desperately in her life.

'I agree the brochures are dull, but the product is surprisingly miraculous. I have one.' And there it was. That power. The reason people like this are influencers. She had their ears.

'When it arrived at my house, I was a little dubious. It wasn't the traditional style of mattress we are all used to, it came rolled up in a long cardboard box. Just so unconventional. And then within minutes I had it set up on the bed.'

They were all listening. Even the wait staff were glued to her words.

'That night I had the best sleep. It was like a secret someone had let me in on.'

Her distraction had worked a treat, she was a catalyst for calm. They were intrigued.

She had the conch.

But what is the brand? I need this in my life. The tall male waiter wished he could ask out loud as he was finishing his shift soon and could buy one on the way home or was it an add to cart purchase? He extended tea and coffee service to everyone at the boardroom table, so he could catch a glimpse of the brochures.

Later the same night he searched back through Solange's blogposts and there it was. Her online explanation described the need for the mattress in a box. Her dilemma - the main bedroom in her new townhouse was on the third floor and her traditional king-sized ensemble simply wouldn't fit around the spiral staircase. Later in the week the hotel attendant slept like a baby, when previously buying a mattress was the last thing on his mind. The power of influencer marketing!

Despite Sonja and her brazen outbursts, they knew she was their money ticket, so they waited dutifully until she returned. Amanda used the time to take a few photos of herself in a high-backed upholstered chair placed conveniently next to the window. The fabric was a unique shade and texture balanced well against the colour of the ocean in the background.

She preened herself instinctively taking the pose and then with her camera on a tripod and her phone blue toothed to take the shot, she expertly took half a dozen photos.

She had moved on from her earlier outburst and was transfixed to her device selecting an image to upload to the appropriate app that guided her through various options to enhance colour and brightness. But there was something else that needed adjusting, those damn lines that had started to appear on her throat. She had once seen an Oprah interview with an actress who admitted she would always wear a turtleneck sweater as her neck was starting to resemble another part of her anatomy. With expert adjustment they were digitally removed as well. Now to find the perfect tagline, hashtags, and the final click to publish. Instantly the likes and comments started to roll in, but she didn't need to worry, her admin support team would sort all of that out for her and no one would be any the wiser.

She looked up from her phone to see Ivy with her hand on her hip staring daggers at Orpheus, he really was an annoying shit and he just looked weird, extra weird today. What was with that? His skin seemed to look a bit yellow from where she was sitting.

Seemingly a million miles away from the aggression in the room, Solange was taken off to her safe place - looking through images of fabric swatches and fan decks of paint colours. She tried to let the childish bullish behaviours of the others wash over her hoping they wouldn't turn on her, they were hunters after all. A pastel colour palate had been selected for the next client and she was contemplating using this for her upcoming series of oil paintings featuring rare or extinct Australian flora and fauna. There was something that resonated with her having lived in Australia long enough to appreciate the island nation and how close to extinction many unique creatures and plants were. The colours and light in Australia had fascinated her, she knew through this collection she would make a statement about how precious our time is on earth, and how there was always someone or something trying to take it away from you.

An email distracted her from her escapist design world, it was the tickets for her upcoming buying trip to France. Two of her favourite antique markets were on in the same week and they were only a short drive to a dozen of her favourite brocantes. She had also set up private meetings with her favoured suppliers of rustic French homewares and had diarised a couple of estate art auctions. This is what she lived for – this was the really fun part of business.

Ivy wasn't going to just photograph the champagne; she took the bold step and cracked it open. The others all gravitated towards her. They vowed safety in numbers and promised this would make for a creative afternoon. Just as Ivy had filled her glass the door opened and as they expected Sonja had returned. Unsure of how she would react they kept composed and took their seats with champagne in hand, the fine bubbles simply mesmerising them into a trance. Sonja didn't miss a beat and walked straight over to the ice bucket and poured herself a giant glass so quickly it spilled down over her hand.

Without a breath, she exclaimed, 'Let's continue, shall we? You have all had time to calm down over the new contract and I know you will embrace it once I tell you about the financials behind it.' Now they were all ears. Perhaps next time she would just start with the monetary side of things and discuss product second. She mentally tucked that strategy away.

With marker in hand Sonja turned her back to them and drew a large circle on the whiteboard. They all knew what was coming next - mind mapping. She would not commence a project without one, so they all resigned to the fact this was non-negotiable and just got on with it. In the centre she wrote the name of the mattress brand Sleepy Box, which was greeted with a groan, then she drew a series of lines radiating out from the circle. She turned to the others waving her pen in the air like she was winding up a machine, this was the indication it was time for ideas to start presenting themselves. Comfort, convenience, value – Sonja wrote them down and then turned to face her influencers and yawned theatrically.

Amanda called it. 'Ultimate unboxing!' At first, they all laughed and then agreed it hadn't been done before. It would certainly get everyone talking. Sonja liked it a lot.

The champagne helped ideas to flow. Orpheus had ideas of promoting the importance of a good night's sleep as a new dad. He could really do with a new mattress, upon reflection the one he had was from his university days. If that mattress could talk.

Ivy was in, she could appreciate the convenience when she moved to a new house the next time. She was never able to stay in one place longer than six months at a time. She didn't want to put down her roots and wanted to remain a free spirit. Sometimes she would even pack up her life and place it into a storage facility. However now with the sharing economy she was thinking a little outside the square and renting her place out on various home share sites while she travelled the world. The thought of a mattress that could just fold up, tied with a piece of string, and transported easily in the back of a car did sound very appealing to her.

Solange was literally already in and was now planning how she could work it in with the latest range of botanical patterned sheets she had collaborated with for a large homeware retailer. This couldn't be more perfect. She could start as soon as the contract was signed.

Orpheus was still left with an uneasy feeling that mattress companies were a front for something else, he really was convinced there was a correlation with money laundering, and he had to admit his reputation wasn't exactly squeaky clean. He grinned, for him being an influencer was a little like being in the money laundering business… a hell of a lot of dirty deals.

Chapter Six

INFLUENCED

UNLIKE THE OTHERS WHO WERE COLLECTED in heavily branded limousines, Solange walked home from the seaplane base, as she lived only blocks away in the tree-lined streets of Rose Bay. A fan of packing lightly, she fit everything into a neat overnighter and ironically, her rather oversized tote. She didn't go anywhere without that handbag. There is something about a woman and the attachment she has to her handbags over the years. Solange was sentimental about a lot of things.

Rose Bay had always been a special place in her heart, so close to the buzz of the city yet far enough away that she could easily escape and walk along the esplanade, stopping to lean on the low sun-bleached rendered wall, staring out at the water and watching the boats drifting past. It really did feel like her part of the world.

One of her guilty pleasures was taking the walk from Rose Bay to Watson's Bay along the Hermitage Foreshore Track and stopping along the way to photograph anything really that took her fancy. She always lamented how so many people were busy tapping at fit-bits or checking emails on their watches while jogging or powerwalking past, missing out on the beauty surrounded them. They really did need to wake up and smell … well, the eucalypts, wattyl and grevillea. While these native plants often didn't have the strong perfume of a florist's cut flower, there was an undeniable crisp, fresh scent. Solange would often stop and close her eyes, slowly drawing in a breath of pure air and instantly feeling the stress drain from her body. She mused that there were so many room fresheners with this scent, but nothing compared to the real thing. Being close to nature even if it was in the suburbs was healing for her.

For some time, she had been working on a concept for her next art series; researching and contemplating her options. What medium would she work in? Would it be textiles, water colours, or oils? So many options, but it wasn't the media that was holding her back, it was something a lot deeper. She really wanted to find a way to use her art as a positive influence for others, to do something special with her talent. She wanted to get people talking.

On her short walk back from the seaplane, she felt an awakening and she opened her heart to the universe. She wasn't sure if it was the fatigue from the outrageous last few days at the resort or a little motion sickness from the plane. And then it happened. Halfway home, Solange sat down in the shade at one of the council benches. It was one that had a particularly stunning view of the harbour, and someone had taped a printed notice on the garbage bin next to it, reminding people to stay on the foreshore track and not to walk on the headland's native grasses. The "urban greens" were voicing their concern over certain flora and fauna losing their habitat if it continued. The passionate writer had continued to add commentary on our children's inheritance, and our obligation to protect it right now for the future.

It occurred to Solange that while the simple act of straying from a council footpath was so innocent, and if only a few people did it the damage would be minimal. If it were a few hundred the results would be bad but perhaps recoverable, however, if it was thousands the chance of total destruction was possible. Such a simple concept when magnified struck a chord with her. Never having identified as an environmentalist or a "greenie" she did give the cause some thought. She really did have to wonder how many creatures and how much plant life the growth of civilisation had really affected.

Mobile phone always close at hand, Solange did a search for extinct Australian flora and fauna. There it was. The inspiration she had been looking for. So many stories that needed to be told.

She clicked on a few more results and it didn't take long for the algorithms to lock in, even her news apps were cleverly picking up her new interest in Australia's lost vegetation and wildlife. Stories on exotic looking creatures and delicate plant life – most with names equally as intriguing. High on the extinct list was the mysterious Thylacinus cynocephalus – the Tasmanian tiger, filmed with its menacing jaw opened wide for a listless yawn while pacing its cage. A formidable predator, yet a rather shy nocturnal creature hunted by man and wild dogs and decimated by the erosion of its habitat and its chosen harsh climate.

Solange watched the clip with intrigue. A lone creature pacing the cage as if predicting its demise, last filmed in captivity in 1933. Grainy and crude, the footage was captivating, and without exception, all who viewed it asked whether there was any chance the animal still existed somewhere today. Many theorised the creature wised up and adjusted to modern man, a step ahead and smartly kept its distance from any sign of civilisation to ensure survival. What if that were true? she pondered. Reading further there were articles reporting sightings over the years. Perhaps the "tigers" were just too clever now, and had become invisible to modern man?

One photo caught her eye. It was a Thylacine with a chicken in its mouth. Quite an achievement for a farmer to get a photograph like this in the 1920's Solange thought. As she read on, it was clear she was not the only one to question the authenticity of the photograph. Tightly cropped and beautifully curated, it seemed the photo was staged using a creature taken from a taxidermist with a fresh plump white chicken wedged in its jaws, the wings splayed open for visual effect. Reading on she noted the source believed the photo was edited to remove the wire chicken fencing, creating an image of the creature in the wild with its spoils. Solange raised her eyebrows. Early example of fake news, she grimaced. But how much power would a photograph like this have had during its time? she thought. The propaganda would have had farmers enraged and on a witch hunt. Previous government bounties would have also spurred on the quest. Interesting yet regrettable, the government introduced official protection of the species only a couple of months before the last known creature died. Too little too late, she relented.

Her thirst for knowledge wouldn't be satisfied on a small screen. Desperate to continue her research, she hurried home and threw her bags on the floor. Kicking off her shoes, she flopped back into the plump sofa while flipping open the laptop. The hunt for information continued presenting the weird and wonderful, like the yowie, yeti, big foot and who ever knows what other fabled creature sightings filled the online stories of country newspapers. There were also plenty of stories about unconfirmed sightings of Thylacines over the years. People had taken photos, but the angles were wrong, the image too grainy or the film not processing correctly. It would be easy to dismiss them as time wasters or publicity seekers. Wealthy businessmen in search of publicity were always more than happy to reach into their pockets and create rewards in an effort to lead to confirmed sightings. But then it gets tricky when you can't trap an endangered species, so confirmations were rare. The game was clearly on, any crackpot with a camera and access to a dark room, or in these days a digital art app could go nuts. The lengths some people would go to.

Familiarising herself with this world of long-lost treasures, a new list of terms entered her vocabulary: status, vulnerable, extinct, rare, fragile category, critically endangered. Others were quickly added.

She read on. If you can't find the creature and there is enough demand or wealthy investors, the next option was "de-extinction". She had never heard of the term. Surely this was the stuff of mad scientists and movies. Apparently, this was a real thing. There was even a TED Talk about it. She knew of Dolly the sheep - but that was years ago. Then there was talk of cloning cows, and whatever really did happen with all of that? The thought of specimens holed up in formalin filled jars reminded her of the preserved Vietnamese Chairman Ho Chi Minh lying in state, just waiting for a scientist to sample and replicate him.

She had to admit she was overreacting and acknowledged the amount of genetically modified food she willingly consumed. She enjoyed seedless watermelons and other fruit made conveniently was available all year round. Guilty even of devouring oven roasted chickens from the supermarket, bred on a force-fed diet of genetically modified grains, growing to a perfect size in a matter of weeks. But like others she would put it to the back of her mind for now.

Maybe, just maybe out there somewhere in the wilderness was a pack of Tasmanian Tigers, happily going about their business and staying the hell out of the way of anything on two legs with a camera. She pondered. What if there had been other creatures put onto the extinction list only to be re-found generations later? How clever they would be to avoid contact with mankind. Even in this modern day of tracking devices, drones, and camouflaged cameras she wondered if it was possible. She asked the question to the all-knowing entity online. And sure enough, a few keystrokes later it answered without hesitation. Yes, this was true and the examples it gave of the "previously believed to be extinct" was magical.

The barking owl, alpine she-oak skink, dinosaur ant and Triboniophorus aff. graeffei, the giant neon pink slug cleverly disguising itself amongst the red eucalyptus leaves of an extinct volcano. They all sounded like creatures out of Alice in Wonderland. The underground orchid, how could there be such a thing? She continued her research. The small purple-pea, an endangered bright lilac plant was once profusely growing in Southeast Australia and now it is unenviably added to "the list". The colour caught her imagination, the image delighted her heart. They all sounded mythical and enchanted, fantastical even.

One story she found was so simple. Diuris bracteata, a species of orchid from New South Wales had been presumed extinct after last being identified in 1888. Then 116 years later there it was, simply re-discovered exactly where it should be, hidden within its own natural habitat, the grassy woodland and forest near Gosford. The more she clicked on each story, the more the system worked and fed her more stories. She was so entranced and had succumbed to losing track of time. Pouring a glass of wine, she threw out any plans she had for the afternoon.

There were other classifications critically endangered, endangered and vulnerable. Those that had been placed in God's "to be processed" tray. Samples of their tiny fragile faded bodies propped up by pins on fading fabric display boards were already exhibited in museums. They hadn't been marked off the list just yet, the clock was ticking until the magic fifty years of unconfirmed sightings had passed and they would be given the unenviable title of extinct. Yet, there was still a chance of the species continuing to exist, hiding in small numbers in obscure places, or even in plain sight!

The list of Lazarus like stories was intriguing and she settled in now totally resigning herself to an afternoon of amateur nature research, when one creature caught her eye and her imagination. One click, and her search engine went into overdrive. This was truly something.

An intriguing name, almost exotic, conjuring up images of long, majestic plumage with glossy rainbow colours, this bird looked nothing more splendid than a portly budgie, the type filling pet shops and ending up in a cage on the veranda at a grandparent's house. All this fuss? She was bewildered. Described in 2012 by the Smithsonian Institution as the planet's most elusive bird, the Australian Night Parrot was previously believed extinct for around one hundred and thirty years.

The description was simple, a bright yellow and green bird with black and yellow bars, spots, and streaks. There was a lot to do about it being ground dwelling, but it still flew, albeit not as high as a normal bird. But here was the thing that really caught her eye. It vanished during the 19th Century. Tales were rife of rare sightings and claims abounded. One sample rotted away to nothing, two live specimens were eaten by cats, and one was found decapitated from a barb wire fence by the side of a desert road. Once again, rewards were offered from rich entrepreneurs, creating media stories of unconfirmed sightings and the whole ornithological world was in a twitter. A gold rush fever of enthusiasm drove the search for this holy grail of birds.

There were plenty of clues, hints and secrets shared about the bird, its habits, speculation over the double ding-diding whistle sound of its call and the locations of sightings. But to no avail. The harder they searched, the more elusive the bird became. There all along hiding in plain sight, living in the spinifex, keeping low to the ground, and only going about its business at night. Despite its best efforts to avoid photographers, researchers were able to capture a couple of photos and a single female.

Solange was already struck by the so-called curse of the Night Parrot. Once you show intrigue you are captured, and you cannot be released from its spell. She wasn't alone. Famous painters, writers, poets, filmmakers were obsessed, specimens were shown at the 1900 Paris World Fair, even the Australian Museum has its own Night Parrot room. This bird had various meanings and representation through indigenous language. It was so much more than just a bird. It had entered her life and she had become obsessed. Thoughts of art, paintings, sketches, sculptures, textiles, and colours flooded through her mind. She was in her space She was creating. And it felt good.

She was now being inundated with options to watch for further information and clicked on the link for Bush Heritage

Australia - Saving the Night Parrot. Solange was hooked and for a couple of minutes was taken away to another place. She felt it was a very special time of discovery as she could see the work and dedication of so many people prepared to make a difference for this bird. The threat of extinction was still very real as they were prone to attack from feral cats and foxes, bush fires, droughts, and poachers. Yes, a black market for exotic creatures was a very real threat.

The video showed the harsh and remote habitat. It was narrated by all types of obsessed naturalists, scientists, and researchers. "It is really a critical time for this species. The Night Parrot could be lost forever if we don't act now", pleaded Rob Murphy the Executive Manager at Bush Heritage Australia. "The responsibility to protect the Night Parrot is the responsibility of everyone, we all need to play a part in protecting this iconic Australian species." She felt her own immediate call to action; this avian enigma had her trapped.

The mysterious bird was known by numerous monikers; Australian Night Parrot, Pezoporus Occidentalis, Spinifex Porcupine Parrot and the native reference of "Pullen Pullen". It was also caught up in a lot of controversy when out of desperation a naturalist and wildlife photographer fabricated a sighting and created a prop of a nest complete with two eggs to photograph. It reminded her of the farmer with the Tasmanian Tiger, history repeating itself. The dishonour of it all. But after all of this and when the world had shunned them, they did it. They found birds in numerous places, cleverly having avoided human contact, and avoiding all of the other predators. If only they could all just maintain a low profile and avoid the threat of demise.

The next part of the article caught her attention. It mentioned the global interest and how this find was so unique and special that not only the location, but the recording of the bird's call had to be kept secret for its own protection. What type of world are we in that we need to put these measures in place? pondered Solange.

It was then she discovered that in the ornithological world the term twitcher referred to a type of birder, which in turn is a type of bird watcher with an obsessive need to see a new species as a ticket or requirement to add to their "life list". There was a whole new world of jargon she felt was best left undisturbed. And there was also a reputation for professional jealousies rivalling anything social media could offer up. Stories of backstabbing (quite literally), scandal, fake photos, bogus sightings to distract others, and numerous other deceitful behaviours. For some reason she imagined Orpheus would make a very good twitcher.

Her creative mind was working in overdrive. She had been consumed by this allegory. What could I do with all of this? Could I help make a difference? What could I create? She had a deep set need to repent, much like Miriam and her need to cleanse the mansion of bad karma. Solange felt this was her chance to save something thought to be lost forever. Her family had done something that could never be forgiven.

That evening she began work on the feature mixed media piece including textiles and watercolours for the Ambassador's residence. She would give the painting to France to absolve the dark secret and sins of her family. An atonement of sorts. It would be her way of making peace with a history that had haunted her. Her rudimentary sketches entailed abstract feathers along with representation of their natural habitat.

Carefully hidden within the art would be the words deception, consequences, death, extinction and sorry. The artists secret message of penance.

Chapter Seven

STARSTRUCK

WHEN SHE LOOKED BACK IT HAD ALL STARTED OUT so innocently. How could she ever have imagined it would end up being so lethal?

A promise. A heartfelt commitment is how it all started. And now she was afraid she would go through with it and finish her off.

She was top of her game and double billed with being known as a nice person, which made it kind of tricky to be the nasty bitch she really was. She had to lock that alter ego up and put her into detention. She always knew there would be a time when she would escape but for now the world was safe.

When she was younger, she had heard an advertisement for an American ice cream company went something like, "Find out what the people want and give them loads of it." She had taken it on as her personal mantra, but little did she know the world could play cruel tricks and that ice cream company went broke a long time ago. Amanda forged on and made a career out of finding the next big thing, the secret to happiness, the intangible feeling could all be purchased by her lending her style and credibility to the product, and in return they would deposit a set fee or a percentage of the sales into her bank account.

While some started out their online careers on a whim hoping one day they might see some money in return, Amanda created a business plan and a strategy. She was in it for the long haul. She went to motivational seminars filled with real estate agents, car sales teams, and any other individual or team that wanted to make money. They would stand on their chairs and shout out motivational slogans along with American evangelical style sales gurus until they were hoarse. High five, swap business cards, cry, laugh and embrace the power of selling. It was addictive, and the influence of the internet was available to those who were clever enough to find a way to harness it. Amanda was clever.

There was no need to re-invent the wheel, the Americans were all over it. She would never forget the moment almost a decade earlier when she saw the effeminate Chris Crocker cry out to the world to "leave Brittney alone!" Fascinated that a man hiding under a sheet probably at his parents' house could find a world-wide audience and go viral as he shouted out his support for a de-flowered music star left her shaking her head at the time. Now she applauded him.

It was the same year reality television started to enter her lounge room and the thought bubble burst. What if?

Amanda was well known for running her business with military precision. Tan on Monday. Nails every Tuesday fortnight. Monday lifestyle blog. Wednesday fashion blog. Friday food blog. Her staff were like Santa's elves hidden away making the magic happen. She was making waves on Twitter, Instagram, Pinterest, Facebook. Her blogs were increasing their hits, the Vlogs went viral and her Facebook live audience consistently responsive and loyal.

'Oh hello… my community. So good to see you all. I'll just wait until a few more of you join. Hi Sharon, yes, I love this blouse, but it is last season and all sold out I'm afraid. Well hello Nikki, nice to see you online today. Thanks for all your support. Just waiting for a few more to come online.' Amanda waved wildly at her screen as she flicked her hair over her shoulder and then paused to read out more comments from her followers, responding in a manner that made them feel like they were receiving inside gossip from the horse's mouth. Floating thumbs up, love hearts and smiling faces flooded the screen.

Tring to keep her tone jovial she shushed to her dogs. 'Keep it down, I'm doing a live.' She had really wanted them to appear, so people could see her designer doggies. More love hearts flooded the screen. 'Sonny and Cher, say hello to everyone.' The screen rotated and then as if on cue, once the performance was over the dogs disappeared. Like a magician it was all smoke and mirrors, they gave the illusion she had the perfect life. The google hits for "oodle dog breeds" skyrocketed every time she would show the dogs through her feeds.

Enough stalling, she could see over three hundred people were now on and watching her. 'Clutch pearls ladies, clutch pearls. There is a new collection I have done in collaboration with one of Australia's top fashion retailers! Want to hear more? I can only give a few hints today as we haven't had the official launch… but …' She leaned into the camera on her computer like she was about to share the secret with it. And equally her audience leaned in to receive.

Unexpectedly the courier arrived at the front door that moment. He could see her through the window of her home office and was waving at her insisting she sign for the package. 'Just leave it at the door.' She whispered and smiled with a thin-lipped gesture, so the audience could register what was going on and then out of camera she frantically waved a dismissive arm to the young guy in his uniform of hi-visibility vest and long scruffy ponytail trailing down his back. But he kept insisting she sign for the package, and he wasn't budging. He must be on commission for the signatures, she cursed under her breath.

Turning the moment into a positive she turned back to the camera. 'Bear with me a moment darlings! More goodies have just arrived, and I am busting to do another un-boxing this afternoon. Stay with me and I will be right back.' Now the dogs were barking as the courier banged on the door again. She could have knocked him to the ground but instead put on her frozen smile and scratched out the quickest signature she ever had. It was just a straight line but none of them cared. He stepped back as she slammed the door, cautious to not get tripped up in the dogs that were now yelping at top pitch. She dropped the package on the table next to her and returned to her audience. Luckily, she had only lost about fifty viewers. The others were hanging around for the gossip. What was the new clothing launch? What was in the box?

She continued the "live" and despite the promises, delivered nothing more than a tantalising tease of what was to come. She couldn't wait to get off air, and immediately phoned to berate the courier company. 'You all know the schedule for the live timings. For God's sake, where was Jerry? He should have told his replacement I do my "lives" during that time. I have a business to run you know.' As she took a breath the receptionist was attempting to explain their version of events when she talked over her. 'Yes, yes but everyone knows me. Tell him to sign the thing himself and leave it on the doorstep. Honestly, I can't keep interrupting my lives for this. Just sort it out.' She hung up abruptly on the receptionist when she asked for her name again and headed to commence an unboxing.

Amanda was in the serious business of frivolous things and opening a box marked "For your eyes only – Amanda Starr" had her titillated. Firstly, she cut open the thick plastic satchel and removed the powder pink box wrapped in a matching satin ribbon. No other notes, messages, or clues to the contents for that matter were visible. Amanda prepared the space on her table and set her phone camera to video in her left hand... and click – record.

'Hi everyone, look at what arrived on my doorstep moments ago. Yes, for those of you watching my live you were all part of the excitement. Lucky for us the courier was determined to make sure we all had an unboxing to look forward to this afternoon.' Reaching out with her perfectly manicured hand to untie the bow there was a little hesitation as she genuinely wasn't aware of the contents of the package. Her unboxings were always as authentic as possible, and after all if it was something crap, the video could simply be deleted, and no one would be the wiser. The bow slid apart without difficulty, like it had been choreographed to do. She continued with her banter about the excitement and unexpected delight at receiving the gift. Then, removing the lid to her surprise it was a new jewellery pouch full of new season earrings in rose gold and tortoiseshell that could all be intermixed to create new looks.

To her surprise, Amanda liked them, and as they were from a local small business, there were points to be scored in promoting fledgling new businesses and throwing her weight behind them. Later that day, Amanda would put the video on her social media and remind her audience the earrings were gifted for editorial consideration, and she was proud to say she highly recommended them and was more than happy to support the retailer.

For Amanda, blogging was a lifestyle agenda. From a blog to a movement – that is what she wanted. Now she had reached the heady heights of an influencer, inundated with restaurant invitations and product samples. It was exciting, fast paced and a constant reminder there was always someone younger, skinnier, or more influential snapping at your heels.

Amanda's schedule was beyond ridiculous as she scrolled through her online diary. A highlighted note caught her eye and made her shudder. She had been putting this task off, it was unpleasant to say the least. "Finalise the arrangements and get her to make a list ready for the good-byes."

Chapter Eight

POISON IVY

IT WAS RUMOURED IN THE INDUSTRY Ivy would stab you in the back as quick as look at you if things weren't going her way. It was also fairly obvious to most that the people saying it were the ones deserving of a good sorting out. These types were always trolling social media celebrities, Ivy didn't give them a minute of her time. Block and report were the automatic response.

One challenge of the dream job travelling the world as a VIP guest is in the art of making it look easy. She had to work hard at maintaining the illusion. Ivy was always aware of the effort required to make everything look so effortless! She was a super organised individual and operated her travel regime with military precision. Very fitting considering life skills gained through certain career choices in the past.

Healing takes time, but it seemed the clock was broken. She decided to own her story. Staying down was a choice. Not her choice. It was time to commit to being in total control of her emotions.

Ivy had a lot of enemies, powerful people that didn't care much for her and her opinion. Her editorial content often made people recoil because she didn't hold back, and she told it like it really was. She was a straight talker and people in this industry weren't used to it.

Gold cards, memberships to executive lounges, presidential suites, views of major landmarks became her mainstay, but she really did grow tired of this. She really, honestly did. There had to be more to her job than this, she laughed out loud at what she had just thought to herself. Upon reflection there actually was something in that. It was time to look at the bigger picture. What did she want out of life? What adventure did she want next?

If you were to google her name, you needed to be prepared. The hits were prolific. If you were searching for a review of most places across the world, Ivy had been there and had rated it, appraised, critiqued, and generally written at length about it. Women planned their weddings around the recommended destinations, men planned golfing escapes from her endorsements, and plenty of legitimate or otherwise, romantic weekends away were strategically arranged on the sterling advice of one Ivy Castell.

But today it was yet another flight to an Asian resort, a new deluxe property opening on Orchard Road in Singapore. She really needed to knuckle down and do her research, but for once she could feel a change coming over her and she really couldn't give two shits. She knew the drill. Welcomed at the airport by smiling staff with her name on a board. Small talk by more nervous smiling staff on the way to the hotel. Speedy check in by exceptionally well-trained staff, refreshing mocktail and handtowel that deceivingly looks like a large mint but when dropped in the water expands to the size of a face washer. The magic was lost on her now, but she always wondered if anyone really did think it was a mint and choked as the towel expanded in their throat. Exceptionally firm handshake by the newly appointed General Manager, an eager Public Relations Manager gently forcing media packs into her hand and then ushered to her room by a porter who looked as if he was told he was escorting the Queen of England to her suite!

As predicted, everything was smooth; flight, airport pick-up, check in, GM, and the terrified porter. The next round of "predictables" was the welcome fruit basket, welcome hand-written note, welcome chocolates and thank God, the welcome champagne. She thanked the porter with the correct currency and cracked open the bottle. She could knock back a few glasses before the welcome drinks in an hour. She felt very welcome indeed. But after all these years she knew the drill and felt a little tainted. She knew there were thousands who would gladly fill her shoes, or the velvet slippers she had just put on – embroidered with the hotel logo of course.

Time to tappity tap. She spoke as if there were someone beside her as she got her laptop out and set it on the beautifully appointed desk. That was quite literally half the problem she acknowledged, there was no one to share these moments with other than her thousands of followers on social media.

She thought it best to start recording her impressions of the property before the champagne took hold. It was moments like this she felt a little like the devious Emperor Commodus judging a gladiator battle. Would it be thumb up or thumb down? She really was in a crappy mood and thought it wasn't fair to take it out on the hotel. She would give them a chance at the welcome drinks as she slugged back the entire glass of champagne with the bottle at the ready to pour the next.

Ivy decided to get the check list out of the way. All the usual suspects were on the inventory. Good lighting – check. She noted the light at the desk was exceptional for working under. The bedside light switch was deceivingly easy to find and included a couple of USB ports. In some resorts she would flick a switch and the bathroom light would go on, or the television, or the balcony light. It would be anyone's guess.

However, this hotel had it sorted, and everything seemed to be exactly where it should be, plus she had the option of voice activation. They had done their homework; she could almost imagine the General Manager breathe a sigh of relief for the high score she would give her room and the amenities in it. The mini bar was a whole next level packed with an assortment of flavoured gins including elderflower and grapefruit made her mouth water. The fruit and dehydrated garnishes were prepared in tiny, packaged containers sitting alongside a variety of artisanal tonics. A tantalising selection of craft beers and lightly flavoured mineral waters was also impressive.

The snacks were a delight as well, she had never seen a rainbow of macarons in a mini bar, they appeared to have been made in-house. She popped open the packaging, breathed in the raspberry scent and without hesitation bit into the small delight. The shell made a delicate crunch and as she reached the meringue, it was the subtle flavour that took her mind away to one of her favourite places in the world, France. She was lost in the moment and in that instant vowed the next flight she would take would be back to her favourite holiday destination, but perhaps staying a little longer and having a lifestyle break. Ivy laughed to herself how a small cookie from a Singapore hotel mini bar was the catalyst for such a decision.

In the finest of moods, Ivy could feel her heart beating a little faster. She felt a spark of joy and she also knew this plan had been lying dormant inside of her, she knew it was inevitable she would do this one day. And now it was time, she felt strangely at peace with herself. It was time to get to know a little more about a sweet young girl named Lourdes. This little girl from a lifetime ago knew a very big secret and buried so many memories. She needed to find her and make peace. It was time.

Ivy subconsciously rubbed at the discrete micro tattoo just above her hairline at the back of her neck, where neat loopy cursive lettering spelled out the words – never ever forget.

Chapter Nine

BUTLER DADDY

THERE WERE THREE THINGS ORPHEUS GENIUNELY LOVED, or perhaps to clarify, he was intrigued by; writing his new novel (the one he hadn't quite got around to actually starting), genealogy and control. As a renowned "Dadpreneur", the main passion one might think is his famous infant son and current lifestyle blogging money-making venture, but even Orpheus could see there was only so long he could milk this cow. There had to be a backup plan.

In the planning phase for his secret manuscript, it had started out as fiction, but he frankly wasn't creative enough for this pursuit, so he re-shaped his space and realised writing non-fiction would better suit his needs. Finding the ever-elusive muse was driving him insane. There just had to be someone of note out there that hadn't been written about. He wanted to break new ground and was already imagining where he would store his awards. He had started a word document for his computer and a note page on his phone with lists of tag lines and hashtags to celebrate his success. But first to find the subject.

To support the research for his writing aspirations, Orpheus took to genealogy as it would provide a roadmap of information once he finalised exactly who his subject would be. He could search back and find out any dark secrets lurking in their past. There had been a spate of advertisements on the television for ancestry related companies now the dreadful Tommy Waterhouse no longer held airtime to ransom educating everyone how to bet on horses. The ancestry businesses were promoting how everyone could be tantalisingly related to Ned Kelly or trace their heritage back to a convict to claim some type of fame.

Why does everyone want to be related to criminals? What was that really all about? He rubbed at the stubble on his chin. It certainly would make for a good book. Do I really need to find someone who could lay claim to a bushranger, or someone shipped off to Australia for stealing chickens? He hesitated. Honestly would people really give a shit and want to read this? Nope, if I'm going to spend my time writing a book, I want to research someone a little sexier than a chook thief. He scrolled through lists of famous actresses, models, and singers, then discounted the thought quickly. They will all be a pain in the arse to try to interview. He wanted a person, preferably female, that he could get close access to, someone worthy of his time and definitely someone good looking.

And so started his cloak and dagger obsession, like a gambling habit kept from your spouse. Orpheus was hooked. He would toggle between screens whenever his wife or his assistant Maddy entered the room and was always deleting history on his computer. He wanted to feel like a detective snooping around picking the eyes out of the evidence. A sleuth reporter, he said to no one but himself. No, actually I prefer detective, that has so much more authority to it.

He pondered the possibility of creating a false identity in an attempt to access private information on his muse. That was easy! He smiled to himself as he recorded the usernames and passwords of his new identities. After forty-five minutes of frustration and a few hundred research dollars already spent it was apparent he needed to define his subject a lot closer before collapsing his bank account any further. An excel spreadsheet quickly ensued with a list of names across the top and a variety of comment boxes including the value he placed on finding something out about their past. He marked off a list of qualities he wanted for the person. They need to be famous and alive which would be a good start. Glamorous is essential, and intriguing - goes without saying is an absolute must. There would be enough bait to ensure his book would be front facing in all good bookstores. He could already picture it.

Orpheus was secretly doing an online writing course and listening to podcasts when he was at the gym. They provided him with many words of wisdom, one really struck a note with him - "write what you know." Yes, he would find someone famous that he knew, and he could use first-hand accounts of their life including his personal interactions with them to fascinate an audience… a big enough audience would pay handsomely to buy his books.

He put this assignment to the side. Next on the list was to task Maddy off with her admin duties when she arrived to start work. So far, he had been able to trust Maddy, she was excellent at producing copy for his blog and her photography skills were fantastic. He had the list of photos he wanted taken with his son and notes about the props required. These days he hardly had to check her work and let her post straight onto his social media. While it saved him time, he always wished she would upload everything faster and he was forever putting the hard word on her. He got the vibe she would do anything for the money. He would keep tapping away at her for that as well.

As soon as she arrived, he put his feet up to watch every episode of Who do you think you are? on catch-up. All in the name of research, improving his investigation skills and a springboard to get this project rolling. Hours later it was hunger that prevented him from pressing the play button for another episode. Walking into the kitchen his mind was awash with new phrases and concepts, fresh discoveries, and money, all the money he would make from this new venture. This was definitely going to show the world he was a serious writer, and they would pay handsomely for the privilege of reading his hard work.

'Maddy!' He shouted with his head in the fridge. 'Can you make me a toastie? I want ham and cheese, but for God's sake don't put any bloody tomato in it. I nearly burnt the roof of my mouth with that piece of lava you gave me last time. Oh, and a milky cup of tea. I'll be in the media room.'

Deep sigh and cursing - every fucking swear word she could under her breath, so the innocent little child sitting in his highchair wasn't poisoned by her. She headed straight to the kitchen and shouted through the door. 'I'm onto it.' Otherwise, he would only have kept shouting to her until he heard a response.

She really wanted to spit on the sandwich, but she was sure he would have a camera hidden in a book spine or something and see her. She wouldn't put it past him. He was a creepy dude, but the hush money - while it made her feel guilty, she certainly enjoyed having it. It was paying off her HECS debt for her studies in architecture. Maddy couldn't wait until she was in a job she was qualified for, and she craved a boss who was actually a decent responsible adult. This guy was a dick.

Feet up on the couch, television downloading the next episode and his alarm set for thirty minutes before his wife was due to arrive home. He was set, if only Maddy would hurry up with the sandwich. He was starving. And the kid could keep it down as well, he thought. Wow the child has a set of lungs on him when he isn't happy. Orpheus smiled to himself. Just like his daddy.

While he waited, Orpheus registered himself on even more websites, anything he could find to do with family research, genealogy, ancestry, he even enrolled for an "Unlock the Past" conference in Sydney next month. He was very careful to use the nom de plume he had created, as his real name was far too conspicuous. He was concerned that his numerous followers might recognised him. He created a few more false names and email addresses, some even under women's names so he could access the variety of programmes several times. A password app on his phone made him feel like a spy, entering all the codenames, passwords, PIN codes and a variety of mother's maiden names and first pet names so he could recall them when needed. He laughed to himself. Gosh if wifey or Maddy found this they would think I was a con man or a transsexual. He laughed at his own joke. The irony would not have been lost on them had they found out.

He quickly glanced at the terms and conditions of signing up to these websites and scoffed at the well outlined requirements and the threats of legal action. How can they trace me, so the worst they can do is cancel my account? That was all the time and energy the legal jargon in the fine print deserved.

His fingers were already twitching and as the coming days unfolded, he could not resist logging in to the various web-based email addresses he had created to see what little gems had appeared. He was disappointed to see the usual spam of welcome emails and junk advertising. He unsubscribed from a few of the sites where emails were flowing through like virtual rivers. This act itself created another email!

There was a joining fee sale ending soon on one of the genealogy tree websites and he didn't waste any time tapping in the details from a travel card he had purchased at his local post office. Untraceable and so clever, he mused to himself. It wouldn't take long until he had memorised the card details and it remained safely tucked away in the false sleeve he had created in the lining of his wallet.

He had created a monster. But he loved it. He had never felt so popular or risqué. Without reading any of the detailed information on ancestry DNA testing Orpheus was beside himself with excitement. Ohhhh…he sighed almost erotically. Imagine what stories I can unlock? Then, a deep chuckle, Oh wow DNA testing. This is going to be frickin awesome. Just like in all the detective movies, all I will need is a strand of hair. He rubbed his hands together naively, not a clue in the world. There was some poor soul out there about to have their life publicly dissected.

Rolling his eyes to the ceiling, he sighed and uttered to only himself. It would be so much better if they were actually dead. He thought about the publicity and the book sales that would induce.

Chapter Ten

MONUMENTS WOMAN

TWO YEARS EARLIER IN PARIS

SHE WAS FEARLESS, A CAMOUFLAGED HUNTER, it was her mission to save the voiceless. The woman herself was a feint, a movement made to deceive an adversary. While some went about their treasure hunt with giant x-ray machines or metal detectors to find treasures hidden behind bricked up walls or down long forgotten wells, Bernadette had other methods. The old-fashioned kind where she talked to people, networked, and got people to divulge information.

When she was younger, Bernadette made a vow like the declarations of a nun who promises herself to God and commits to do everything in her will to uphold all the church represents. Why is it we imagine such conviction is only ever present for religious people? For this passion and commitment also pulses in the veins of those who are entrusted with ensuring the safekeeping of their country's culture and heritage, the signposts of their history and way of life. While some countries sell off their antiquities for cash injections or to fund war machines, France has always known art is part of its identity and must be preserved for future generations. Bernadette's vow was to maintain this identity, she was a believer, and she lived and breathed a world of culture and heritage. Vive la France!

At art school she learned the names of precious works of art and their famous creators verbatim. She had an excellent recall for dates, locations, and muses for each piece. Bernadette breathed this world. She also understood the importance of keeping these precious works protected; safe from damage, decay but most of all safeguarded from theft. Art theft happens in so many ways, brazen snatch and grabs, or cleverly concocted scenarios that involved timing, resources, and bribes. But most of all, her all-consuming task was as an agent for the French Culture and Foreign Ministry. This was two-fold. In the first instance she was an agent for the Art Recovery Group reporting on suspicions of art theft, and secondly, more of a personal mission was to assist with the identification of original owners and surviving heirs unaware of their rightful claims to art stolen by the Nazis during the Second World War. Of all her occupations and pastimes, this one she carried out with the most pride.

Talks by museum curators, procurement officers and directors dominated her early education as a student of art. All explained the tremendous effort that went into researching the provenance of each piece and in certain cases ensuring the art had no evidence of forced sale. Special reference was always made of the Nazi art plunder. Full due diligence was necessary to ensure reasonable steps were taken to comprehensively appraise each piece. Bernadette often wondered if it was merely lip service that obliged them to give these lectures, as surely, they would not genuinely want the lost owners to claim and remove any precious piece of their prized collection, simply to be hung on a wall in a house, placed in a locked vault away from an audience or worse, sold to a foreign museum. It would be like breaking up their family, plus they were always referring to limited budgets and resources. It was as if they were saying quite simply, "We will be the guardians of these works until the owner claims them." Which was becoming more and more unlikely.

She had recently returned from a private viewing in the temperature-controlled, darkened storage facility at the Louvre featuring a small sample of their collection of orphaned looted artworks. All items listed on the inventory with the Musées Nationaux Récupération (National Museums of Recovered Artwork) or the "MNR" with a moniker crudely stamped on the back of each work. However, these were only a few of over eight hundred paintings looted from Jewish families by the Nazis during the Second World War entrusted to the Louvre.

If only these paintings could speak of the many times they had changed hands, of the walls they were snatched from and the quiet, dark places they were hidden in during the war. Then she thought of the fate of their owners, the families who had fled or been deported or worse, and the harsh reality of their demise. For the owner of an item of such beauty it may feel like a curse to be in possession of such a work for fear of what others are prepared to do to take it away.

"That terrible war had deprived the world of considerable art, history and identity", the academics proclaimed. The chronicle of events leading up to one of the biggest occasions of art theft and destruction in history also alluded to one of the greatest subterfuges – the emptying of the Louvre prior to German occupation. It was stinging her memory. For it was the heroic actions of the Director of France's National Museums during the period that prevented the loss of over four thousand items of cultural property. Monsieur Jacques Jaujard prevented Hitler from taking the world's most famous paintings to his planned Fûhrermuseum in Linz and Leaonardo da Vinci's Mona Lisa was to be among his top trophies. Jacques was a step ahead of the French pro-Nazi collaborators who were eager to assist their oppressors. Aware war would likely bring bombing to prominent landmarks such as the Louvre, Jacques had to devise a scheme. He also factored that once Hitler had taken his pick of the collection, the confusion which followed would include destruction, theft, and pillage of anything remaining. His task was simpler in words than actions - to evacuate most paintings, sculptures, and artefacts. Each item would be painstakingly wrapped and packaged during a cleverly arranged three-day closure, thinly disguised as repairs to the Louvre.

The prized Mona Lisa was carefully placed into a custom poplar case lined with luxurious red velvet. The only marking on the box was three red dots along with the code MN in black and L.P.0 in red to signal a Louvre painting. This was the only painting to be given the prestigious three red circles and was transported by ambulance to avoid detection.

Bernadette knew the coding for the crates – yellow for valuable, green for major works of significance and red for world treasures. Two red circles showed the items were very important works. She agreed the Mona Lisa was indeed worthy of her three. This important lady almost needed a passport as she was off on a significant journey of many miles. She was moved a total of six times and with a secrecy that defied belief. This was certainly precious cargo. If only Da Vinci knew the trouble he would cause!

Jaujard was relieved when the BBC broadcast a very special message 'The Mona Lisa is smiling.' This was his code she was safe.

The Winged Victory of Samothrace was one of the final pieces for Jaujard to evacuate from the Louvre. At eight feet tall, over two-thousand years old and weighing almost six tons this was quiet an effort. Bernadette couldn't resist researching the images of the removal of her beloved sculpture on her laptop. Wrapped in cream sheeting and tied with ropes the large sculpture was more to Bernadette than simply a figure of beauty. The marble statue is believed to commemorate a victorious battle, it conveys action, honour, and triumph. To Bernadette the cultural icon represented everything she stood for in life.

Now with a sigh, Bernadette turned her thoughts to the pieces that hadn't made it home. Were they bombed and destroyed? Are they sitting in the vault of a corrupt person? Or worse, are they rotting away behind a bricked in façade where they would never see the light of day? Her search was to continue, and there were two-hundred and fourteen very good reasons why.

After the evacuation of paintings to the South of France during the Second World War, there were many items still unaccounted for by the French authorities. It was now common knowledge that hundreds of works from the Green Circle Collection had been intercepted by a team of Nazis assigned to the Art Theft Division known as the Einsatzstab Reichsleiter Rosenberg, simply abbreviated to ERR. German intelligence passed the details of the last known storage location of the artworks to First Lieutenant Wilhelm Fünten and his specially trained task force who soon found themselves at a deserted grand château in the Languedoc region.

In more recent times, Château du Créapsy had been sold as part of a historic trust restoration project and had come to Bernadette's attention. She was already aware of its significance during the war, however the version of the story she had been recounted told of the occupants fleeing the château days ahead of the advancing German troops. In a rush to secure the artwork, the Nazis packed paintings throughout the night when a kerosene lamp had accidently been shattered, quickly spreading fire through the château. One German soldier lost his life as the fire raged, and others escaped with minor injuries. It was reported all the paintings were destroyed, the fire so intense it caused the roof to collapse severely damaging the château.

As part of her current role, Bernadette insisted on overseeing the renovations albeit remotely and proposed a team to assess the planned works. She was very curious and had thought she may wish to visit the site herself if her schedule allowed. She poured herself a glass of rosé which always reminded her of warm summer evenings and laughter with friends in her younger days as she clicked open the file on the fairy tale château. All the usual bureaucracy, forms, copies of ancient documents and plans, more forms, letters requesting a relaxation of renovation restrictions needed to be attended to.

Good luck with that! she grimaced at the screen as she allocated the obnoxious administration tasks to various team members. It was then she noticed another letter had come in accompanying the original documents. It was from the Maire of Caunes-Minervois, Monsieur Pierre Guichard, who had found an item he believed would be of interest to the historic trust group.

As the first stage of clearing the rubble from the worksite had already been permitted, the builders were under strict instructions that all memorabilia were to be separated from the general debris being thrown into the large industrial sized skip bins and reported to the Maire. He was a man with a sharp eye and a wit to match. He couldn't keep away and had been frequently visiting the site as it had already been agreed several of the outbuildings were to be used for additional administration space for the municipal offices of the hôtel de ville, as the townhall had outgrown its space for document storage. During his last visit the project manager handed him a large box containing an assortment of rusty, derelict items that usually would simply have been thrown out.

Pierre was always recycling or repurposing before it became fashionable. The village featured a collection of memorabilia in a museum to ensure it featured on the tourist map. The display was housed beside a café overlooking a small marble fountain and he fondly thought of it as his second office. The people in the village did not need to make formal appointments to see the Maire, all they had to do was buy him a café au lait… and depending on the time of day a pain au chocolait or any delicious treat on offer. The local doctor had started warning him he had to watch his cholesterol intake. Pierre would simply nod in response like one of those bobbing head dogs on a dashboard and the doctor would laugh through a wheezing cough and walk off as he lit his cigarette! "Do as I say…"

Today on his third coffee and looking through the box of treasures in the dappled shade of the plane trees, he took a little longer when he came to a small, charred metal box with clasps that overlapped and had held the contents safely over all these years. It was the size of a tissue box and in the light, he could make out a name that many decades ago had been thoughtfully and purposefully etched into the surface with a small sharp blade. Pierre moved the box around to catch the best light as he polished the name. It was not French… but German

- Wilhelm Fünten. The box was light, and he could feel the contents shuffle about as he placed it on the table.

He went to open the clasp but there was no chance. It was fused shut after all these years of dereliction and the ravages of fire. He reached into his pocket and pulled out his Swiss army knife, handy for everything from cutting cheese, opening stubborn bottles and now obstinate tin boxes. Careful not to remove his fingers as well, he gently pried the first clasp open and then the second. The force almost made the box fly through the air, he quickly caught his grip and said a prayer of thanks the blade was facing in the other direction. He marvelled at this special moment, no one had laid eyes on these contents for over seventy years.

Like a child with a new meccano set, he carefully placed the contents in a neat row on the table in front of him. The items were simple: a small, perished notepad had been used for sketching but was now yellowed with age and smoke damage, two pencil shaped charcoal stubs, a postcard from a nearby village folded neatly into quarters and some faded red coloured thread. Pierre snapped a photo of each item from different angles with his phone and added it to the email that detailed his find.

As instructed, and through all the correct channels Bernadette received the email with the photographs and description of the small tin box and its contents. The correspondence requested if there was no official use for the find they would like it donated to the Caunes-Minervois memorabilia collection.

Something caught her eye; it was the sequence of events she had been waiting for. The name Wilhelm Fünten did indeed hold great significance for Bernadette, she had been anticipating this moment for a very long time. Her index finger quickly scrolled down the track pad of her laptop, she zoomed in on each of the photographs and re-examined the details in the email that identified the items and the location where they were found.

She was exhilarated and had so many questions regarding the contents. Why was the postcard folded into four? Would the sketch pad hold any clues? The charcoal, professional artist quality or the result of the fire? Red thread? What Army officer would need red thread? To repair uniforms, kit bags, perhaps? But surely not red? This baffled her, but she knew it would fit together like a well-designed jigsaw puzzle. The pieces always did.

As a covert research agent for the Office Central de lute contre le traffic des Biens Culturels (Central Office for the Fight against Trafficking of Cultural Property) she knew it was time to start wearing her other hat and investigate the find as there was more to it than just a rusty box found by chance. The contents were designed to be found by a like-minded person. But what exactly they all meant was beyond her at present.

Yes, she knew the name Wilhelm Fünten, and she knew what he should have been... would have been, if there hadn't been a war. There was no doubt in her mind that Wilhelm would have been the world's leading expert in French Renaissance art. He had topped his class in art history at the University of Berlin and had been given the rare privilege of spending time to complete research in France. This man had the scholarly expertise and a photographic memory for dates and details. From everything Bernadette had researched, he was hardly a man at all as he was only twenty-eight and yet he was so respected and held in such high regard. His love of art was so well known she imagined he would no sooner wish to break a stained-glass window than to loot the prized artworks of France. She knew only too well how the pressures of war and the threats to your family and their welfare would make men do many things that in times of peace they could not imagine possible.

She nodded her head in disbelief. This strapping young man… intelligent, I imagine well-spoken and kind, ending up as an officer in the ERR? As a select team of art thieves organised by Hitler himself, their mission was to confiscate pure art, deemed sufficiently worthy destined for his planned Führermuseum in Linz. Simply another part of the propaganda machine, he was ensuring works would fit within a strict set of criteria to ensure the purity of art for the future of Germany. Other items deemed to be "degenerate" were either sold off to profit the war machine or line the pockets of high-ranking officials, or simply burned at mass public burnings.

She had to search through her computer, but she knew it was there, the file on Wilhelm. Yes, she was spot on, he was exactly who she thought he was. She really did have pity for him as she imagined for someone who had dedicated their life to art and its preservation and conservation, it would have been torturous to then be assigned such a task. She imagined he would have had a strong sense of morality and justice. He was a Catholic but also came under the influence of his military father, and his early involvement with the Wandervogel – a German Scout association and part of the German youth movement.

What chance did he have? She pondered. Just why did he allow the château to burn down and destroy all the paintings? It just didn't ring true to her. It never had. She had a copy on file of the report he had submitted advising of the destruction of all the property and the loss of one soldier. And the further advice they were moving out to the next posting station. However, Wilhelm was only to survive another couple of weeks before dying from a lung infection, and other members of the original squad had all been killed in action at later stages of the war. None would ever tell the story of the evening's events when such rich cultural history was taken from the people of France.

It only took a few days for Bernadette to clear her schedule and travel to Caunes-Minervois. It was a dry and arid landscape just starting to reveal signs of spring as the rows of grape vines showed the first buds bursting from the gnarled wood. It would only be weeks and the colour of the countryside would change almost daily. She marvelled to think how this harsh shale ground could produce such beautiful wine.

Pierre had agreed to meet her in his office in the village where he would show her the small collection from the tin box. Then he would host a quick morning tea at his local café and ultimately, they would head to the château. He was excited about the visit and had ensured the office was dusted, flowers were put in a vase and his large smartly carved desk freshly oiled for the auspicious guest.

Bernadette appreciated the gesture and could smell the teak oil as she walked in the door. It was a familiar smell; it indicated the care people had for their belongings which was very important to her. It also demonstrated the esteem in which she was held. Pierre had already laid the contents of the tin on the table, and they were all there, just as he had found them. He gave Bernadette a moment with the items before he spoke any further. He could see she was in a zone, like a parent staring at a newborn baby for the first time or a loved one farewelling their partner. She put on a pair of white conservator's gloves and gently picked up each piece inspecting it slowly. Holding it close to the desk lamp and then to the sunlight that streamed in through the window.

He recalled just how mesmerised he was when he first saw the items and how gently he had held them in the same respectful gesture. But the white gloves? A little extreme? He wondered what other items they might also find at the château. It dawned on him the find might not be a good thing and may in fact cause significant delays or perhaps even prevent the re-building of the property. He remained calm and waited for the immaculately dressed woman to speak.

Bernadette continued to examine each item almost unaware he was in the room with her. She saved the notebook until last. She sat down and pulled the lamp closer. Carefully, page by page she looked beyond the obvious drawings and markings, seeking any other clues in deep hope the small book may include more than it was prepared to give up at first glance. And there it as. A name - Adeline Lanquetin, it simply had to be a relation of Solange Lanquetin the designer from Australia and Bernadette was on the mark – just as she had predicted.

Capable of containing her emotions, she really would have been a great poker player, she turned the page and kept looking at what followed with the same interest. She had burnt Adeline's name to memory and had no need to write it down.

As she finished inspecting the items she put on her charm and thanked Pierre for upholding the honour of his position and alerting the authorities to this find. She assured him the items would find their way to a museum of sorts and would keep him updated. She also assured him he would get a mention on the plaque that described where the items were located.

To a Maire these accolades were important. He wanted to leave a legacy of his time, and this showed his responsibility in honouring the correct preservation of historic buildings within his region. Plus, he could take his grandchildren to see the exhibition knowing they would take great delight in seeing his name.

He wished he had given his car more than a quick once over with a wet rag that morning. To put such an opulent creature as this woman into his car embarrassed him to the core. But Bernadette would hear nothing of his apology she was perhaps enjoying the happiest moment of her life and wouldn't have minded walking all the way.

As they drove out of the village and eventually down the long pathway past the large rusted wrought iron gates and the overgrown hedging, Bernadette couldn't help but imagine the place in its former glory. What a magnificent entrance that must have been. She drew a breath as they approached the property, for the building was in a genuine state of ruin and disrepair. Nature had reclaimed the living area and seemed to have taken up residence. The evidence of the fire was obvious even after all these years. They were greeted by the sorry sight of blackened window shutters that seemed to defy gravity as they hung wearily from the façade.

As a token gesture Pierre offered Bernadette a hard hat but she politely refused, instead having to control herself from pushing past him to look inside. As she had expected she could see only signs of ruin and decay. The beams of the roof had fallen in due to the fire, spilling debris across many of the rooms and there was clear evidence something else had happened during the disaster as she could see an indication of walls that had not caved in but had been smashed through. One thing was certain, whatever precious secrets the beautiful old building had protected they had all been given up a very long time ago.

Chapter Eleven

JUDGEMENT CALL

AFTER A SHORT REVIVING HOT SHOWER, she stepped into her black cigarette pants with a crisp pleat pressed into the front, a silk blouse and the highest of red patent stilettos. A delicate china cup of fragrant peppermint tea was waiting for her on the side table, the steam curling through the sunlight. Bernadette smiled at the efficiency of Sandrine, she was probably one of the few people that did impress her, she seemed to be able to pre-empt her needs. Always faithful and ever dependable Sandrine.

Looking at her reflection she marvelled at the superb array of ever so pale muted tones her colour consultant had arranged at her latest hair appointment. It looked like a selection of pastel crayons from an artist's palate - hues of rose pink, a gentle touch of lavender and a soft platinum (never to be referred to as grey) complimented her short pixie style and was part of her signature look. She took a moment to reflect on the task she was about to undertake like a general preparing strategies.

The lobby entrance was grand and gently lit. Bernadette flashed her first smile since arriving. The young woman that stood before her had achieved so many accolades and was indeed a gifted and talented individual. She had read widely about her achievements and her family history. Bernadette had memorised her portfolio, she was intrigued to at last finally meet the designer, Solange Lanquetin. Such a strong following on social media especially Instagram with over two hundred thousand followers – a global sensation. The choices of art Solange selected for her projects brought a smile to Bernadette. Cheeky and brave, she mused.

Bernadette had two dossiers on Solange, one for her artistic achievements, photography, and design work and the other, a substantially thicker file contained the details of her French ancestry going back five generations. Bernadette was curious to find out exactly what Solange knew about her family and their history especially during the horror of the Second World War. She was also interested in how it was that Solange purchased her art and antiquities for the interior design assignments featured widely in magazines. This would take some gentle prying, but Bernadette was skilled and very patient in this field. She would get her answers eventually and would ensure she had the evidence to back up everything. She was after all one of the finest covert art thief hunters in Europe.

Mathieu cleared his throat in an act supposed to draw attention to himself but awkwardly made him sound anxious and nervous. He projected his voice like a circus conductor announcing the next act. 'Ah Madame Bodelle, we are so very pleased you have travelled so far to join us today. May I present Madame Lanquetin.'

Solange had been watching Bernadette walk in and despite having done her own homework from a recent spate of magazine articles, found herself observing just how elegant and confident this woman was. She mused at Bernadette's amazing hairstyle; she had not seen such a co-ordination of colours so chic. Despite her age, the woman oozed style. The thoughts burst through her mind as she surveyed this striking woman. Her body language remained the same, calm, and reservedly friendly as always.

'Pleased to meet you Madame Bodelle. I have admired your work on many occasions. Mathieu tells me you have only just arrived from France a few hours ago.'

'Enchantée. Solange let me assure you, the pleasure is mine. Monsieur Arnaud has thoroughly briefed me on your work here in Australia and I am looking forward to hearing more.'

He scoffed silently to himself about the suggestion of him having briefed Bernadette, she hadn't said a word to him since her arrival. Mathieu escorted them to the drawing room. He had met her before on a few social occasions and was an admirer of her work. She however couldn't have picked him out of a line-up.

It was impossible not to recognise the French influence in Solange's work, and yet the way she was able to combine Australian modern and country styles ensured she had many adoring followers. She was the darling of Australia's design industry and yet so humble. It seemed she just wanted to do her thing – design and art, but this was the social media era, and much more was required. Her life was scrutinised, everything she wore or ate seemed to be available for sale by the simple click of a mouse.

'Please take a seat, Madame Bodelle I have arranged for tea and refreshments while we discuss…' he was gesturing towards the sitting area as Bernadette cut him off.

'Solange, please call me Bernadette.'

Mathieu bristled when he heard Bernadette encourage Solange to use her first name as she had never offered the option to him.

'I am interested in your use of Australian heritage colours when all the other designers are slaves replicating minimalist Scandinavian themes. The use of all white would simply make me feel like I was in an institution.' Bernadette ushered Solange to one of the plush high back chairs and then she set herself in the chair beside her leaving Mathieu to sit on the whole lounge by himself. It seemed that in one manipulation Bernadette had set the appearance of Mathieu being interviewed by the two women.

'Thank you. You are too kind. I work with the amazingly talented team at a boutique paint factory, and they assist me to create my own colour palate that seems to be timeless.' She sat in the luxurious chair and noticed the obvious blanking the Administrator was getting from Bernadette, she felt awkward about the exchange.

'Yes, I have seen these colours, and I have been following your social media pages. I admire the way you create such a refreshing mix of old and new without the kitsch of a theme. This indeed is a natural talent.' She paused. 'But what I really want to hear about is the story of the Harris-Gerwel mansion. I hear this was your first real break in the industry. Such an inspiring story.'

Solange sat back comfortably in her soft chair. This story while well-rehearsed was one she loved to tell, and she wanted to savour the moment. 'Don't worry I never tire of telling the story as I am so fond of that house. Let me set the scene. It all started with a chance meeting about fifteen years ago. I had been living in Rose Bay for almost a year and in between study and my part time work I would enjoy sitting in one of the promenade cafes in Double Bay the next suburb towards the city. It really was a charming village atmosphere and people watching was a delight.'

She recalled the ladies weighed down with large gold linked necklaces and matching bracelets chatting over layered tea cake stands, and parades of glamourous people with pampered pooches and luxury cars crawling past hoping to be seen. She would make a cup of tea last for over an hour to justify her taking up a small table and chair to the side. The mixture of glamour and excess gave her creative energy to draw and draught design ideas into a sketch pad that seemed to go everywhere with her in her square edged cane basket in those days.

On one occasion there was another lady also sitting by herself taking tea, looking sad and forlorn. She gestured to Solange to come and join her. Without hesitation Solange scooped up her collection and carefully balanced her tea set on the next trip and joined the woman. They struck up a conversation and agreed to meet weekly each Saturday at ten o'clock for morning tea.

Solange loved to hear the stories of Miriam as she spoke fondly of her Owen – a name she pronounced with endearment. He was her beloved. In his lifetime he was also a highly sought-after game hunter, a pastime from a bygone era. Owen was a giant man, not only in size but reputation, he had guided famous actors, wealthy businessmen, past Presidents, and the odd high court judge to bag, net or lay claim to any number of the top ten big game. His speciality was African and North American trophy hunting. The big five are the African lion, African elephant, African leopard, southern white rhino, and African buffalo. Add in a couple of giraffes for stamps and a giant American black bear, Owen had it just about covered. All his clients went away with a trophy to display in the office or if they were addicted the ever-needy trophy room.

Owen and Miriam Harris-Gerwel were quite a couple in their day, a period long overtaken by society's drive to right its previous wrongs. Miriam had only ever known their lives to be filled with taxidermy animals of some sort, even as a child her own father had a collection of moose heads above the fireplace. They were forever staring into space with a fixed expression on their face. Glassy eyes stretched fur and a faint smell of formalin. It always gave her the creeps but somehow, she felt they were safer with her family than out in the nasty wilderness. She had such a gentle, naive approach to life.

As she explained, it wasn't long after they were married that Owen, who had trained as a driver was quickly picked up as an assistant hunter. Inevitably return hunters then requested Owen to lead the hunt. As his prowess as a hunter became more widely known and in demand, their small Double Bay apartment grew into a three-bedroom house on a quarter acre block and then less than a decade later, the mansion. Owen needed somewhere to display his collection of photos with the famous hunters and a series of rooms with giant glass doors that represented each of the continents: the Africa room, the North America room, and the Asiatic collection.

When a visitor arrived at the mansion they were greeted by an enormous sweeping staircase, the balustrade featuring a variety of iconic animals. The thick woollen carpet and the flocked wallpapers were also in a safari theme. There was simply no doubting whose house you were in.

Owen had always insisted on Filipino maids, and it was a non-negotiable they wear the traditional maid uniform. There was no funny business going on, he just felt it was what rich people had and therefore, that was his world. Miriam was always kind to the small team of cooks, cleaners, handymen and gardeners. She enjoyed stealing them all into the dining room with her when Owen was away, and they would share meals together and stories from their very different lives.

Miriam was so lonely, and she genuinely enjoyed their company. The two maids, while fiercely loyal were superstitious about the animal spirits, highly angered at the world their physical representations had entered, trapped inside their dried-out fur, attached to trophy boards in this mansion so out of touch with a modern lifestyle. They were just not able to go into the trophy rooms. They tried hard, but they just couldn't, terrified something bad would happen in their next life. Miriam, ever understanding and so very kind obliged. Whenever Owen was out of the house, she would go into the trophy rooms to dust and vacuum. She would talk to each of the creatures while she danced around them ensuring she kept good vibes in the space.

The gates at the entrance to the mansion were ornate but they were also secure, and they needed to be. Animal rights groups were targeting Owen and the jungle of preserved lifeless animals he had stored within his glamourous surrounds. The groundsmen were forever picking out leaflets stuffed into the mailbox and the maids were continually hanging up on abusive callers. Miriam was protected from the outside world and the reality that it had changed since her childhood. Owen had shielded her from the real world, and her warm environment was a safe place.

Predictably, like all who make dangerous pastimes their living, Owen's demise was inevitable. It wasn't a wild animal charge or a stray bullet, but the tiniest of scratches made worse by the unsanitary conditions of the African bush. Not wanting to disrupt the hunt, Owen treated the small wound superficially and bandaged it. The infection spread so quickly that before the sun had set, he was feverish and starting to lose consciousness. Later, doctors would have more technical ways of explaining how his body had simply shut down and he didn't have a chance.

When the news reached Miriam, she found herself quickly surrounded by an ocean of floral tributes, cards, and letters from the celebrity hunters. The memorial service was well attended and Miriam looking like a sweet ballerina in a simple fitted black dress accepted words of condolence. Then to the house for refreshments and shortly afterwards it was just Miriam, her flowers, the stuffed animals, her ever faithful staff... and the growing collection of overdue accounts for payment. This was a world to which she had never been exposed. She was about to be overwhelmed by the line-up of hands held out after money. Money to service loan repayments on foreign assets she didn't even know they had to pay wages, utilities, and maintenance. Solid financial advice along with an administrative assistant enabled her to settle this world of sharks quickly.

Life became quiet for Miriam. Gone were the lavish parties, receptions, and households of guests. Those animals weren't talking, and the staff were anxious believing they would soon lose their jobs.

A year later, the house remained a museum to a darker time in environmental caretaking, the staff were still loyal, and Miriam continued cleaning those giant rooms dedicated to a previous life. She found herself at a local café needing to leave home to take in some fresh air and a little retail therapy. And that is where she met Solange! The rest as they say is history.

After meeting every Saturday for almost three months the friendship blossomed, and Solange received her golden ticket – an invitation to the mansion. It was like a film set and a natural history museum. Miriam just didn't know what to do next with her life. The animal activists' brochures were finally making their way past her mailbox and into her conscience. She wanted to see the house full of life again and she now understood the damage her husband had done. The scar he had left on the world had to be made good, and she needed to make amends. Community attitudes had taken a giant leap and had left her guilty with a house full of antiquated trophies from another era way out of step with current expectations. She asked Solange, a woman with a shameful secret of her own to assist her with the re-invention of the property. Together the women concocted a plan.

'It was clear Miriam was a good person and wanted to give back to the world in some way. The sweet woman felt she and her husband had taken so much. So together we created a plan to donate the majority of the animal collection to museums and open the house as an artist residency retreat, with a large number of individuals able to attend due to scholarships funded in her husband's name. She felt this really did make amends. I was lucky enough for Miriam to ask if I would design and oversee the refurbishment of the house, and it was the most exciting liberating moment of my life. The staircase was divine, the wallpaper heavenly so I already had so many features that didn't need a lot of work. But it was my own art along with a collection I bought while in France from a variety of markets, brocantes and vide greniers that made a jaw dropping gallery feature wall. Pictures of all shapes and sizes, frames bold and gilded, or simple black frames. The art all naive, nothing of note, mainly the work of novices, but there was true beauty in the imperfection of it all! A magic in the way they were put together and displayed. The residency is featured globally in the media, and it is usually the photograph of the main staircase you will see.'

'Yes, I have certainly seen it and it is marvellous. You have an eye for the eclectic. It is something unique and you should be proud. Didn't I see it on the front cover of...?' Bernadette tapped her manicured nail on her front tooth. Of course, she knew where it was featured.

'Vogue, yes it was the Vogue Mansions, Manors and Estates special magazine and when I found out it was to make the cover I was thrilled.' The smile wide on Solange's face at the memory of the moment she picked up the magazine from a tall glossy pile at her local newsagency. She had wanted to shout out to everyone in the shop this was her work featured, instead she hugged it to her chest as she paid.

Sounding more like an interview than a social exchange, Bernadette then asked, 'With so many successes quickly following that design project you have been a very busy lady for the last decade or so. What are some of the latest projects that you are working on at the moment?' Another question she needn't have asked as she already knew the answer.

'So, my latest project, a renovated group of ex-military buildings on Sydney harbour has taken a lot of my time, energy, and resources. I worked on this in collaboration with several architects, builders, and landscapers. It is called 'Harbourside Base' a name that is reminiscent of the buildings' historical naval connection. We were able to incorporate aspects of naval history into the design framework all cleverly integrated without being too kitsch. I can send you the portfolio for the project if you like?'

'Yes, I have been following the progress on your Instagram page. The building and interiors are truly something that you should be proud of. I would appreciate that, and I would very much like to be kept up to date on each of the completion stages. This will assist me with my briefings back to the French Foreign Ministry's Office of Cultural Heritage and Decoration. They will want evidence of your sympathetic use of historical decor.'

Mathieu shifted in his seat and felt a little awkward at their exchanges. He still hadn't said a word and he felt that the meeting was moving a little too quickly. He hadn't had time to even outline the project requirements or mention that Solange was only one of a selected few that were being considered for the assignment. Remodelling of an Ambassador's residence was one of the biggest events he would undertake in has role during this posting. Yes, he had assisted with large events such as the French Festival that featured across Australia at different times of the year. He had overseen large exhibitions at the National Gallery and most of the other major galleries. He had met just about every French person of note that had visited the country to promote a book, film, or product. But this time it was personal. He wanted to know the detail of this project, as his time was limited in this role and after another few years in the French civil service, he would have completed the renovation of the house of his dreams, full of art and clever design features that would stand as his status symbol for a well-earned retirement.

Bernadette had already made her mind up that Solange was to be awarded the contract. Equally, Mathieu had to admit that Solange was the perfect candidate, she was French born and had lived and worked in Australia. She was the perfect blend, so typical of political correctness. But he was also a stickler for the rules and the guidelines for an Ambassador's residential refurbishment stipulated that there must be at least three businesses interviewed by the Administrator and a representative from the French Foreign Ministry's Office of Cultural Heritage and Decoration who would also supervise the overall project personally. He resigned himself to the fact that he would merely be paying lip service to the next two candidates providing quotations.

Mathieu desperately wanted to join the conversation but every time he interjected; Bernadette shut him down. He recognised he was not a part of this discussion which seemed to be about everything except the embassy upgrade! It was fruitless that he should stay any longer. He would have to talk to Solange separately, without Bernadette snooping. He stood up as it was the only way to get attention. 'It has been a pleasure to meet you Solange and I look forward to hearing more about your work in the near future. I will discuss matters relating to this assignment with Madame Bodelle and I will be in touch to confirm details.' Mathieu politely shook Solange's hand and gave an official nod to Bernadette, then turned rather quickly, and departed.

Bernadette continued to talk with Solange as if nothing had happened. 'So, tell me more about where you got your artistic talent from. Your parents? Where did you study or were you self-taught?'

They both knew there was some type of game afoot. Solange was aware that Bernadette would have seen her resume, but she played along.

'My parents were not really artistic at all. My father worked in a factory in France and then came to Australia as a winemaker, apparently following his father's trade.' She was extremely cautious talking about her family. It had been a very long time since she had spoken publicly about them.

'He came out from France on a fixed term contract then met my mother here and the rest is history.' They both laughed a rehearsed type of laugh that sounded a little stilted. Bernadette knew exactly what type of factory her father had worked in and she wondered if Solange did as well.

'I grew up in Sydney and went to a school that encouraged my artistic interests. I had a few enthusiastic art teachers that opened a new world to me. They showed me how colour and light can be used, and they introduced me to oil paints and most importantly to the art gallery. I studied visual arts at the National Art School in Paddington.'

Bernadette was intrigued, 'And so with all of this exposure to the art world you only ever worked with oils, or did you expand you interests?'

'Well during my studies, I have covered everything from working with resin, clay, wood, and a lot of other media. And as you might know I have developed quite an interest in photography.'

'Ahh such a talent and the ability to vary your skills. I am impressed. I imagine that your parents are very proud, and I am sure that they have a beautiful home full of your work.' Bernadette was poking the bear as she knew the sad truth.

'It is unfortunate that my parents didn't get to see me even grow up. They both died on the same day. I was there, and I watched it happen. It was my doing.' Solange surprised herself that she had talked about this subject at a meeting to discuss design. How had this woman managed to get her to open up about such a sensitive topic? Perhaps she had also trained in psychology. But now was not the time to talk about such things. She didn't want to share such a tragic tale here and now.

Chapter Twelve

INNOCENCE LOST

WORKING ON THE NEXT STORY FOR HER TRAVEL BLOG, Ivy was staring at a large, stylised map of the world wallpapered to her study. She had a packet of ruby red marker pins and took great delight spearing them into each place she had travelled. Her standout favourites were marked with shining gold pins, these were the places she dreamed of returning to. Next, she lay out a large sheet of cardboard, coloured highlighters and pens planning to brainstorm ideas for her next story. She spoke out loud in a voice like a quiz show announcer. Would it be a guide to the top rainforest walks? Perhaps wellness spas in Queensland? A farm stay in New South Wales or the best cooking class retreats in Europe? Scribbling ideas onto the cardboard, she stepped back to review her options.

Maybe it is time for a simple family style holiday in a retro redecorated caravan? She glanced over at her to-do list stuck to the refrigerator with a glossy magnet promoting one of the many places she had visited as a child. The magnets all had special memories and reminded her of growing up around the pineapple fields of Bundaberg in sunny Queensland or the blood orange orchards of Griffith in New South Wales, known for its dark rich soil and comradery amongst the growers. But her favourite of all the magnets was the one from their cherry-picking adventure in the country town of Young a couple of hours drive east of Griffith. A friendly place that appreciated the help of the transient fruit pickers. The harvesting happens during the lead up to Christmas and so there was always excitement and parties, the weather was hot and dry but there was always a chance to cool off with a swim at Chinaman's Dam. She smiled at the memory of her mum packing a hamper for them to head off for picnics on their days off.

Ivy shuddered, remembering a time when her life had been a lot simpler, as a little girl travelling around Australia with her parents. It was also a harsh reminder of a time when she was known by her birth name, Lourdes. A name that had been packed away a long time ago, and for good reason – the painful memories and a shocking secret.

*

1978 QUEENSLAND

IN A TIME BEFORE THE INTERNET AND GPS, when people used maps to navigate and read local newspapers to find out what was going on. Her childhood memories were of her two devoted parents who had lovingly called her Lourdes Guadalupe Magdalena Castell. They were interested in a different type of tourism to those pictures in the glossy brochures. To experience a little more of the lifestyle and culture that came with each small town away from the tourist traps. Always happy to be offered work in orchards picking glorious plump fruit that made their mouths water and their backs ache. Meeting people from other countries and cultures made the hard work worth it. They certainly didn't do it for the money. As a mechanic her father was always able to pick up additional work while they travelled supporting their gypsy lifestyle.

'Look at the rows of strawberries Lourdes, they look delicious. So plump and the smell is making me hungry.' Her father stretched his arms out to emphasise the scale of the farmland that lay before them. 'It goes on for miles and it's protected by these tall and imposing rock faced mountains. They look like guardians protecting the precious fruit.'

Lourdes loved nothing more than when her father told stories that transformed something quite plain into a magical wonderland. She sighed and snuggled closer to him. 'Tell me more Papa.'

'Tomorrow when all the other pickers arrive, the little barrows will line up in neat rows and ever so steadily move forward picking off only the ripest fruit. By the time we are done tomorrow tonight, and come back again the following day, the sun is so strong that a new batch of strawberries will be ready to pick.' He smiled at his little girl who was growing so quickly and had a thirst for knowledge.

Back in the caravan at night, Lourdes always thought of it as an adult sized dolls house. Pale pink gingham curtains were tied back with beautiful tassels and the kitchen table folded neatly into a padded banquet seating area lovingly handstitched by Claudia her mother. The sweetest collection of cushions and bolsters in mismatched fabrics somehow all combined to create a unique and appealing space.

Her parents' room was an oasis of calm, always so neat – everything in its place. The ceiling air vent was popped open, and a cool breeze channelled through, the air was fragranced with the scent of her mother's signature jasmine perfume. Even out in the hot fields, orchards or vineyards she could find her mother with her eyes closed. All the other mums smelt of cheap deodorant or more often body odour.

'Mumma, when I grow up, I want to smell just like you,' she said while hugging her one night. They were lying on the bed while her eyes started to grow heavy with dreams.

Claudia tucked her daughter's ebony hair behind her ears and looked deep into her daughter's almond eyes. 'Oh, but Lourdes. When you grow up you will find your own special scent and that will let everyone know that you are in the room. It is something that will be unique to you.' And with that she continued her story that mesmerized Lourdes with tales of flowers, spices, wood and balms used to create the magic of perfume.

So much magic in the world, dreamed the innocent ten-year-old girl as she nestled into her parents' dreamy bed plumped with feathers and down. Moments later she was in a deep sleep and so relaxed it almost made her mother envious. Later after her parents had finished their meal and tidied the kitchen, they would lower the dining table and place another padded mattress over the space. After creating another fluffy haven, they ever so gently transferred their precious bundle into her own sweet bed.

The next morning, like every morning was filled with adventure and surprise. Where the other fruit pickers complained of low wages and scorching sun, her parents marvelled at the beauty surrounding them. Perhaps this is where Lourdes got her special talent for noticing things others overlooked. She had a way of seeing life through a filter that highlighted the beauty. Her attentive mother, a secondary teacher from Spain, had always insisted that Lourdes continue her education while they were travelling and worked double time to ensure that her bright daughter was set up with a lesson plan under the shade of the van's awning. Lourdes was never out of sight of her protective mother.

And then, at the end of the day the sound of sulphur crested cockatoos screeching at sunset would make her heart race and her eyes dart from tree to tree. It was indeed the golden hour when the sun would gently start to sink behind the mountains and the sky full of rippled clouds would turn a glassy pink. Looking past the trees that were constantly rustling with their noisy visitors, Lourdes would stare at the black dots that would appear. One by one they would dart past like shooting stars with their wings outstretched and their sharp claws retracted. The flying foxes were on their way home to settle for the night, but these little bats would also put on a show and squabble and shriek while jockeying for position in the large fig trees that lined the fields. These magical noises were now a part of her evening routine, homework should be completed by the time the last of the bats were darting past. It was impossible to concentrate as the sight always mesmerised her. It was time to pack up books and set the table.

Always curious, Lourdes was keen to ask questions about the history subject that she was studying. She had learned about a girl a bit older than herself who had to secretly live with her family in the attic of someone else's house during the war. At dinner that evening all Lourdes talked about was war and fear.

Her father gave Claudia the "I told you so" look. He had been concerned that she was studying material that was too old for her. 'My sweet girl, that war that you are learning about happened a long way from here in a country on the other side of the world. Look, let's have some of this nice dinner mummy has made.'

The distraction technique didn't work. She was still agitated and worrying about bombs, soldiers, and future wars. A decade earlier, her parents had experienced the same concern, her dad had already completed his time in national service. Paranoid and overly concerned that tensions might escalate once more, he didn't want any part of it, so they decided to leave Europe.

They had met in the stunning province of Girona on the Costa Brava in Catalonia and had made a pact to move to the other side of the world to begin the adventure of a lifetime. For now, that was subtropical Queensland for the strawberry picking season. They loved the warm weather, the beaches, and the social life of Australians, there was always an excuse for a beer or a wine. And this perhaps sadly is one of the reasons that the little girl's life was about to change forever.

The day had been so hot and humid that even the shade of the small cloth umbrellas over the picking trolleys was not enough for them to escape the sun. As fast as they drank the water from their cooling thermos flasks it was flowing out of them. The sweat ran in rivers down their backs and along their hairline. Her mother had a cotton scarf tied around her hair to stop the sweat running into her eyes, she refused to wear the big floppy towelling hat that her husband had pleaded with her to put on. Claudia was far too proud to allow herself to be seen in that, but her husband didn't hesitate and secured the ties under his chin to ensure it stayed in place. He had a big day ahead and then had taken on a job after work to help a motor mechanic nearby.

As they had their caravan onsite at this farm and there were others doing the same, the environment lent itself to communal dinners or shared drinks with picnic blankets and camping chairs scattered about. This was usually homework time for Lourdes, and they would sit quietly at the dinner table finishing complicated maths problems or practising languages. Spanish, French and English were the three languages they had shared with Lourdes since birth. This little girl only knew a world that was multi-lingual. She easily slipped between the three but always dreamed in French.

The hot day had taken its toll on Lourdes and her eyes were rolling in her head. Her mother simply closed the books and gently announced, 'Enough my sweet pea,' she smoothed her hair away from her face. 'It is time for you to sleep. Your little body is growing so quickly that you need to rest now.' There were no protests from Lourdes, she happily climbed into her parent's cosy bed and was asleep within minutes of her head hitting the pillow. 'No shower tonight. Oh, dear we have missed our chance.'

Opening the door to let some breeze in now that the mosquitos had died down, the laughter and chatter could be heard coming from the other workers. One of them caught Claudia's eye and they held their wine glass in the air and beckoned her to come and join them. She hesitated briefly, then on a whim scooped up a glass and took a bottle of chilled wine to join them. It would be such fun when her husband was back to join them after labouring over a car engine.

She positioned herself to see the van in case Lourdes woke and needed her, plus she could also see the path her husband would soon walk down on his way home. The group were welcoming and there were new faces who had joined recently, that she hadn't met. There was another couple that spoke Spanish and she nestled up closer, so she could easily chat and find out their background. Moments like this it felt like the burdens of life were lifted off her shoulders and she had not a care in the world.

The candles were burning lower, and the wine drained at a rapid pace, some people were getting louder and started singing. Some of the songs were a little off key and not exactly as tame as she would have liked. They were a little suggestive and dirty. One couple were starting to behave a little aggressively towards each other with a few angry words and shoving. There was a whisper of drug use amongst the group. Not at all sympathetic to the needs of people behaving in this way, Claudia used the excuse it was time to check on her daughter, but the group made fun of her and pleaded with her to stay for another drink.

'One more and then I really must go.' She had to admit that she was enjoying herself. Feeling lightheaded from the long day in the sun, the oppressive heat plus the overbearing responsibility of being a parent who needs to be up early to start the day. Regrettably, after the next glass of wine she took her leave and wished everyone a good night, joking about the headaches they would all have the following day.

Slipping into the caravan Claudia checked on her daughter and watched her breathing, something she had always done at night. That final check. She gently slid closed the concertina doors of the bedroom not disturbing the child as she set about converting the kitchen table to the little bed for Lourdes when she heard the door open.

In that moment, she knew that something was not right. It was not her husband walking in but one of the women that she had just met. One of the new couples that had just arrived that day. There had been no knock, she had just opened the door and walked straight in.

'What are you doing? Why are…' Her frightened whisper was cut off.

'I know women like you. I see what you do.' The woman stared through her. The dilated pupils indicating trouble.

'What are you talking about? What are…'

'Shut up. Just shut shut shut up! You stupid woman! You think you are better than me... think that because you are more educated, because you come from another part of Spain to me. You think you are...' The woman tripped up the stairs and fell awkwardly clearly hurting her shins. She continued her tirade. 'Don't think you can talk to my man like that. Laughing with him while you play with your hair. I'm not invisible I could see the way you were looking at him and then looking back to your van. You are not as good as you think you are.'

The air was hot with the smell of sweat and fear. The woman's shins were bleeding. She was speaking quickly, and her movements were erratic. Her behaviour was different to when they first met a few hours ago. Something had changed, and she had become unreasonable and aggressive. Pleading now, terrified, Claudia's legs were weak, she stepped between the woman and the space where her daughter was sleeping. A mother's instinct kicking in.

'Stop. What are you saying? I don't know what you mean? Stop. Sto…' She was still trying to keep her voice calm, but it broke, she was panicked.

Then the stranger without any hesitation or warning picked up a carving knife from on the draining board and hysterically started screaming more abuse and began to frantically stab at Claudia. The protective mother caught between the woman and the delicate concertina wall of the bedroom. There was nowhere to run, and she instinctively put her hand up to her face to protect her from the blows but to no avail. The first few stabs instantly put Claudia into shock, the severed artery made her lose consciousness and this didn't deter the intruder who continued her stabbing frenzy while issuing a warning to stay away from her partner, clearly unaware there would be no chance of that.

Two little eyes peeped through the joins of the divider while the air took on a sharp smell of metal and her life would never be the same.

The adrenaline in the woman caused her mind to go into a zone where she could not begin to comprehend what had happened. She simply dropped the knife and walked away rubbing at the blood that was splattered across her chest with curious wonder. She stumbled off into the darkness now that she had sorted out that problem.

The two little eyes continued to stare.

It would be another thirty minutes before her father would arrive home greeted by flashing lights and sirens. His whole life altered forever as he saw one ambulance drive past him and another with a second stretcher set up at the door of his van. There was so much noise and yet he could hear nothing. His hands were still covered in the sticky oil that was stubborn and couldn't be washed off as he pushed his way to the policeman stationed at the entrance of the caravan.

'What has happened here? Where are my wife and daughter?' His pleading was frantic. 'Oh my God, what has happened here?

The police tried to hold him back explaining that there had been an incident, and they were still trying to get a child out of the bedroom. He looked back to the ambulance and without hesitation forced past the police officers and into the van. The sight of blood everywhere, dark crimson spread across the floor, footprints of where the ambulance crew had been. The little haven that had one been a safe and happy place now resembled a slaughterhouse. The smell of death was offensive.

Two police officers inside the van had been trying to coax Lourdes out from under the bed when her dad had burst in slipping on the floor, his arm flailing in an attempt to steady himself. The officers instantly braced up to stop him from entering any further, but the man was not to be reckoned with. They all tried to calm him, and he could see he was surrounded with the policeman from the door behind him now. His body simply slumped, and he thought that he was about to pass out. But he could hear a little voice.

'Papa?'

One of the police officers shushed and pointed under the bed.

'Come out my little one. Come to Papa. I am here to keep you safe. Come. Come.'

The little girl crawled out from under the bed. She was pale and shaking in shock, but her feet stopped as she edged towards the first of the blood and she recoiled. The taller of the two policemen scooped her up and swung her in the air straight to her father's open arms where she gripped onto him, wrapping her arms and legs tightly around him. She did not cry, she simply stared into space.

As they walked out of the van the crowd that had gathered started to clap as they saw him with his daughter. It was enough to drown out the policeman on his radio. In a whirlwind of gloved medics and machines, Lourdes was taken into the ambulance where she refused to let go of her father. The doors were shut, and they were on the way to the hospital.

It was to be a long journey ahead for both of them. How could they ever function? What did the future hold? Lourdes' silence and fear endured.

Named after the city of healing and miracles, over time Lourdes found her voice again. She used her imagination like a filter to blank out that terrible day. She never spoke about it, but the effects ran deep. As she grew up, she made herself a promise that she would never allow another person to threaten her, she would be strong both physically and mentally. Judo and self-defence classes ensured that her personal safety was paramount, and she would stop at nothing. She would leave behind the little girl who watched her mother die and become a fearless courageous version of herself.

Chapter Thirteen

COERCIVE CONTROL

JUGGLING SO MANY TASKS, he sighed to his infant son. 'If I was in an office now there wouldn't be any interruptions. I could just get on with my work, how on earth am I expected to keep on top of this?'

The boy just stared back at him without expression. It kind of gave him the creeps.

'This week's story feed needs to be finished, take the photos, think up punchy taglines, attend the launch of some travel bag company that Ivy is hosting, and still have time to write my book. And then all you do is cry about it!'

The boy just continued to stare.

'Maddy, can you sort this out? I really don't want to get food on me at the moment.'

The young woman popped up out of the lounge chair, she had been curled up in it like a cat as she tapped away on the screen of her phone. She always resented the way he referred to his child as "this" or "him" and never by name unless they were filming. 'Sure, what did you need?' Her tone was simple and just matter of fact. Then she started to coo at the little boy. 'Aww come on sweet boy. Time for lunch, Maddy will find something yummy for you.' And with that she scanned the kitchen cupboard for something that could be plopped into a bowl and nuked in the microwave. 'Can he have baked beans yet?' She shouted into the pantry.

'I don't know, Google it.' Orpheus rolled his eyes at the interruption.

She already was, and the answer was yes as her screen glowed with the response that it would be okay from six months but select the ones without artificial sweeteners and to keep an eye on the salt content. Blah, blah, blah! From six months is all I needed to know. She grabbed the tin, snapped open the sharp lid and poured the contents into a bowl decorated with blue puppy dogs. Less than thirty seconds later with spoon in hand she set about attempting to get the contents into him.

Orpheus had committed himself to post online every day to satisfy his social media following. He wished that he could employ some "real" staff, shouting out ideas in a brainstorming session each month like Sonja did, and then the staff would just scurry off and get shit done. For the time being he would have to keep using Maddy on the sly. Camera in hand and laptop open, first, he took a quick look at what the other daddy bloggers were doing around the world. He reassured himself that they were all covering old material. Topics like "How to break into the mummy groups. Why am I always so tired? Oops Emergency Ward again!" No, he was above this type of chatter, he covered subjects like how teaching foreign languages from an early age assists with the child's ability to absorb learning, and outings to galleries that stimulated the mind, and yes, a few recipes that he had Maddy try out. He always had flash cards that featured in his photographs – a Spanish girl waving hola, a French girl with her baby doll poupee… and numbers, lots of counting in foreign languages. There was a pack for almost every language as he was the brand ambassador for Peek-a-Baby flash cards. In return for each purchase that was made by clicking through the link on his Instagram or Facebook post he would receive a decent twenty percent commission along with a couple of grand in retainers.

'Maddy, can you tidy him up now? I am going to need you to take some flash card photos with the two of us.'

He selected five cards, a couple of props and worked out his locations. Maddy had to change the boy's clothes for each shot, so she had them all lined up on the kitchen table next to the appropriate flash card. Next, she dragged out the large potted fiddle leaf fig from the window near the front door, hopped up on a short ladder and hung the background sheet for the images. The client required a non-fuss approach, they really wanted their cards to stand out. They had this routine worked out and they knew that their time was precious. An infant will only tolerate so much jiggling and a few outfit changes as it was almost nap time.

'Hold your chin up, and turtleneck.' This was her cue to get Orpheus to not show any chin shadow, he hated it when he saw an image of himself, and it looked like he had a double chin. She had been blasted about that enough in the past, so she knew the drill. 'Look, look… look over here.' She jangled a noisy bell toy next to her shoulder. The camera was on a tripod, so she had to zip it up and down to get a few different angles. Shortly her work would be done, and she could put the sleepy boy back to bed.

'Right. Okay sort him out now and when he gets up, I want to shoot the lamb's wool throw promotions. Those colours are awesome. I want the photos with them draped over his cot. Remake the bed with the pale blue pinstripe sheets.' He held up moss green, ocean blue and cream throws imagining how he was going to incorporate them all in one image.

Maddy didn't even reply, she just did as she was told. Why argue when you are being paid three times what an average babysitter gets? Hush money, she laughed to herself, that is exactly what he called it. What a pompous pain in the arse he is!

These photos are alright, but she really needs to do a course or something. Could be better! He downloaded them straight to an app on his computer. Ahh now let me work my magic. A mouse click here, a colour enhancement there. He scratched at his short stubble beard while scanning for the next option that would put magic into the photograph. And with the final click on the spot healing brush to remove that extra crease line on his forehead. Where on earth did that new line come from? He stepped up to look in the mirror and practiced some fake smiles and there it was again. This was an inconvenience, but he would investigate it and book an injectable later in the week.

Next, he directed Maddy to program the release of the images, their catchy titles and hashtags ready for their 5:00 am post each working day next week. It was time for a cup of tea or perhaps something a lot stronger, but he would make the sacrifice and wait until his wife came home. Then he would open a bottle of shiraz to enjoy while she was making his favourite sticky pork ribs and a sweet slaw salad on the side. She was attractive, intelligent, and most importantly amazing in the kitchen. He often gloated that he had hit the trifecta when he met her.

Under the slight glow of her phone, Maddy sneakily eased herself back into a chair in another room. She was more than happy to just hide away from the child's crying and Orpheus' orders. But it wasn't long before a sliver of light came from the hallway as Orpheus beckoned her out of the room with a long list of things to prepare for the afternoon, along with the usual command of. 'Tidy up this place before my wife gets home or she will freak out.'

With Maddy safely tasked off, he ducked into the bathroom and pulled out his toiletries travel bag, he dug around and pulled out a bottle that was hidden behind one of the fabric pockets. He was rushing and didn't concentrate properly to unscrew the safety lid, it infuriated him causing him to knock his bag off the counter. He stared at the door expecting someone to come in and catch him but there was no sound. He tried again and focused, releasing two large, coloured tablets into his hand then tossing them straight into his mouth. He held the pills on his tongue until he managed to sort out his bag and hide it back inside the cabinet and only then did he take a mouth full of water to swallow them. Orpheus flushed the toilet for effect and then felt obliged to wash his hands again before opening the door and venturing back out into the house.

While Maddy straightened the house and dragged the fig back into its happy place – she thought to herself about just how temperamental those plants were. One odd look and the thing would drop all its leaves in protest. A bit like Orpheus!

Orpheus now had a short window of time to explore his new obsession with genealogy. He had only just logged in when he stopped typing and stared up to the ceiling as if to thank the Lord himself. The idea had landed. Yes, that is it! Perfect. Yes, I know who I need to research. This book will make me a fortune. The choice of subject couldn't have been clearer, and he had complete access to her. Someone who intrigued everyone and was photogenic, it was also a bonus that they had such a mysterious past. The writing detective could begin his work.

The innocence of it all, he marvelled. Solange would never know.

Chapter Fourteen

ALMOST PERFECT

'I KNOW I AM VERY BUSY. Yes. Yes. I will. What? I don't know about that. How could I possibly?' This was the usual phone tag banter that she conducted with the staff at the care facility for her mother. 'We have spoken about that.' She used the same tone that she would with a ten-year-old child. 'Okay, well, yes, I said I will. Okay. Talk soon.'

Amanda hung up and clicked a second button on her steering wheel to activate the Bluetooth again for her next phone call. 'Call Brianna.' The phone rang out. She tried again. Straight to voicemail. She clicked the button again. 'Call Steven.' He answered immediately. She rolled her eyes at his efficiency. 'Where is Brianna?'

'I'm well. Thanks for asking Amanda.' His sarcastic response was always the same. 'Brianna is sitting her French exam. Do you even know what time it is?' He shook his head wondering if Amanda did have any concept of time and responsibility.

'I haven't heard from her this week.'

'She has been busy studying for exams.'

'Tell her to call me.' She disconnected the call.

Strumming her fingers on the steering wheel, she moved her left hand off the wheel and turned on the stereo, choosing an album from her playlist. Her eyes spending more time on the music selection than the road. She hated these visits, and they always made her feel so responsible for what was happening – the tension was building. She was feeling heavy, like a cloak of guilt had wrapped itself around her for not keeping a promise to her mother. She had sworn that she would have done what her mother had asked, but her schedule was overloaded, and she was forever chasing her tail just keeping her head above water.

Her silver BMW leapt over the speed humps at the facility. She ignored the slow signs and the no parking sign as she edged into the tight space. I won't be here long, and I can afford the fine. The defiance building up in her like a lawyer heading into court.

They knew she was coming, the green light flashed to announce her arrival. Pushing open the glass doors, the airlock pressure sucked at her eardrums. The next green light flashed and then the pungent smell of disinfectant and pending doom offended her nostrils. The carpet, she sarcastically imagined was one of a fine selection of two available from the hospitals and nursing home "floral range" in some dusty catalogue. Designed to hide urine, blood and whatever other body fluid was destined to find its way into its pile. She shuddered as she pumped her hands with the disinfectant that was screwed into the wall fixture. Even touching that gave her the creeps.

Her feet led her in the direction of room 304B, not that they had three hundred and four rooms. This was a special ward on level three, room 4B. She considered buying a bronze plaque for the door "Eleanor's room". The woman was due a long service medal for surviving the cream paint and hard mattress. But lately Eleanor wouldn't have had a clue if her arse was on fire. Most of the time she didn't even know her own name.

'Ruth!'

'Amanda, Mum! I'm Amanda.' It had started already, the confusion and repetition.

She walked straight to the window in an attempt to open it, the smell of old people and unwashed hair made her feel ill. Forgetting that the window was safety fitted to only open a few inches, she nearly put her neck out as she yanked at it but to no avail.

She cleared a chair of old magazines and sat down. 'Mum, you know Orpheus - that guy that sort of does the type of work that I do?' The elderly woman stared blankly back to Amanda. 'Mum, you only met him yesterday. How could you forget a shit like that?'

'Ruth watch your language. What could that young man possibly have done to…'

'Amanda Mum. I'm Amanda!' She just rolled her eyes and sighed loudly. Today she had no patience for traffic, her renegade daughter, her arsehole of a husband or her dementia burdened mother. 'Mum where does your brain go?' Amanda knew that her mother was already too rattled to get upset any further.

'I told you about him yesterday. Remember me telling you I went to the launch of a new pram?' She waited to see a spark of acknowledgement, but nothing was coming. The stair pram… she thought to herself. How does a shit like him get to promote products like that? This thing was about to be the new must have for every new mother. He was going to make a fortune and all he had to do was turn up and put the kid in a damn pram. He has the perfect child. She could only imagine if she had taken Brianna as a baby. There would have been tears and vomit. How does he manage to pull it off? I wonder what commission rate he is on?

So many unanswered questions spinning around her head. There were times that she envied her mum and how quiet her mind was. Eleanor was just sitting quietly, staring at a bird that had landed on the window ledge. Innocent to all the stress in the world, naive to everything that Amanda had to do to get by. I have to hustle to get every contract, hustle, hustle! Her thoughts turned hateful as she reflected on Orpheus and how contracts just kept getting handed to him on a platter. It isn't exactly like he is the only guy on the earth to have ever stayed at home to look after his kid. Jesus, they treat him like a rock star. She lamented to herself.

Amanda had taken her mum along to see the launch to conceal the fact that she wanted in, she wanted to see him in action and see how he pulled it off. At the office he always seemed so well put together and showing no signs of lack of sleep. She remembered back to the days when Brianna was a baby and there would have been no chance that she could have fronted up to a promotion like that. She would have had sore, leaking nipples, and been unable to sit or stand for that amount of time regardless. It further confirmed her theory that she just hated men full stop.

'How do you know this man dear?'

'Mum I work with him. Well not with him but sort of with him.' Now she was talking like her mum in a type of confused state. 'He is a blogger like me. We sometimes work on the same projects. We collaborate...' She cut herself short at that word. Collaborate. It was the evil nemesis of bloggers, basically the word that defines everyone working together looking like everyone is enjoying themselves. When all they are really thinking is, "If only I had this contract to myself, I would be able to do so much more with it… but oh no I have to share!". Bloggers, like children with lolly bags… don't really like to share.

'That's nice. Do you have a baby as well? Is that how you know him?'

'Okay Mum. We are both bloggers; you know how I write stories and put them on the internet? Mum, you know this.' Her blood pressure was rising. She needed some air. This place was really suffocating her. God kill me now if I ever end up in here. Breathe. Jesus just breathe.

'You don't sell prams?'

'Mum. Mum, no I don't sell prams, Orpheus does.' God now she was doing it again. 'No Orpheus doesn't sell prams, he promotes them. He is like an advertisement that you would see on the television, but he does it from his computer and people who have babies follow him on the computer program.' Looking to the ceiling for divine inspiration she wished she could find an analogy that would help? 'He is sort of like someone that writes stories in your favourite magazines... but they are just on the computer and not on paper. And people can buy just by clicking on the story.' Okay stop now. She thought to herself, mum is staring at the bird again.

The knock at the door signalled that it was the nurse coming to collect her mother for afternoon tea. A lady who coloured her chickens in fluorescent dyes was coming to entertain them.

'Amanda felt like asking the nurse to take her blood pressure. She was almost seeing stars at the frustration of the visit.'

'Goodbye Ruth.'

And at that moment she felt a blood vessel pop in her left eye.

Chapter Fifteen

LIGHTING THE FIRE

THE RESTAURANT WAS AN UNUSUAL CHOICE for a diplomat. It was in the suburbs on the "other side of the bridge". Balmain was lovely and while the restaurant was quaint, it was also a little hidden away for those who usually like to be seen dining. No-one would notice them here. Solange knew there was more to this meeting than discussing the refurbishment of the Ambassador's residence.

Mathieu had arrived early, he wanted to be prepared and not rushed. It was important this meeting went to plan. He was growing impatient, and his time was limited, he had received notification of his next posting for the following year. There were a few gaps to fill before he was ready to leave.

He had arranged for the invitation to be hand delivered by a silver service courier. A little old fashioned but he needed to impress. The service was paid from his own private card, it was simpler that way, no need to process claims on the expense account.

He stood up to greet her with the customary kiss on either side of the cheek. 'Bonsoir Madame. So lovely to see you again. Yes, well I was in Sydney for a couple of days and thought that it would be a perfect opportunity to see you.'

Solange felt a little awkward at this exchange. It all seemed so cliché. She kicked herself for not researching if Mathieu was married or not. Did it ever matter? This is the exact reason she really did not like dinner "dates" with male clients.

They always wanted more out of her than she was prepared to give.

'Monsieur Raymond it is indeed a pleasure to see you again. I appreciate that you have taken the time to meet with me.' Keep it formal and distant. She reminded herself.

'Ah Solange, please call me Mathieu - we don't need to be so official today.'

She glanced around at the other patrons in the restaurant and the waiters, her eyes almost signalling an SOS. She looked like a trapped bird, so fragile and totally at the mercy of her menacing predator.

'How has your week been?' he asked while nodding to the waiter and then without even giving her time to answer he ordered a bottle of champagne. Real champagne, from the region of Champagne, not the sparkling wine Australia presents on its wine lists, sadly lamenting days past when it was able to use the title.

Without waiting for her reply, he started on claiming some story about the origins of the vineyard and how his family owned a house nearby and how he would holiday there as a child. The pompous way he transferred the information was simply straight out boasting and held no bearing other than to attempt to further escalate his status.

Once the exchange with the waiter was complete and he had finished reminiscing about his childhood she managed a reply, not actually sure if his question was still open to answering but she attempted. 'Busy as always, so many projects happening at the same time.' She stopped herself short to add. 'Of course, my design work for the Ambassador's residence is always top of mind but I am waiting on the final samples to present to Madame Bodelle.' Keep it sterile and professional.

His air of approval was dismissive; however, he did react instinctively when she mentioned presenting the samples to Bernadette and not him. How had he allowed this chain to take effect? He forced himself to shrug off his pride for after all, this meeting was merely a feint to conceal his real motives.

'Yes. Yes. I have no doubt that you are doing fine work on this project.' He leaned forward. 'But tell me what other…'

The waiter returned with the selected bottle of champagne and after the pageantry and ceremony surrounding the opening and sampling of the contents he continued. 'Pardon.' He cleared his throat theatrically and leaned in again. 'As I was saying. Please tell me what other projects you are working on now?'

Solange sensed he may be hinting he didn't want her to be working on other projects. She felt a little unsure how to answer but continued. 'Well, I always have several projects on at the same time. It helps me maintain my creativeness as I often find something that presents itself for one project will be better suited for another. Take for example the fish scale tiles I was planning to use for the…'

Mathieu's face showed his instant disinterest. It was obvious that he wasn't really listening, just hearing noise.

'Oh!' she giggled nervously. 'Oh, that really does sound rather awful but let me show you a picture. It really is quite lovely; they are very on trend.' She realised it would be terrible manners to pull out her mobile phone in a restaurant and she hesitated, but he gestured for her to go ahead. He leaned in closer again and she felt the awkwardness of her wanting to pull back. He was in her personal space, and she could feel his breath on her face.

Scrolling through her photos took only a moment before she presented the image. Her face glowed from the reflection of her phone. 'Here, this is the one that I wanted to show you. These are the tiles that I am planning to use for the Harbourside Base multi-use space at Sydney Harbour. You remember the ex-military building on Sydney Harbour that I mentioned during my interview?' She hesitated as she handed her phone to him, so she didn't need to remain as close to him, but he stayed leaning in.

'You certainly have an eye for beautiful things Solange. I would never have imagined something that reminds me of a fish could look so striking.' He handed back the phone slowly so that their hands touched.

'What other projects are you working on?'

The discomfort of the meeting continued as now she felt a little confused. Was this a combination of an awkward unwanted first date mixed with a job interview? Her nerves were getting the better of her, she was extremely uncomfortable. She was about to rattle off her portfolio, clearly not understanding what he was asking, when he continued.

'You see, I have a couple of private houses, I would describe them more as exclusive residences that I am working on, you know, renovating. These, along with a small number of fashionable restaurants and I am also continuing my own art, photography and I am working on a private commission for a range of textiles.' She seemed to blurt it all out very quickly. She picked up her champagne and took a decent sip, more like a glug. It was delightful. She did have to admit that if the story was true and his family holiday estate was near this vineyard, he was indeed a lucky man.

'I believe that you also travel to France three of four times a year. Do you still have a house there?' The interrogation continued.

'Actually, I go to France on buying trips. This is one of the parts of my work that I especially enjoy. I attend the furniture and art markets, visit brocantes and as many vide-greniers as possible. I'm always on the lookout for furniture I can have re-upholstered, or lamp bases that I can put a new lampshade on. I would say this is one of my design traits. People recognise my work through this.'

But he already knew that. He knew she had been to Lyon in May to visit Les Puces du Canal, where for three days she scoured the hundreds of vendors. Many items were purchased and carted off to a nearby waiting hire truck. They were then transferred into a shared container for the long journey back to Australia. Again, in August she visited other second-hand dealers and markets in the south. He noted she owned a small house near Carcassonne in the south and stayed for almost three weeks. He believed that by now, he already knew every single thing about her.

She unconsciously continued to volunteer information. 'Yes, and I still have a small house in the southwest of France. It is on my project list, but for the mean time it is habitable and still quaint and rustic. It is my dream to one day block out my diary and dedicate time to bringing this charming petite maison back to its former glory.' She felt like she had exposed something far too personal to this man who she did not trust. How did he know about the house? She had never told anyone; it was her little secret a private escape and very personal to her. It was like telling him that she had an illegitimate child. She didn't want him knowing too much about her. She always tried to keep this side of her life private. There were a few loose ends in France, and it was better to keep that on a low profile.

They continued chatting; however he didn't ask her anything more about her house in France which was very unusual as most people were curious and fired away loads of questions. He didn't need to ask her as he would do his own reconnaissance and find out the details he needed when it suited him.

This time it was his turn to talk. He told story upon story that expressed his importance and the exclusiveness in which all activities were conducted through the Embassy. His role was to oversee all and to see all. Nothing got past him.

She got the message. He was important. Yes, I know exactly what you are doing. Setting the scene about how noteworthy you are, that special delivery for the invitation, buying dinner and now clearly painfully trying to buy a ticket into my pants! She was steeling herself for a firm response to let him know she was not at all interested.

During the meal he continued to talk about the work he did, all the events he attended, and the famous people he had met. He continued to self-promote, telling of the many gallery exhibitions he assisted the curators with and then, just as she was lulling off into a stupor, he asked her a very direct question that caused her to silently choke.

'Now that we have all the social chatter out of the way. I am curious. Tell me about the stolen art you import.' He casually continued to eat his meal.

Holy shit. Stolen art. Did he just really say that?

'Mathieu, I don't know…'

'Yes, you do Solange, you know a lot about it.' He still didn't bother to look away from his food.

'I don't know where this is coming from. I do import art, but it is from flea markets and from the grandchildren of deceased estates. I have receipts from... well I have receipts.' She didn't have receipts and she didn't ever really question the provenance of the art.

Shit what does he really want?

He just kept eating and sipping on his merlot that had arrived to accompany the main course. Swirling it in his glass and watching it under the light he was really showing what he was made of and how he wielded his power. He reminded her of a boy torturing ants with a magnifying glass and enjoying every moment.

'Am I being accused of importing stolen art?' She was sounding frantic.

He continued to investigate the wine and sighed at her like she was about to receive a reprimand for being a naughty girl and spoke calmly. 'Solange, as I said before, nothing gets past me.'

Stalemate. They both sat there in silence. Her mind was running a hundred miles an hour. What does he really know? How could he know anything? Is there any way that I could test what he knows? But what she simply really wanted to ask is What do you want from me?'

Silence.

And then Mathieu spoke. 'I think we will keep this simple and skip dessert. I will be in touch.' And with that he simply stood up and left the table handing a couple of hundred-dollar bills to the waiter as he walked out the door.

*

IT HAD STARTED OUT A SIMPLE RESEARCH EXERCISE. He always did a thorough investigation on any new supplier or person of importance related to the Embassy. It would never happen on his watch that the gardener would be found to be head of a crime syndicate or supplier of amphetamines. Not on his watch - ever.

He scrolled through the files, all the usual material supporting a young French family moving to Australia for work in agriculture, settling at a vineyard in South Australia before moving to Sydney and working in art and design. Interesting career change, Mathieu thought wryly to himself… and that is exactly what made him so good at his job. While others would think nothing of it, he looked a little deeper. The Australian government had put out a call to European agricultural specialists to assist with the cultivation of their vineyards during a reinvigoration of the industry. They needed the expertise from Europe, in particular France as the perfect place to get the skills and knowledge. However, just because you are French doesn't necessarily guarantee you are an expert vigneron. And why the move straight into the commercial art world after the required period of time to gain residency in Australia? Something was odd about this. He picked it.

Reading on, the researcher identified that when Solange was twelve years old tragedy struck. The family was enjoying a simple day at Coogee beach. He could imagine the tasselled umbrella fluttering in the sea breeze, coloured beach towels like on a movie set. The water would have looked tantalising to the uninitiated, and the foamy white tips forming mesmerising patterns on the water.

Her mum was first in the water, she was all prepared and had put her swimmers on before leaving the house. Solange had packed hers in her basket and needed to wiggle about while her dad held her towel around her like a privacy barrier. The sand was getting into her swimmers, and she was getting tangled up trying to flick it out. They were both so preoccupied trying to maintain privacy that when they turned around, they were shocked to see how far her mother had moved away from the water's edge. As their eyes adjusted to the brightness of the reflection of the sun off the water it dawned on her father that something was not right, and his wife was in trouble. Little did they know or understand the power of a rip and how deceptive the water could be, luring you in and quickly sucking you deeply out into the ocean.

Panic took hold of her mother and the more she tried to swim in the cruel sea, the more it seemed to be pulling her back. She tried to shout for help, but her mouth filled with the salty water of the ocean, forcing her into a vicious cycle as it hit her lungs she would cough and suck in more of the briny water. She had never learned to swim and really didn't have a chance. Her feet were kicking as the water lapped across her face, she was quickly growing weak. Through the foam of the waves, she could briefly see her husband running into the water but couldn't hear his scream or her young daughter crying.

So much noise, so much drama. And then suddenly, the only audience was a little girl. Standing at the water's edge not letting the deadly water entice her to an early grave. She stood there frozen, staring at nothing but blue water and white foaming waves. Nothing else, they were both gone.

He flicked forward a few pages impatiently. As she was now a dual citizen and with no living relatives in either France or Australia, she was put into foster care for about six months. Her parent's possessions were sold off to pay for their funerals and nothing other than an old trunk with a few heirlooms and her clothing remained. The house in France was small and derelict, the title would be transferred to her name. Moved, moved again, another family, another school, and finally an adoption to a family in Sydney.

High school, then university graduating with a degree in Fine Arts. What else? He sarcastically rolled his eyes. She started hand printing designs on tea towels and tablecloths and selling them at art and craft markets where she was discovered by an art magazine who published a small article on her. The projects grew in size and intensity, there were awards and increasingly commissions for work that had her career moving. Then she decorated the house of a wealthy woman in Double Bay that was now an artist retreat, he had all the media clippings in front of him. This was picked up on by an interior design company that was looking for fresh input for their design team and the rest as they say is history. It wasn't long before Solange had the courage to break out and start out on her own where she could have the freedom to create art, photography, textiles, and interior design. She really did have a talent for picking a look that was edgy and usually shared a unique message. He did like her work.

Her social media platform ensured her status was securely cemented. That is until Mathieu dug up a little something else about her. On her frequent buying trips to French art markets, Solange would gather together a shipment of art and curios to be used on consignment for her design projects. Yes, she had told him this already, but he took it upon himself to understand the style of art she was selecting. This was important. And then it struck him that something was not as it seemed. For in the house of an apparently wealthy yet middle class family was a piece of art that caught his eye. Deceptive in its naive style and simple framing. Most would not even give it a second glance as it sat amongst a cosy collection of still life oils, painted by enthusiasts or portraits colour enhanced by amateurs, the effect none the less very effective.

But there was something about the way this unique little piece stood out for Mathieu. He recognised the style immediately and with a little more research he confirmed that it could well be an original Henri Rousseau, in fact he had little doubt.

What was this slight seemingly harmless woman up to? Surely, she would know her art styles and periods. She would know the provenance of every piece. Was she sloppy in her purchasing or was there a little more going on that slipped under the radar? Or was it a completely innocent purchase where even the new owner was not aware of the value and provenance of what may be hanging on the wall?

He reflected on how that one simple sentence had rocked her. Tell me about the stolen art that you import? There was no stepping back now. She knew that he knew. And if she had done it once, she would do it again.

The other thing that caught his eye was the string of abuse Solange received online from followers on social media with strange names like @watchingu and @lifetrader. They had been intimidating and threatening, yet she did nothing about them.

Now Mathieu was not picking up on this for the good of mankind, he was not about to alert the authorities and have her investigated. He was interested in it for the good of Mathieu.

At first, he had simply wanted to pick up some design tips as he was planning his own renovations on his family estate in Brittany, and he wanted nothing more than to hear how this woman was going to plan the Ambassador's residence.

Previously it occurred to him that he might consider hiring Solange for his own project. He dreamed of a house filled with original artworks that all had a story, he didn't want prints, copies, or photographs. He had decided that only original artworks would grace his walls. His personal collection was growing, but he wanted to expand it with a few key pieces that were not available on the free market. However, the time to discuss this was not over dinner, he would pick the right moment. But he had sown the seed of her role in this plan.

Chapter Sixteen

GASLIGHTING

IT ALL STARTED WITH A SINGLE EGG. Most creation does. Along with a whole heap of other factors. On this occasion it was not life that it was starting, but trouble. One egg thrown at your front door in the middle of the night signals the start of something very rotten indeed.

Solange cleaned up the reeking mess as quickly as she could. She didn't want prying eyes asking questions. People were always trying to make more out of anything and everything. Often referred to as tall poppy syndrome, Solange knew it as her own personal burden to bear. Rubbish disposed of – out of sight and out of mind. But then it didn't leave her alone and kept playing on her mind. It is the sort of prank that school leavers played but it wasn't the end of the year. Just bored kids. She kept telling herself. But the other voice reminded her of all the recent events that had occurred.

The series of vile online comments were far too personal an attack for just a simple disgruntled follower. The messages had been sent not always as comments to her posts but as private messages directly to her from a variety of profiles. The messages were all extremely personal.

"Why so shy? I enjoy knowing all the things you hide from others?"

"Tell me why your family bolted to Australia?"

"What are you hiding in that sweet mind?"

"I'd like to get to know you a whole lot more."

"I'm coming over some time."

"I know what you have done."

Over time the messages got a lot more peculiar and threatening. Solange was frightened and panicked, these people were stepping over the line, they were clearly crazy. She knew that she should go to the police or at least report them, but she had secrets that she didn't want exposed. She took screenshots to look back on them, to torment herself over, and over again.

Then fake profiles of her social media sites had started popping up, she had been hacked. They were all legitimate photos of her, and the front pages looked identical, but when her followers clicked on content they were led to other pages with, well very dubious content. It worried her a great deal.

Who are these people targeting me? Are they trying to make money from this? She wondered as she exited from her screen. Perhaps they are competitor designers? She just couldn't understand it. While she hesitated at reporting messages, she didn't delay at report the fake profiles and have them removed.

Was it the Russians? It always seemed to be the Russians... or was it the Chinese now? She would check in with the mobile IT guy that helped her out. Or could it even be him? She had watched a television series about a serial killer who had been the home security installer. Usually the person that you trust. She shuddered.

He was always telling her that she sounded like a sixty-year-old when she kept saying that she had been hacked. He explained numerous times to her that hacking was different to people copying your profile, which was what seemed to be happening to her all of the time. To her it sounded just as evil and predatory.

It started happening a few weeks ago and it was Sonja who called to let her know her profile was being used by someone else and she needed to sort it out. Solange didn't even register what Sonja was talking about and was promptly instructed to google her name. Sure enough, there were about a dozen hits, and they all had the same profile picture and looked exactly alike. But when she clicked on them, some of them sent you to porn sites, others to plumbing sites and one even went to a funeral home.

Why would someone do this to me? Solange was baffled. They are just trolls. But why pick on me? What have I done to them? She thought hard about who she must have annoyed now? She always tried not to step on anyone's toes, but it was near impossible. There was always some tree hugging group sodding off at her for supporting timber products or non-organic brands, but sometimes despite her best effort it was impossible to find an eco-friendly option. They were getting more creative in their cruelty. Last week they had superimposed her face on a dead koala at the side of the road. Saying that she was responsible as she was driving them from their natural habitat, it gave her nightmares.

There was no doubt anonymity lowers inhibitions, one writer commented to her. "Click on this link. It will show you how to kill yourself." She remembered that her response was so physical that she literally tossed her phone across the room. This was some high-level abuse. But she had convinced herself that if she just ignored it, it would go away.

You just don't speak to other humans like that. If you were face to face, sure people might swear or say a passive-aggressive remark that would burn. But unless they were high or drunk, would they instruct you to go and kill yourself? She was clearly spending far too much time overthinking all of this. Cyber safety was not something she had been given a lesson on and was naive and raw in her approach.

She had experienced petty hatred when at school. These teenagers had been capable of despicable things. Nasty, verbal, and physical acts that were demeaning to her. She always felt because she was orphaned at a young age, people would take pity on her and be especially kind. But with her striking features and shy nature, Solange became a target primed for torment. It was so much a part of her life she had been groomed to take it.

Out of all the menacing events from the past few months, a few seemed to match up. There was an obvious pattern appearing around the words. "I know what you have done."

Starting to hyperventilate, she gripped the arm of the chair. Her whole body started to shake until it had reached an uncontrollable tremble. She considered calling someone but there was no one, honestly no one she wanted to be with. The only friends she had were Ivy, Amanda, Orpheus and maybe Sonja, and there was no way she was admitting to them she was being bullied online by so many people.

It started to eat away at her, and she felt powerless. A wild sea had formed, and she was drowning. Overthinking everything, like the large new dent on her car. Deliberate or just a shopping trolley pushed by a blind person? Is it time to talk to the police or am I just overreacting? Yes, she convinced herself that she was being a bit dramatic, after all worse things happen to other people all the time.

Sitting down to a refreshing cup of herbal tea it occurred to her that she had other suspicions. Had someone broken in last week or am I imagining it? I am a stickler for turning off all the lights, and yet the bedside light was on when I got home. There were missing items from my beauty kit… and my hairbrush? Have I just misplaced all these things? She had searched everywhere for them. Maybe I just left it in the last hotel? She retraced her day. But I am sure I used them this morning. It was like wondering if you had left the iron on as you were boarding the train to the city.

That reminded her, that her mailbox wasn't locking as smoothly as it used to. She would have to get the handyman to see to that. As she drained the last of her tea, she looked out of her kitchen window and swore she saw something. Was someone watching her? The kitchen window was on the second floor, so she had never felt the need for curtains or shutters, but suddenly she felt extremely exposed.

Keep calm, keep calm. Her pathetic mantra was of no use. The feeling of being watched was unnerving. Solange had already let the whole world in to her private life. They knew what her kitchen table was like, what furniture she had on her patio as well and she covered her mouth and closed her eyes. They know what my bedroom looks like. They even know what sheets I sleep in. She had posted a photo to Instagram last week to show how the new fabric from her range looked as a doona cover that would be available for sale in the coming months.

It was time to get a security plan, a type of strategy. She spent some time looking online for blogs on the topic as she knew she wasn't the first person on social media to have some weirdos living out their fantasy by following her a little too closely or bullying her in such a publicly humiliating way.

She was still perplexed and a little bewildered that so many of her online trolls were making the same comment. 'I know what you have done.' The words ran over and over in her mind as she stared at the yellow envelope sitting in front of her. Another hand delivered message and the only contents, a simple set of hand-written instructions.

Chapter Seventeen

WORKPLACE DYNAMICS

THE IMAGE SHE HAD POSTED THAT MORNING had attracted a strong feed of positive comments. It was a shot of her morning yoga in the tranquillity room at the hotel spa. The staff had closed off the space especially for her and were thrilled with the result. Very "insta-worthy"! There was something very special about the shot that had resonated with thousands of her followers. Perhaps because it was a deliciously peaceful calming influence during the hottest and most stressful time of the year. Those weeks leading up to Christmas were always filled with false promises and looming deadlines. Looking at a soothing image just resonated with her followers. Except for a couple. The usual smart-arse comments by avatars with ridiculous provocative names. Most influencers were emotionless to them and just ignored or blocked them. One of them stood out for two reasons. The name was very targeted @watchyourback and the second – what they had written. 'I know what you did.' There it was again.

Solange had recently engaged two job share administrators, who assisted her remotely to respond to comments and questions on all her social media. Both had immediately highlighted this one to her as they felt it was unacceptable and felt very uneasy about it. They both also discreetly commented to her, asking if there was something they needed to know about. What had she done? She must be having an affair with a married man as it is exactly the type of behaviour a jealous wife would respond with - a public humiliation campaign. Secretly they also thought this would be very exciting as Solange was so squeaky clean and it might be good for her image to get a little roughed up. No such thing as bad publicity was a number one rule of marketing.

Solange simply messaged them back to say she had it under control, then she took a screenshot and instantly deleted the comment. On the inside she was crumbling. She knew what she had done, and she knew the devastating effect it would have on her reputation and her life. It was that clear cut. The end.

Panic attacks are strange creatures and sometimes enjoy taking their time to stir around and work themselves up. She used to think she could control them, but it was merely a case she could only delay them. Her breathing became a little shallow,

The look of absolute horror on her face when she answered the phone. She saw the name appear on the screen and knew there was no use hiding. She had to take the call. She also knew she would not be required to do any talking – just to listen. She was silent with the phone to her ear, and she was nodding obediently. The only word she did utter was, 'Yes, I understand.' And then she completed the call by pressing the end call button. She didn't say goodbye. There was no frantic note taking. Just her pale face and shocked slow movements following the call.

No one else but Orpheus observed it, he was noticing a lot of things about Solange lately. She was acting very strangely. Her usual calm and composed demeanour was only slightly ruffled, but he noticed it. The others went on talking over the top of each other if that was possible over the sound of Sonja harping on about financial projections and deadlines.

Following the phone call, Solange discreetly removed herself from the room. She was not one for a scene and she certainly did not want anyone asking too many questions. This was not for public broadcast. Biting back the tears she quickly fled to the ladies' room. Although there were easily twenty stalls, two of them were occupied. She quietly locked herself into one furthest away from the other occupants and tried to control her breathing. She would wait for her companions to leave before she would let out a deep moan, almost a type of chant that would expel the negative energy from her body.

Clearly these women were in for the long haul and all she could hear was the occasional woman clearing her throat and the other rolling off reams of toilet paper.

For God's sake just finish your business. Solange wished she could call out but instead she just counted the seconds in her head, resting her left foot onto the toilet lid and leaning over onto her knee. Despite being beside herself, she didn't want to touch any surface. The last thing she needed was a bout of diarrhoea.

The next sound she heard was someone knocking on the main entry door to the bathroom. The stalls fell silent.

Then one of the women giggled and called out, 'Come in.' Her voice was comical and the other laughed in unison calling out her name and a further silly comment. Clearly, they knew each other well. Next, they heard a man's voice.

'Hello. Is everything all right. I have just come to check on you. Erm, ahh… this is really awkward. But are you alright?'

The two women burst into laughter, chatting amongst themselves. Solange could just hear a few phrases from the women about not needing his help and cracking up laughing.

Solange wished them all away. But the man would not recede – she knew he was not the type to give up easily.

'I know something is wrong. I saw your face when you took that call. I am worried about you. Oh, this is very strange. But I'm coming in. I am making a complete fool of myself but I...'

With that the two women burst out of their stalls in hysterics, wiping the tears from their eyes to stop their mascara from running. They were clearly a little tipsy Orpheus observed by the way they were wobbling out on their high heels looking like newborn foals. Either that or they were high as kites he thought. Now it was his turn to laugh. The women straightened themselves off while looking at their blurred reflections in the mirror and stumbled past the stunned Orpheus.

'Good man. You go win a heart.' The taller one slapped him on the shoulder blade causing him to cough. He waited until the show was over and then went to the only stall with the door shut. The red engaged sign warning him off, but he insisted.

'Solange. I know that is you in there. I can tell by your shoes. Well, your shoe. I don't know why you are standing on one leg. But I want you to know I am here if you need someone to talk to or a shoulder to cry on.' He knocked again and waited, then watched as the door slowly opened.

She looked very pale like she was going to pass out. He grabbed her by the arms and sat her down on the toilet lid. They both winced but she was thankful as it was that or landing on the floor.

What Orpheus would give to find out who was on the phone. He loved a bit of gossip. Who said what? Now he had to be patient and casual.

'Hey there. Just breath normally. Whatever has just happened. It will be fine. Look I feel like a complete dick standing in the ladies' toilet. This is…' As he was delivering his "I'm a nice guy" speech they were interrupted by a new arrival, they could practically hear the woman screech to a standstill when she saw Orpheus.

'Oh. Hi. Look we are busy here right now. Can you just give us a few minutes and we will be all done here?' The woman raised her eyebrows and backed out towards the door.

Now Orpheus felt like asking Solange to move over as he was feeling a little flushed in the cheeks. He really felt like a chilled Sauvignon Blanc or a cheeky little Pinot but now wasn't the time. Or was it?

'Solange, why don't we go to the bar. I am sure a quick glass of bubbles will help. It seems to be a cure-all for most ailments.' He held out his hand.

His pleading eyes seemed to win her over and she reached out to accept his helping hand to steady her. She appeared very frail, like the delicate shell of a former prima ballerina. A very tall ballerina. She was easily a foot taller than he was. He reminded himself to investigate those men's shoes that have a discreet platform built into them. He was forever seeing advertisements for them in airline magazines and now because he had searched for them online, they were always popping up in the advertising bars of his feed.

Solange insisted on washing her hands well with soap and then splashing some water on her face. Orpheus followed suit, and this made them both laugh. At that moment the main door opened again and this time it was a security guard who instantly recognised the VIP duo. The images of these guests had been burned into his retina. He was under all kinds of instructions of how to look after them, but he didn't think he would find them in this predicament. He just kind of stood their staring at them as he pondered what to do. It was an awkward moment like walking in on your parent's mid act.

'Hi.' That was all he said and gave an awkward type of fan wave.

'Oh hi. Yes. We are all done here. All good. Yup fine.' Orpheus who was easily half the man's size just skirted around him.

And with that Solange and Orpheus excused themselves and headed for the bar. The sadness and emotion of the moment washed away as they laughed at what the security guard must have thought. Solange felt her shoulders drop and she genuinely left the phone call far behind as she took the first sip of the tall cold glass of bubbles in front of her.

They chatted for over an hour about all their upcoming projects and of course about Orpheus' infant son. He went on about how they were inseparable; their lives were one. However, Solange did note she had never met the child and noted that Orpheus was so often out without him.

He was still busting to find out who had been on the phone. So, he went there and just asked her outright. 'I must ask. Who was on the phone that made you so upset?'

She stared at the bubbles rising in her glass and wished he hadn't gone there. 'Honestly it was just a ghost from the past.' She simply nodded her head and flicked her hand as if to brush the bad news away.

He wasn't letting her get off with it that easily. 'No, I mean you were so disturbed. Who did this to you? What did they want?'

He isn't going to let this go. That little devil of worry sat back upon her shoulder but she genuinely hesitated. This could turn south very quickly, but he was so nice and a sincerely caring person. No, she would keep up the act - everything was fine. She was good, and she would be able to look after this.

'I really appreciate your concern and your chivalry chasing me down to the ladies' toilets. Now that was a very brave act.' They both laughed. 'But the phone call was just a client pushing for more than I am prepared to give. You know that sort of thing happens all the time.' It was now or never. Start the escape plan. She shifted herself off the seat and gulped down the last of her champagne causing her to burp unexpectedly which gave them both a laugh and on the momentum of frivolity she continued to walk and talk. 'Time to head back to Sonja. I must see her about a few items from the planning session. Then I need to get ready for the dinner. These photos don't take themselves you know.'

She promptly thanked Orpheus and before he could convince her otherwise, she took off in a tiny run blowing kisses from the palm of her hand and mouthing her thanks. He was astounded at just how quickly that had happened. She had just disappeared. He ordered another drink and let the curiosity eat away at him. He didn't want to go back into the dragon's den, he wished he was done for the day.

They were the best of frenemies although Solange, who was clearly not expert at reading into body language or comprehending sarcasm, genuinely believed they were all her friends. Well, they were... but not exactly the type of friends you could really be that open and honest with. Solange was desperate to rally Ivy, Orpheus, and Amanda into her friendship group. She was prepared to take the friendships to the next level and make a genuine commitment. She had a plan.

In their world of all things glamorous and shiny, she felt the best gift she could give them at Christmas was one of deep sentiment. What could she give that would really leave them with the understanding that she felt they were like the siblings she never had? The family that she longed for and a genuine friendship group, like those she envied when watching sitcoms? She had worked out the perfect gift and was prepared that her loss of these precious items would be her gain through the friendship that it would help to foster.

Sonja was annoyed at the delay and showed her impatience when Solange and then finally Orpheus returned to the meeting room. She had an announcement to make, she loved the good news stories and this, while it was a given, was certainly good news.

'I am delighted to announce our superstar fashionista Amanda has been invited to be the ambassador for Culture Constructions.' She clapped her hands and encouraged the others to join her, then she read from the email. Amanda cringed at the use of the outdated term "fashionista". 'Culture Constructions is a forward-thinking fashion label that promotes the unity of world fashion. Their new season range is to be called the Ikebana Collection and Amanda will be the face of the range, featuring stunning oriental printed fabrics with a modern infusion. Amanda has been selected to wear the key piece of the collection, the padded cape kimono. She will make headlines in this; it will take our breath away.'

Of course, they all knew who Culture Constructions were, but Orpheus laughed out loud. 'They sound like a building company with a Japanese florist... oh, oh, and the modern infusion sounds like something from a menu.' He laughed at his own joke, and it was so bad the others couldn't resist laughing, even Amanda had a laugh. More at Orpheus who was looking rather odd and just blabbing on.

The afternoon had fallen apart on Sonja, she had been cornered by an overeager and a very drunk Orpheus trying to convince her she should be pushing for him to appear on Dancing with the Stars or a cooking competition show. He had even tried to persuade her he could be a wild card entry for Married at First Sight. Despite the fact he was already married, he believed the producers would like the twist it would bring.

She literally threw her hands in the air and told everyone to go forth, do their thing, enjoy the resort and post about it. They would meet back at the rooftop bar for cocktails and presents. They had arranged a type of Secret Santa and were all very curious as to what and who they would get a gift from.

Sonja was shattered, her hot flush seemed to be blowing off the Sahara. She was imagining sliding into one of those ice baths she had seen footballers jump into after a rough game. Then she dialled the internal phone in the conference room directly to housekeeping and asked them to prepare a bath of chamomile tea and ice. Yes, ice! she repeated. She also requested a bottle of champagne – not sparkling wine! Champagne! She shouted into the phone. Without further hesitation the housekeeper started the process to ensure their VIP guest did indeed have everything she wished for. Behind the scenes food and beverage staff were filling large tubs of ice and placing them on room service trollies, then covering them with crisp white linen cloths. The others were steeping enormous tea pots of their finest. The bar staff simply popped a bottle of Perrier Jouet Grand Brut into a polished silver ice bucket and debated on taking one or two glasses. They discretely packed the second one – just in case. When Sonja arrived in her room twenty minutes later, she could smell the lovely tea permeating the room. The air conditioner had been set on a comfortably low temperature as requested. She was suitable impressed; the bath was exactly as she imagined, and the Perrier Jouet was indeed the Champagne of Champagne. Then she gingerly lowered herself into the bath and could almost hear a sizzle like a fire being extinguished.

Parfait! She exclaimed in her limited French to no one but herself.

An hour before they were all due on the rooftop. Solange had arranged a private meeting in her suite for Ivy, Orpheus, and Amanda. They were all curious as hell to learn what she was up to and arrived within minutes of each other.

First thing they all did was check her room was no larger than theirs. Which proved to be true. They were all given exactly the same sized suites, luxurious apartment sized spaces with deluxe bathrooms, divine balconies and fabulous entertaining areas. The sound system was remarkable, and Solange had her favourite playlist on of gypsy jazz which instantly put them in the mood for fun. She also had the staff fill the room with candles which added to the atmosphere. But the thing their eyes were all instantly drawn to was the bar set up. The largest item was a glass water dispenser with a small tap on the front. A row of ornate antique pale green reservoir glasses. Displayed in front of this was a stack of coffee cup saucers, a glass pot of sugar cubes and an ornate silver device that looked like a small cake trowel. Oh, how they all loved a surprise, and this had them all intrigued.

Solange was also excited she had been planning this surprise for a while. When they were all there, she made her announcement. 'Well as it is Christmas, I have a little surprise planned for you all.' They looked at her with wide smiles and eyes like small children being told a story. 'I am going to make you a special cocktail. It is made with something that was banned for many years but has made its way onto the market again.' Their minds boggled until she walked behind the counter and produced a bottle of Green Fairy Absinthe.

'Awesome.' Orpheus was clapping his little yellow hands. This was the same excitement he felt like when he had his first cigarette behind the school gym, only that didn't end well and somehow, he felt this might not either, but he was in. For this spirit had a reputation for making people crazy. He was all up for that - surely a little crazy never hurt anyone.

Amanda asked everyone to make a pact. There would be no photos or posting of this on social media. She had a reputation to uphold.

And all Ivy wanted to know was what was taking so long. She wanted to taste the Green Fairy. She had heard that Ernest Hemingway was all over it and had even named a cocktail of his own creation. 'Death in the Afternoon'. She almost shivered with anticipation and was surprised at Solange for making this suggestion as she was the most conservative person she knew.

Solange was quick to point out it was actually legal. Their faces looked doubtful but not wanting to ruin the moment of intrigue she felt she had to assure them that a 500ml bottle was only seventy-five dollars at Dan Murphy's. It wasn't often the four of them were silent but at this moment they all went on an adventure together. Wide eyed they all watched Solange as the show began. She held the glass in her hand. 'This is called a Pontarlier glass or reservoir Absinthe glass. They are designed specifically for this drink alone as it has a reservoir to aid in measuring out the spirit. I am sure you recognise them as they are the most iconic glasses from the Belle Époque. The choice of glass is very important as it will enhance the experience of tasting the absinthe.' Next, she expertly placed the silver slotted spoon over the top of the glass, which she advised them was called an absinthe spoon. They were entering a new world, an unchartered exciting new world of cocktails, new phrases, and accoutrements. An absinthe spoon! They all wanted one now. Amanda had already decided she was going to buy a cocktail bar to match her Hampton's style furnishings and an absinthe spoon would be proudly on display so she could tell people all about the process. She wanted to recreate this moment for herself.

'It is an all-natural spirit but at a very high proof. It is about 50-80 percent alcohol.' She tried to stress this to ensure that everyone was onboard. They all nodded as if she was about to inject them with truth serum. Then she placed a single sugar cube on the slotted spoon and moved the glass under the chilled water tap, ever so gently releasing the water so it gently dropped onto the sugar cube dissolving it before their eyes. The Listerine green colour started to fade and was replaced by an opalescent milkiness.

'Adding the sugar to the water opens the spirit up, it helps the fragrance to blossom.' They were mesmerised watching the chemical fusion before their eyes. Patiently, glass by glass she created a little serve each for them.

Orpheus who was still confused about what a Belle Époque in fact was took a big gulp and coughed at the strong unexpected burn, he believed the drink tasted and smelled like paint thinner he had been expecting something more like a crème de menthe flavour.

To Amanda it looked and tasted like medicine, but it was also fashionable, and she wanted in. This was so new but old. Suddenly she felt a jolt and her legs felt a little wobbly. Clearly it was also fast acting. This felt so liberating.

Inhibitions were thrown to the wind and Ivy usually over cautious and vigilant, felt she was in a safe enough environment to let her hair down a little. She too experienced the instant buzz the little drink with a big punch supplied.

On their second round they were all laughing about the events of the day without any reserves and Sonja was an easy target. 'She got herself in such a fluffy state.' Amanda's tongue felt a little heavy and she mispronounced the word fluffy, so it sounded like ph-warph-fee. She tried to say it again and mangled it. They all laughed, and Ivy even snorted. This set them all off in hysterics.

Popping a bottle of champagne Solange declared she had an announcement. She had their attention when the cork popped out with such force it hit the ceiling and left a slight mark. Like naughty children they all covered their mouths laughing.

'I have been wanting to tell you all something for a while. Shush… shush!' She wobbled about in her heels with her index finger across her lips. They stopped chatting and started to listen. 'I want to tell you how special you all are to me.' She continued to fill up the glasses and handed them out while she was talking. 'As you all know I am a single child. In fact, I am single in so many ways… no husband, no boyfriend and sadly no parents. I really have no one in my life other than my work.'

They all looked at her as if she was about to turn up the lights and tell them to leave, the party was over. But quite the opposite was true.

'I want to tell you how much you all mean to me. And even though we have only known each other for a few years, and well you Orpheus as the newest in the agency... well I still feel like I have known you for years as well. So, I need you to know I think of you like, well this is going to sound very daggy, but I think of you like siblings. Yes, we have our moments, and we get shitty with each other, we get a bit jealous but on the good side we all get it. We get how hard this industry it. We work in a world that everyone thinks is so luxurious and easy. It is anything but easy. It is the hardest thing I have ever had to do in my life, and it has been the most stressful being in the public eye in this way with so many people judging and saying awful things. At times honestly, I have just found it way too much. But then we catch up together each month and I see I am not alone, and it isn't just me.' Her head was starting to swirl a little bit, perhaps she should have used a nip measure rather than free pouring the absinthe.

'I want to give you all a gift that money can't buy. A gift from my heart. A gift from my past.' And with that she walked into the room beside her and came out with three beautifully wrapped gifts all the same size and same wrapping. They didn't have a card and there was no way to distinguish them. She simply handed them out one at a time. When they had all taken a sip of their champagne, they thanked her and were very keen indeed to see what the gift was that money could not buy. Orpheus was first to unwrap, and the look of disappointment was clearly evident. Amanda looked at him and imagined what a little shit he would have been every single Christmas morning.

Oh, his poor parents. But then she looked at the gift in front of her with confused eyes and saw the same expression on Ivy's face. They had each been given a very old-fashioned hand embroidered picture in a frame that smelt like an op shop and didn't reflect Solange's style at all. They all just looked up to her for explanation for there had to be a good one.

'These three tapestries were handed down to me from my great grandparents to my parents and eventually to me. They were in with a large box of other items that hold a lot more significant memories for me. But I felt because there were four of them, if we each had one, we would always be connected.' She hesitated and then awkwardly added. 'Like siblings.'

The gesture was not lost on them. They all did a group hug and by now most of the glass of champagne was already gone. They were becoming all emotional and expressing feelings they would normally never have shown. It was a unique moment for all of them. A time when they genuinely did feel like they all belonged together. It was special.

Orpheus thought his allergies might start playing up and he could feel a tickle in his throat. Was that the absinthe or the start of an asthma attack? 'Honestly, I don't know what to say.' He was about to tell her it really wasn't his thing.

He was going to decline the gift when she embraced him gushing. 'I know. It was a big decision, but you are truly worth it. Our friendship means this much to me.' She even kissed him on the cheek.

He was a little star struck at that moment and dulled down his strong filter as he sat possibly the ugliest thing he had ever been given beside his chair and struggled to think where on earth he would put the damn thing. It was a nice gesture, but it wasn't going on display anywhere too public in his house.

The other women were genuinely touched at the gesture and vowed to remember the moment forever. While Amanda had reservations as to where she would display such a gift, she was a lot kinder in her approach. She had recalled reading how the Governor General was forever being gifted items that would only ever go on display when the dignitary or a representative from that country was visiting. She decided if Solange ever visited her house, she would put it on display during the visit and then keep it safely tucked away at other times.

Ivy on the other hand was delighted as she already had a gallery wall of all the quirky things she had collected over a lifetime of travels, and they made up a wall of curiosities as she had often referred to it. The wall was now consuming almost every wall in the house and made for a conversation starter. This was a very welcome addition to the collection.

As usual Solange did not pick up on these thoughts and felt relieved that everything had gone so well. She poured another glass for everyone, and they all agreed a quick round was a good one as they had to meet Sonja for drinks at the rooftop bar. Luckily for them Sonja was feeling a little cooler, well she would describe herself as comfortably chilled. Plus, she had enjoyed the whole bottle to herself. They were all on par when they met up and none of them suspected the other for being a bit legless.

Once again, they all agreed they wouldn't put any posts up about the night as it was private and special. They wanted to keep it in their clique. The one photo that was permitted was when Ivy, Amanda and Solange held their drinks in the air to salute a fun evening. The city lights were twinkling in the background and for once the women were not putting on their usual "duck" faces performing for the camera. They were genuinely relaxed, and it showed. Orpheus was tasked with taking the photos while Sonja was siding up to a terrified waiter her hormones obviously out of control. One phone at a time he snapped a few shots and then with Solange's phone he did something else. With deft fingers he quickly manoeuvred to an app, clicked a few settings, shut down back to the home screen and placed the phone down on the table.

The evening was one of the most memorable they had all had together, laughing and sharing the funniest of tales until the staff were yawning and gently reminding them of the noise levels a number of times until it was evident, they needed to politely dim the lights and close the bar. The team were really none the wiser, they all stumbled off to their beautiful suites to sleep the night off under their plump feather down duvets and high thread count sheets dreaming of green fairies.

Luckily the following morning was breakfast at leisure which interestingly enough was all taken as the room service option with double coffee orders on most. Late check out was also the order of the day. And for the first time in a very long time. Amanda had forgotten to pre-set up a post for the morning. Her followers were a little confused they were experiencing "fear of missing out" big time!

Chapter Eighteen

HIDDEN IN PLAIN SIGHT

IN HER WILDEST DREAMS Solange could never have imagined her research for her next design collection would open her mind in this way. She continued exploring the world of extinct or critically endangered Australian native flora and fauna but could not escape the intriguing night parrot – she was caught in its spell or was it a curse?

Believed to have been extinct for over one hundred years the Australian Night Parrot had caused quite a stir with ornithologists across the globe. Millionaires had put a cash bounty for a bird - dead or alive. Currently only three people had been able to say they had spotted a bird alive. There were tales of lies and deception, false hopes and dishonest behaviour. The world had gone mad, and it was irresistible not to investigate further. She dived in with the innocence of a child.

Living in plain sight amongst its natural habitat of the harsh spinifex, the bird continued to torment experts who came to remote arid landscapes equipped with the latest gear to photograph, record and for some, potentially trap a specimen. And yet a live bird hadn't been identified in over one hundred and fifty years, or had it? The reports had her confused. She was also puzzled as to how an extinct bird could be given so much attention. After all extinct meant final – gone. However, as she discovered this clever little bird was now actually on the endangered list.

So, while it had previously been added to the extinct list, was the fact it had been found make it de-extinct? She Googled to see that there was such a term and pondered as to what that really meant to her. It had simply been there all along. We just weren't looking in the right place for it. And now that it had been found there was still a great deal of mystery surrounding it for certain photographs had been discredited and the recording of the bird's call falsified. Solange had made enquiries and was prepared to travel the great distance to see the environment and perhaps catch a glimpse of the rare bird herself. But as she soon discovered she was not the only one. The mysterious bird was to be kept as just that for a while - elusive to outsiders.

The location is a 56,000-hectare reserve purchased from a cattle farmer by Australian Bush Heritage. It has been named Pullen Pullen Nature Reserve for this was believed to be the name given to the bird by the traditional owners of the land, the ancient Maiawali people.

There is a cloak of secrecy around the distinctive haunting "ding-ding" call made by the Night Parrot for fear that by releasing recordings of the call would allow poachers to potentially trap the bird. There were many that were so desperate to hear the call this was a truly special moment in history, but the conservation group prevented the release as the bird is critically endangered and needs to be given time to build up numbers in the wild without any disturbance. She could understand this need for privacy as she herself was feeling threatened and flighty.

The bird has many enemies, and it was no wonder. It was a miracle that it was rediscovered and should be protected and allowed to thrive. For all its time on earth it has been threatened by many predators; wild raging bush fires that destroy its nesting areas in the spinifex, years of successive droughts depriving the bird of fresh water, foxes and wild cats picking the birds off, stalking them every night. Predatory poachers tempted by cash would steal birds and eggs without regard for their future.

Obsessive twitchers with a vast intelligence network would be prepared to go to extraordinary lengths and travel long distances to see a bird as rare as this so it could be ticked off their "life list". Serious birdwatchers would give anything to be able to spend time in the presence of this elusive creature to write their carefully constructed notes; and while respectful and considerate they would undoubtedly arrive in their thousands inadvertently trampling through the sun-bleached spinifex and stirring up the desert sands.

The harshness of this landscape was already painting a picture for her. She had a reverence for this place, a place that could be home to such a colourful sly creature. It astounded her. She was searching for atonement herself for the sins of her family which seemed to be the same for Bush Heritage Australia, they wanted to give the bird another chance. For it was the interactions with humans that almost caused their demise in the first place and this was a way to make it better.

Guilt followed her around like a shadow and this would be a perfect way to give back for something she felt responsible for destroying. Like a life for a life. She would beg her forgiveness from the universe for the wrongs of the past and make amends in this new way. The Night Parrot was calling to her.

She would offer to create a series of paintings of the bird and its habitat, to tell the story of something found. She would call the collection "De-extinction" for this was her phoenix rising from the ashes of the arid harsh desert of the Australian bush. Solange planned to donate all proceeds from the collection to a nominated charity for the bird. She had already commenced painting the hero piece at the Ambassador's residence and it was named "Atonement" - her encoded message of apology for what she had done to aid the destruction of cultural heritage of her homeland. This was her silent peace offering. Little was Solange to know the impact the legacy of her decision to paint and feature this rare bird in such a way would have.

She would wash away her dirty secret and her guilt by supporting a worthy cause. This she believed would bring her reprieve from the sins of the past, the recompense she was so desperately seeking.

Chapter Nineteen

SECRETS

IVY WAS FIRST TO ARRIVE AT THE RESTAURANT. She was always early. She wanted to select the table and especially the seat. Ivy would never sit with her back to a door. She wanted to see them coming.

Instead of scrolling through comments on social media, she kept her phone in her satchel and retrieved one of the five books she was currently reading. It was by no accident she had the book open with the following quote highlighted.

"Appear weak when you are strong, and strong when you are weak." – Sun Tzu. Yes, she was reading The Art of War.

Solange wasn't sure if this was a warning or advice. But it had the desired effect, and she felt the air heavy around her. What does she know? It was a game of cat and mouse, and sly self-conscious Solange was most definitely the latter. Why has she agreed to meet me here? She had always thought of Ivy as a friend but there was something about Ivy that had always put her a little on edge.

Ivy was always so confident and self-assured. She didn't seem to ever need to ask, everything was always offered. Was it out of fear that people reacted like this? It was the same reason Solange agreed to meet for lunch, she simply would not have refused.

Solange felt they were friends but knew the threshold and would not step any further into it. She was okay just where she was. A little nervous she knocked her glass and spilt it across the table. Waiters rushed over, fussing over the two women – they knew exactly who they were. The manager had to stop all the staff from trying to have a peek. He tried his best to keep everyone calm.

'Oh, I'm so silly. I am a little tired as I didn't sleep well last night. I have so much on my plate at the moment.' Solange kept putting her hair behind her ear, a nervous tick Ivy had observed her doing on many occasions. She kept repeating the action as if to distract herself. Then she straightened out the replacement napkin the waiter had just placed on her lap and began to fuss over matching the edges. It didn't go unnoticed with Ivy, in fact it was distracting and very annoying, she reached her hand out and placed it firmly over Solange's hand.

'Solange get a grip. Honestly you need to sort yourself out. You are looking a little ragged. This just isn't you at all.' Ivy was looking straight at Solange, and she seemed to be showing genuine concern. 'I noticed at the Christmas party you were even more withdrawn than usual. Is it the workload? Is it Sonja? She can be a right bitch… well all the time. What is up?'

'No, honestly, I am just tired I am working on too many things at once. I am just not good at managing my time.'

'You do have people to assist you behind the scenes? As in not just the interior design stuff. I mean admin. You do, don't you?'

'Yes, yes, I have a small team helping me with… helping me to keep all of that on track. But at the moment they seem to be bringing more…' She paused and picked up the wine list deciding it was not the place or time to be airing her dirty laundry. Smiling she instantly changed her tune. 'How about a lovely bottle of rosé? Here is one from the Languedoc region of France. It should be delightful. Do you know they are very strict about the standards of wine making in that region? They are part of the AOC, the Appellation d'origine contrôlée which ensures a protected designation of origin, like a certification. They have very strict rules and prohibit the use of irrigation.' She was about to continue her nervous chatter when Ivy stilled her by lowering her menu with her hand.

'Solange. We have known each other for several years. I know something is up with you. If it is Sonja just let me know and I will sort it out for you. It is her - isn't it?'

She knew there was no escaping this line of questioning. 'Look. Let me order a wine and then we can talk. I really need a wine. Will you share a bottle?'

The waiter that was hovering nearby moved quickly. He knew the look of a couple of women in a hurry to get that first glass of wine under their belt before they ordered lunch. Within moments he had two glasses of pale pink wine poured and the remains chilling in an ice bucket beside the thirsty women. He gave them a moment before he hovered again for their orders.

She gulped a little too quickly and her eyes watered. 'It is just the comments. I don't know how to deal with some of them. They are shocking. Actually, a little disturbing.'

Ivy raised her body up within her own frame. She knew how to deal with these types. She had her fair share of jealous keyboard warriors criticizing her and her dream job. They all mentioned how nice it would be to get paid sipping cocktails by the poolside or being given all sorts of gifts and gadgets relating to travel. They also mentioned she didn't deserve any of it and most of them used words like sucked, elitist and bitch. Ivy took no notice. She never did, not even from the first word of criticism she ever received. She simply hit the delete button. She didn't need to do a course or read a book to teach her how to deal with these types of bullies. She simply ignored them and just like that they went away. Well of course they didn't go away, they persisted, but to her they went away every time she pressed delete. In fact, she took great delight in doing so as it reminded her, she was the one with the power. The other thing that reminded her of this was every time she saw a new deposit hit her bank account.

'Just get your team to delete them. One tiny button. They don't even need to tell you they saw anything. Just delete them.' She was very firm, but Solange persisted.

'You don't know what they are saying. I am afraid, like actually frightened. I think there are a few weirdos out there who might attack me. They could be following me home for all I know. I keep getting a weird feeling someone is watching me and some of those messages... well they are saying things that...' She hesitated.

Ivy picked up where Solange had left off. 'Okay so to be honest, at first, I actually used to reply. I tried to reason with them, I explained how hard my work was and the sacrifices I have had to make. The hardest part of my job is making it all look so easy. But it fell on deaf ears. In fact, it even enraged some. So, in turn I got incensed and started threatening them, oh Solange some of the things I said I would do to those people was shocking and...' She hesitated. 'Very illegal. They were very, ahh... let's say forceful acts. I took delight in telling them I knew how to find them, and I would hunt them down and make them apologise in person. Wow I was like Liam Neesen in a movie, nothing was going to get in my way of finding these people. Then one of the spineless bastards reported me for my threatening behaviour and various social media outlets blocked me for twenty-four hours with something like a cease-and-desist notice. I was the victim, and I was the one they were telling to back down.'

Solange wished for a world of innocence, where people were nice to each other. A world of people like Mother Theresa, the vibe you got at a heath retreat spa, where people would gently greet you with 'Namaste', rather than threats of beating heads to disfigure faces. Yes, that would be preferable. She jolted herself back to reality and back to Ivy telling her how she had been hunting down trolls on social media. No wonder she had always had that vibe about Ivy.

'I'm telling you to just delete them. Report them. Block them. Delete them.' She shook her head. 'Seriously half of these people are just idiots who are stuck in dead end jobs. Board at work and probably being undermined by bosses that are just weak pricks who enjoy their power and use it on their staff. So, the staff want to get their revenge on the workplace and the boss, they want to assert themselves and so being the spineless pricks they are, they take it out on innocent good people like us. You are an easy target Solange. You really do open your soul online. Perhaps you need to be a little more cautious with your content. And showing pictures of your house is just inviting crazies into your life. Literally… people do know where you live.'

Solange wanted to throw up. That is exactly what she had been thinking about. That damn series of photos had included the front of her house which was so distinct, and all those photos of her bedroom. She shivered just thinking she may as well have put her actual address online. She wanted to move. She wanted to run away from all of this. She would put her house on the market and learn from this mistake. But that still didn't stop all the messages.

The waiter returned to the table and thought the lovely lady with the French accent was looking a little ill, like she might throw up. He enquired about her order, and she simply ordered "the" salad. Despite there being five salads on the menu. He thought better than to ask. He would tell chef the lady just wanted a garden salad and to put a few dressing options on the side. The other woman with short sharp black hair ordered the fish of the day. He had already had the whiting for his lunch and knew it was an excellent choice.

'I knew something like this was up. I just knew it. Seriously Solange don't let these little fuckers get to you like this.' Her use of such harsh language shouldn't have shocked Solange but in a restaurant like this, other patrons were listening in. How could they resist?

'I think I need to see a psychologist. I need some strategies to cope with all of this.' Solange put the palm of her hand to her forehead, then she reached out for her waterglass and placed it on the pulse of her neck in an attempt to slow herself down.

'Now, no need to be a drama queen. Sure, go see a phycologist, I'm all for it but I would also recommend you go and see someone else. Someone with a little more pow!'

Solange was left wondering if Ivy wanted her to go and buy a gun. This conversation was quickly deteriorating and going down a dark path.

'Oh God you think I mean like a gun or a hit man. Oh no, no, no… better.'

Solange really wanted this conversation over, although she was very intrigued. There would be no way in the world she could enter into anything untoward.

'I think you need to learn self-defence and not just the physical but the mental strategies as well. We work in a super competitive environment and now we have the added burden of weirdos feeling like they have the right to take a piece of us. Well, let me tell you they have no right to us at all!' Ivy slid her copy of the Art of War across the table. 'Okay, well maybe this is not exactly entry level reading, but I am sure we can find something for you.'

'Have you done self-defence classes Ivy? I did see that weird arm hold you put Orpheus in at the Christmas party while we were all laughing. I think secretly he was crapping himself.' Both women laughed at the memory. Orpheus looked so pathetic.

'I went way further than just self-defence classes at a YMCA. I learned from the best. I didn't want to buy a twelve-week course. I wanted in. I hired some nutcase personal security trainer, he was mental - but that was over a decade ago now.'

Solange physically sat back from the table. 'How did I not know this? You have never mentioned it. You never write about it. Wait up. What? Are you serious?'

'Solange I am serious. This was a turning point in my life, and it gave me the skills and confidence to stand up for myself in all circumstances. How on earth do you think I travel to some of these places solo and still walk out with all my belongings? I have been confronted physically many times and people quickly get the message not to try it on with me.'

'Like Orpheus. He stopped messing about with you.'

'Exactly' and she couldn't resist adding. 'Stupid fucker.'

They both laughed until Ivy spoke again.

'There is more I need to tell you. I think you are someone I can trust, and I am going to tell you something that not many people know.' She leaned in. 'Ivy is not my birth name and… there is a reason I had to change my name. I would never have been able to have the career I have if I didn't change it. A search on my birth name would tell a very different tale.'

'What did you do Ivy? What is this about?'

'I will leave it up to you. Search my birth name - Lourdes Guadalupe Magdalena Castell and you will see why I needed to shed that name and start again.' With that Ivy held her hand out in a stop motion, signalling this part of the conversation was over. The ball was in Solange's court if she chose to investigate it.

Her mind in overdrive and having never been confronted with a situation like this Solange knew not to pry any further. Ivy had given her permission to look into her soul and her fingers were itching to check her device but that would have to wait.

'Lourdes is a beautiful name. Isn't that the name of Madonna's daughter?' Solange had a quick laugh at herself for what she had just said as clearly Ivy was not the offspring of the world's most famous female singer. She regained her composure. 'It is just so calming and peaceful. It reminds me of… well obviously Lourdes but ironically that place is hardly peaceful at all. So many pilgrims, lining up to see the grotto. So many sad, sick people wishing for a miracle and so many stalls selling plastic water bottles in the shape of the virgin Mary.'

'Yes, it will be no surprise to you my parents were Catholic. My mother told me a story of how when she and my father were visiting the grotto it was the first time she felt me kicking in her belly. So of course, what else is a good catholic couple going to do other than call their baby Lourdes?' They both laughed.

Since Ivy had opened up about her past, Solange felt nostalgic and couldn't resist sharing her similar tale. 'You might not know exactly where from France I am from. But it is just a tiny village called Caunes-Minervois in a wine growing region in the southwest of France. It is the Languedoc-Roussillon region, but it has just become part of a new greater Occitanie region. You would like it as this area grows a third of France's wines.' She laughed at herself sounding like a tourist guide. 'There is a river that flows through the village and the water is said to originate or form part of ... well I don't really know but it comes somehow from Lourdes. Interesting hey?'

That was in fact very remarkable, and Ivy was all ears.

'In fact, there is a tiny church in one of the valleys and carved into the rock face are a series of reliefs, and in them are different statues of the virgin Mary. All in differing stages of disrepair. But they are a marvel none the less. It is a special place. Maybe...'

'I should go there.'

'Yes. Ivy, I think you would love the adventure. It is a little off the tourist track, but it is a magical little place. Whenever I go on my buying trips to France, I visit the small house that used to be owned by my great grandmother and was handed down through the family. I have it decorated it in a simple style and let it out on home share sites. Actually, I have nothing to do with that side of it. I have a local manager and cleaner for the house, they just run everything and the little place ticks away quite nicely. I prefer that it is lived in as it keeps a positive energy in the house. It feels loved.'

Ivy could already picture herself sitting by fountains and streams, sipping a chilled rosé and sampling local charcuterie and fromage. She also knew that by the evening she would have her ticket booked and would have found out where Solange's petite house was and would have booked it without Solange knowing. What a surprise Solange would get hearing about her adventure. What a surprise indeed!

Ivy finished the last of her wine and insisted on paying the bill. She had to rush off as she had a deadline to submit an article and felt the creative juices flowing. She felt a trip to France next on her agenda and couldn't wait to start planning. Now this was next level. There was nothing in this other than a personal adventure and the possibility of opening her mind to go back to the beginning, going back to her roots for a while. In fact, she would love to have a house of her own somewhere in a place like that.

This would be one of the first times she would put on her "out of office" message on her emails. Her staff could handle everything – they talked like her now. They knew what she would want from them, and she would ensure they had the tools to do it while she was gone.

They did the European double cheek kiss with ease and then Ivy gave Solange a genuine hug but held on just a little bit too long and looked her in the eye. 'What I told you is between us yeah? I have told you because I need you to know.'

Solange took a moment to pour herself the last of the wine and forced herself to drink a large glass of icy water. She looked around to ensure that Ivy had left before she googled her name. Her face told the story. This was not something she could repeat. It sent a chill down her spine and would never be spoken of again.

Chapter Twenty

WHAT HAPPENS ON TOUR

IT IS SAID THAT A PILGRIMAGE IS a religious journey of significance in one's life. Usually what is left unsaid is that it is done to atone for unspeakable sins and beg forgiveness.

Like a voyeur Ivy had researched the Camino de Santiago walk from St. Jean Pied de Port in France to Santiago de Compostela in Spain never once with the slightest intention of actually allocating the thirty days it would take. A lot of her followers had been urging her to take on the challenge as if it was like the Tough Mudder five-kilometre endurance even. It would take a lot more convincing than that, as she knew taking on the challenge of the "Camino" would probably break her, not the physical challenge but the mental self-flagellation that would occur with every step. Ivy knew at some stage in her life she needed to repent - but it would be on her own terms.

Ivy had created her own system of rituals to atone for her crime and it was a pilgrimage of sorts, but this journey was to mean so much more. She had questioned her religious beliefs many times and she supposed it was out of fear she didn't fully renounce her Catholic faith and upbringing. She considered herself a realist and there was just so much of the bible that didn't ring true for her… well she just had to look at the theory of evolution for a start and 'BAM!' as they say, 'the rest is history'. While she didn't doubt there really was a man named Jesus born to a woman called Mary, she did doubt a whole lot of other things. Like just what were the crusades all about? How could the Catholic church, or any church support killing in the name of God? And cancer? Well, what was that all about as well. She shook her head. Why not just let everyone get along and be healthy? Imagine a world like that?

But Ivy's world wasn't like that, it was full of memories of death and violence, of jealous people who were prepared to take away the most precious of all things - her mother. Then for her to turn her rage and to take the life of another. She knew that by doing this she was going to hell if she still believed in hell. She wasn't even sure of that. But right now. Today. Of one thing she was very sure. She wasn't going to let any of this get in her way.

While she was used to long haul flights, she had been upgraded, which for some is an unknown luxury but for Ivy it was almost part of her job. She would definitely be writing a blog about the amazing service on board the flight. It was exceptional, and she loved the serendipity of discovering something new. This flight had been the delight of discovery for someone feeling a little jaded with the whole luxury industry. Maybe it was the non-alcoholic elderflower flavoured gin – that way she felt like she was drinking but was able to arrive without a hangover.

Shifting to the new time zone always took a little bit of adjustment for which she allowed time but was impatient with herself. She had hired a local driver, so she could really sit back and relax. They headed straight for a tiny market village nestled at the base of the Pyrenees. If a miracle would happen, Ivy felt that visiting the Sanctuary of Our Lady of Lourdes after all it was her namesake, and she felt a calling that it was time to be cleansed. The holy waters that flow from the spring in the grotto have been claimed to cure people. She needed all the help she could get.

Lourdes was a couple of hours drive from Blagnac airport at Toulouse. This would give her time to catch up on some sleep in the airconditioned comfort of the luxury car. When they arrived, the driver cleverly had arranged to enter via a service entrance with the help of his brother-in-law who had the contract for rubbish removal. A lot of tourists equalled a lot of rubbish and the brother-in-law had become a very wealthy man. Others were out with their small stalls selling plastic bottles in the shape of the virgin Mary filled with water gathered from the stream. Jostling for every tourist dollar, the brother-in-law simply sent in a monthly invoice for services rendered. Plus, it gave him access to special entry passes making him a very popular person in the family especially with limousine drivers.

Ivy was impressed. They were there, and he had a car park in the shade. He offered to walk with her and take her on a fast track through the crowd, so she could see the statue in the grotto, and they could be on their way. She declined his kind offer and slipped him a fifty euro note to wait and leave her to herself, which he more than happily accepted and climbed back into his air-conditioned car, reclined his seat, and fell asleep in an instant. He had been booked as a set fare to drive her all day, so this was a cash bonus he tucked away, thinking of the bottle of Pastis he would buy later tonight.

She wanted some time to herself to absorb all that was around her and to understand why this place had such importance to her parents. Despite the heat and the crowds, she could feel it was a special place. She started to block out the distractions of the others around her, the sadness and despair she could see. So much sadness. People who were sick with physical injuries and in ways that couldn't be seen. She didn't want to categorise herself in this way. She was after answers. She wandered through the grotto in the snaking lines listening to people praying and begging for miracles. She could smell the wet earth, the sweat of the people around her and sickness. They were tired and worn, seeking forgiveness like her.

Quickly making her way back to the car she wrapped her knuckles on the window of the car and the driver shot to attention unlocking the car for her. The cool air helped to calm her unease. She asked him to drive her to a new location, which caused him to raise his eyebrows as it would be at least three hours' drive. Most people just stayed in the local area. He didn't hesitate though as it wasn't his car or fuel. He was just the driver. They headed off and he knew he would have plenty of time to get back to the depot by the end of his shift.

Once again Ivy made herself scarce as she caught up on much needed sleep and two hours and fifty minutes later they arrived at the destination. The Abbey carpark of Caunes-Minervois and this is where she would farewell her driver – a more than pleasant chap who knew the rules of when to speak and when to just drive. The tourist guides describe the village as a small medieval town in a distinct wine and olive growing region. The cobblestone roads were everything she had hoped they would be, their hard surface worn smooth with all the years of mainly foot traffic, for most of the roads were inaccessible to cars, which added to the charm. The driver helped to get her bags out of the boot of the car and offered to walk them to her accommodation, but she politely declined. She wanted to take in the atmosphere of this delightful village without interruption or unnecessary conversation. She thanked him and assured him she would give him and the company a very good write up. He smiled and set off on his journey home.

The local manager of the house was a woman named Célia who also worked at a local vineyard. She had messaged Ivy to say the key was in a lock box and she was free to arrive whenever she pleased. Célia would pop in and check on her over the next day or so to see how she was getting on but made a note she could call her at any time if she needed anything. Ivy enjoyed the casual nature of the message in "Franglish", it was worlds apart from the structured formality of her usual five-star world. She breathed in the fresh air and was a little startled as she heard the Abbey bells chime. She was standing right under the bell tower and just stared up like an innocent child watching the show. It was as if the village was heralding her arrival, the sound reverberated through her lungs. She felt deliciously happy.

As she had mastered the art of packing lightly, she was actually very thankful as she could only imagine having to pull a heavy suitcase across the cobblestones and down the narrow street to the house. Her French was rusty, but she was quickly greeted by a middle-aged couple arm in arm. 'Bonjour Madame. Quelle belle après midi.'

She returned the greeting with a simple, 'Bonjour' and a very generous smile. Did they just say something about skiing? But it is spring, and the weather is divine. She thought it was time to move the translation app to the front page on her phone.

Walking along and taking in the architecture of the co-joined villas all with their windows opened to the fresh afternoon breeze she could hear the sounds of young families laughing, of music playing and muted voices chatting. A few fluffy felines greeted her and curled around her ankles. They were irresistible, and she stopped to pat them enjoying the light down of their baby fur. As she walked, they followed her, the curious little creatures enjoying their new play friend. Calculating in her head, what stage of life one becomes known as a crazy cat lady, she wondered what life would be like with a pet.

And then she stopped. The soft scrolled blue letters signalled she had arrived at her holiday house, La Maison d'Art. Placing her bags at the door stop, she stepped back to marvel at the beauty of this lovely romantic home. The shutters were painted in a delicate shade of duck egg green and the stone point work on the front of the house was the work of a true artisan for it had stood for hundreds of years and was simply magical.

The neighbour Amy was at her kitchen window putting away her groceries from the market as she noticed yet another happy guest arrive next door. She knew that look. The traveller who had made the effort to find this special place and the look on their face was the reward of how it was worth every minute. She would pop over later with an invitation to morning tea as a welcome to the village. As a New Zealander who had now made France her summer home, she had always vowed to make every effort to make everyone love her new country like she did. She often took people to markets or to events such as onion festivals or olive oil tasting in neighbouring villages.

True to Célia's words, the lock box was discretely tucked away and once the code was entered the container popped open to reveal an ancient key with a pressed metal tag with the same font as the La Maison d'Art sign. The key really was ancient as it was part of a very old-fashioned long bolt opening mechanism. She did as instructed and turned the key three times clockwise and when she felt she could turn no further she twisted the handle and the door opened. The lights had already been turned on for her and when her eyes had adjusted, she could see all of the decorative finishes.

'Oh, little house you are truly divine.' Ivy was in love. Genuinely in love. 'There was absolutely no doubt you are the work of one Solange Lanquetin. She will be so surprised to learn I am staying here.' She shuffled her bag inside and closed the door. Walking further into the house she entered the small kitchen and dining area, filled with finds from brocantes which she knew as an equivalent to an antique store and vide greniers - the empty attic markets. There was nothing that shouted modern or factory made, except Ivy noted with appreciation, the washing machine discreetly tucked away behind a designer floral fabric curtain. The one thing that struck her immediately was that all the artworks in the house were originals. They were absolutely delightful, some in gilded frames and others in simple dark wood frames. Some were signed prints and others were the size of post cards.

The bed was soft and fluffy, the small library filled to the ceiling with books and magazines, the delicate working desk would be a treat to set her laptop up on. The shower enormous, the staircase heavenly. But it was the parlour on the top floor that took her breath away. The stone wall pointing once again a feature as were the French windows and the French double doors leading to the flower filled terrace. She whispered to herself while gazing out the window. How could Solange ever want to leave?

She was thirsty and made her way down to the fridge to put in a bottle of wine she had purchased on her way out of the airport as it was hot and would take a while to cool down. She was desperate and prepared to put ice in her glass if required. But when she opened the fridge she found a delightful bottle of local rosé with a note from the owner, she instantly recognised Solange's signature and beside it was a small charcuterie platter from the local restauranteur welcoming her to the village. Minutes later she was on the terrace with her cold glass of wine and her platter listening to tiny sparrows flying overhead, fussing about, and getting ready for their evening rituals.

This is heaven on earth. She said aloud to no one but herself as she sat back, closed her eyes and relaxed, genuinely relaxed for the first time in her life. I could do this. I could move here today and start again. She was startled for a moment as she thought she heard a slight banging sound. Oh, shit I didn't shut the door properly. She was second guessing herself, assuming the slight breeze had kicked the door open. She went down to the next floor and stuck her head out the window. When she heard a voice below.

'Allo, Bonjour. Bonjour Madame. Je suis Amy. Je suis de la maison de l'autre côté de la rue.' The woman wasn't dressed in a floral frock and apron as Ivy had imagined a neighbour would be dressed. For some reason Ivy felt she was in a time warp since she entered the house. The woman was dressed in a pair of beige chinos with a crisp white linen shirt and the collar pulled up against the afternoon sun. Her sandals were beaded nude and rose gold, glittering in the sunlight – just like her. She seemed like an oasis against the grainy cobblestones. Her hair was a dark bob of glorious unruly curls, and her skin had a glow that seemed to be an all year tan. Oh, what Ivy would give to have that hair!

'Ahh bonjour Madame. Je suis Ivy. Enchantée.' She was reaching the limit of her French. She still didn't have a clue what else the woman had said. Perhaps the kitchen was on fire for all she knew, but this woman looked like she had just stepped off a Ralph Lauren catwalk.

'Ahh forgive me but is that an Australian accent I hear?'

'Oh, is my French that bad?'

'Un peu – just a little. But it is so nice that you are trying.' They both laughed.

I'm Amy from across the road. I hope you don't mind but I saw you arrive, and I wanted to say I am going to the local restaurant in an hour for drinks and some… well… like tapas style food if you wanted to join me. I'm meeting up with some others, so it should be a fun night. They have some great live musicians and…'

'I'm sold. Let me just take a quick shower and I will be ready.'

'Oh great. You will love it. It is such a beautiful night, and you can't miss it. Mind you this sort of thing happens almost every night here in the summer so strap in for a fun holiday.'

'Perfect. Just knock on the door when you are ready to go, and I will be there.'

'Parfait. À bientôt.' She waved at Ivy and turned for the three steps that would take her home.

'Sweet.' Ivy returned to the terrace, drained her glass, and went to shower and wash off the day's travels.

True to their word Amy knocked on the door and Ivy was ready. They walked together the whole five hundred meters to the restaurant. The tables and chairs had been set up around the fountain under two enormous plane trees that Ivy was advised (and by many more people over the following week) were planted by Napoléon himself.

The evening was a delight, the music amazing and the food simply divine. The restauranteur and his wife were amongst the most hospitable people she had ever known and ironically none of them knew who she was. None of them were after five-star rating or feedback, they were just genuinely wanting to ensure she had a fantastic time and a celebratory welcome to the village.

During the evening Ivy had enquired about the river flowing through the village. She was curious to know if it was true the waters came from Lourdes. She suspected this might be a local secret and so she approached the topic with caution. George, one of the British men who lived in the village, immediately volunteered to take her there in one of his cars in the morning.

'One of your cars?'

'Yes, I collect them. They are all vintage sports cars and in perfect condition. I am a mad keen car collector and take them to car shows and drive or trailer them all around France and Spain. A right lot of fun that is, I'm telling you.' He looked a little like Richard Branson's younger brother and he seemed harmless enough. Anyway, she could hold her own, so she took up his offer.

As agreed, he collected her at eight the next morning, but she wasn't expecting the car at the door. He had selected for the trip a classic French car, a Citroën 2CV in sky blue. These things were designed to fit into tight spaces. He told her it basically ran on the engine of a souped-up lawn mower. And that is exactly what it sounded like. Someone revving their lawnmower at the front door at the early hours of the morning. She was sure there would be someone tsk tsking her at their doorway, but they all waved her goodbye with cheery shouts to have a good time.

He had the soft top roof off and as they sped through the empty streets, she felt a thrill like she was a teenager again. He was funny and sweet and totally harmless. They went to the Catholic church beside the river. The Notre Dame du Cros was an ancient stone church with a simple gravel entrance, and it seemed deserted. They parked at the entrance and to their surprise, there was a Mass going on, even with only five people in the church – including the priest. None of the worshippers took much notice of them as they were used to visitors popping in and marvelling at their little hidden gem on the hillside.

Next, they walked past a type of brocantes, but Ivy noted it was nothing like the usual charity stores in Australia. This was filled with treasures that looked more at place in a museum. The whole place ran on an honesty cash box sitting out the front on the table not even tied down. The innocence of this place had won her heart.

As they walked to the rear of the church the area looked like nothing more than a graded gravel carpark. Her kind guide motioned for her to keep walking and it wasn't long before they saw a stream and then the river. It was enchanting, and she could hear the water bubbling and gurgling as it made its way past the reeds. They continued to walk, following the natural path of the river for a few minutes when they came across a designated seating area.

'This is where they host the weddings, or you can just bring a picnic here if you like.' George commented.

'This is next level.' No need to hire arbours, nature already had that sorted. The light dappled space had a divine feel about it and Ivy knew it was very special magical place for someone to celebrate an event.

George didn't quite understand if next level was good or bad, but he could tell from the look on her face, she was mesmerised. They continued for another few minutes and he had to call her attention to the rock face on the hillside. Meters from her face Ivy could see a series of reliefs cut into the hillside, each of them featuring statues of the virgin Mary encased in glass just as Ivy had read about. At that moment Ivy so desperately wanted to believe, she wanted to believe the world could be a good place, that she could be forgiven for all the bad things she had done.

Later in the week Ivy was talking with Amy and the restauranteurs about their lifestyle. Amy was very direct, she lived in the village just for the warmer months, every few years she would have a winter there but overall, she would spend time in Spain or visit friends and family in warmer climate. She had had enough of cold weather growing up in New Zealand. This had Ivy's mind racing. She wandered past the real estate agent's office in the village, but it was as if time had stood still. The photos were all faded and the corners rolling. The descriptions were poor and the photos even worse. There were photos of indoor drying racks with underwear on them and kitchens full of dirty dishes. These people needed to attend a real estate sales course.

She went home and cracked open another chilled bottle of rosé. Google would help her, and it did. Within minutes she found five great options well worth a view. She could easily spend three or four months living in this tucked away oasis, she could still work from here writing as required as her business was ticking along well, and her product range was strong. The price of housing was so affordable in this part of France. This was truly living the dream and she wanted in.

After viewing a few of the properties she felt she needed to establish a solid relationship with a trusty notary to assist with legal matters, so she asked around her new friendship group and they all pointed in the same direction. The reputable Jean-François Dubois in the neighbouring village. The funny thing was that when everyone said his name to her, they all raised their eyebrows and smiled a cheeky all-knowing look. When she met him, she knew why! He was the most handsome thing she had ever laid eyes on, plus he was smart, he was single, and he was French. That accent was killing her. She loved it.

Jean-François met her in the reception area and shook her hand guiding her into his office. He pulled out her chair. Wait up! She thought. He just pulled out my chair! After that she would have signed anything he put in front of her, she was hopeless, and her legs felt like jelly.

Her attempt at making polite conversation was met with a bemused look. 'Est-ce un peinture de notre enfant?' Ivy pointed to a small child's painting in a frame on his desk. It was clearly of a man with dark hair in a striped t-shirt looking a little plump.

So charming was Jean-François that he took a moment to compose himself before he politely explained it was a little mix up with her words. Her translation was a little incorrect. "Is it a painting of our child?" Was perhaps not what she had meant to say. She had used notre which translated to our, when he believed she meant to use votre – your! Then he further explained actually neither were correct as he did not have children and he subconsciously pointed to his ring finger while nodding his head signalling he was not married. And now he was equally embarrassed.

To compensate Jean-François further explained, 'My nephew painted this picture of me at his school, but we all laugh as it looks more like Pugsley from The Adam's Family, and I hope that I…'

'Oh no. No, no, no, you look absolutely nothing like Pugsley. Far too handsome.' And with that she physically slapped her hand over her mouth to prevent any more brain spillage while giggling like a child herself.

This was not how he had expected this meeting to go, but this woman with the wide smile and infectious laugh made him feel a definite spark of happiness.

Jean-François had left the same impression on Ivy. Imagine what Solange will think when I tell her about all of this. Yes, just imagine.

Chapter Twenty-One

LET'S TAKE A CLOSER LOOK

DISTRACTIONS WERE EVERYWHERE, clawing at him for his attention. The baby was sorted, but the incessant clicking coming from the phone of the babysitter as she tapped out numerous messages was driving him insane. She was such a time waster. He had two hours before his wife would return from work and the babysitter had already put the slow cooker on for dinner. Technically he was free to keep writing, but there was something else that had been distracting him - Solange.

What was it about this woman that didn't quite fit the portrait she painted of herself? There was definitely something she was hiding, some dirty little secret she didn't want exposed. She was just too perfect. Her profile picture showed her looking down and away from the camera. He thought about that as well. She didn't ever really look into the camera in her photos. At first, he thought it was just her look, but now he wondered. Was it guilt? He had the imagination of a writer, and it was taking him to dark places. He had to find out and he knew he couldn't ever directly ask her.

What is that you are hiding from? What little secret do you have that will break you if it ever gets exposed? He smiled to himself and thought how a little research would get his creative thought process well under way. It might even help him to eventually tackle the three thousand words he had promised to write today. Yes. He would do a little digging on Solange for an hour and then he would dedicate a solid hour to writing.

He was writing the book in secret from his wife who he knew would not be impressed as he was supposed to be working on freelance jobs that would bring in a much-needed immediate cash injection. Producing a commercially successful book was like winning the jackpot and she wasn't a gambler – she had never bought even a scratchy in her life. The working title of his book was still to be determined however; he was already convinced he would write under the nom de plume Sterling James. He felt this name had quite a ring to it and would stand out – not this his actual name didn't. He always enjoyed the reaction on people's faces when they would ask for his name when he was making a reservation or signing up for a loyalty program. They always typed the name as if they had dyslexia, not sure what letter came next. He enjoyed making people feel uncomfortable. He enjoyed how it separated him from the mainstream.

He looked around to check Maddy wasn't watching him, but she was comatosed in the glow of her mobile phone. He typed in the web address of one of the many ancestry websites he had seen advertised on the television and was momentarily distracted by the first listing to present itself. Find out your past with our DNA testing. The message continued to explain that for only $135 excluding shipping/postage costs he could uncover all of Solange's secrets. Ordering the kit was easy but getting a DNA sample from Solange was going to be difficult. How on earth was he going to get it without her knowing? He tapped his index fingernail onto his front tooth while he pondered this problem.

Then he read on, watched a video, skipped over loads of fine print and detail including details on privacy statements, data collection and records. He also skipped over the detail explaining the test was for saliva and not hair for which he was already prepared. He was however pleased to read that once he had received the results, he would request they delete the DNA test results and destroy the physical sample. He felt confident nothing would be shared with third parties or link him to the data. He could barely contain himself with excitement, he felt like a spy on a covert mission. He promptly signed up using his pseudonym and the associated email address he had set up. He was secretly working on the web site but felt he had enough projects on the go so he put that on the backburner. Welcome Stirling thanks for joining us, let's start our exciting journey together. Your DNA test kit is on the way. He also had a post office box he kept private from his wife. He would now start to check it every day.

Again, he checked the time and now it was eating into his writing time, but he promised himself this one last task and then he would write. He texted Maddy and heard her groan as she got up off the couch. She glared at him as the coffee machine burst into life. She knew not to grind the beans while the baby was asleep, so she had prepared some earlier. That smell - he was in heaven. He reduced the screen and tapped away at an article he was writing and trying to sell to newsagencies on the "rise of the blogger" and "how buying habits have changed due to the trust they have in their social media brand ambassador".

Back to the really fun stuff, he took a guilty look around and typed the word "drones" into the Google search bar. He whistled out loud when he saw the prices. Wow there is some serious coin involved here! Up until now he had been using his mates' drone and was very skilled with it. He had been using it for a few months now, so it was time to invest in his own piece of kit.

Orpheus knew some of these things were so smart they were being trialled to deliver parcels, even fast food. He rubbed at the stubble on his chin and contemplated for that type money he would need to do a lot more research. Quadcopter, app-controlled robotics, camera and video drones... and I would be a drone pilot. He really liked the sound of it. But how on earth was he going to get this one past his wife? Father's Day was coming up and it was only a week before his birthday. Yes. He would combine both and tell her he would save her the trouble of looking for a present.

He would put $100 on the main debit card and the other couple of thousand on his private credit card. He had the statements emailed to himself which he kept on the low down. She didn't even ask so he didn't ever tell. He opened up his diary and rescheduled his book writing until tomorrow under the code name of a made-up news article. So many codes and secrets but he had a very good memory, he put this down to the fact he always insisted on having at least nine solid hours of uninterrupted sleep. To achieve this, he slept in the spare room while his wife was up and down to the baby.

His research was interrupted when an alarm went off on his smart watch to remind him he had an appointment. Lucky, he had set the alarm as he hadn't written down the details of the meeting as he really didn't want anyone else to know about it. He shouted out to Maddy to put his coffee in a take-away cup, then deftly saved documents and set his computer to sleep mode. He was in the car in no time and with hardly any traffic on the road he was in the car park at a large shopping centre precinct.

'Okay lady - are you stupid or what?' He said out loud as he strummed his fingers on the steering wheel. 'Right, now for the third time you are going to attempt to park your giant four-wheel drive. I bet the thing has never seen a dirt track in its life.' He shook his head and gave an over exaggerated sigh. 'Seriously, if you stuff it up again, I will get out and park the damn thing for you.' Now he slammed his hand onto the horn and threw his hands in the air. The woman seemed very frantic, and the sound of the horn didn't help. She seemed to be talking. 'Get off the bloody phone, seriously one thing at a time lady!' And with that he screeched his car around hers in a very dangerous manner. He had had enough.

Inside the car the woman was rattled enough from her frantic morning and had usually made it a policy to not talk on the phone while driving. She couldn't ignore the caller when that number appeared – the school nurse - she answered. The brief exchange quickly became a blur.

'Are you still there Mrs Bolton? … are you there?' It was just all too much for the anxious woman to handle. The phone call had arrived while driving to the airport, she was due to fly out for a conference, plenty of time to spare… and then the phone rang.

It was the school nurse. 'Hello is that Mrs Bolton? This is the school nurse. Now, there is nothing to worry about. Tom. Is. Fine.'

All mums know how these phone calls work, the calmer the nurse – the higher the chance that things were not fine.

'Yes. What has happened?'

'Mrs Bolton, Tom had a little accident at rugby training. Everything is all right. It sounds like you are driving at the moment. Can you pull over and I will let you know the details. But everything is fine.'

Her senses sharpened and all she could think was that he was most definitely not fine. She pulled into an outdoor shopping centre carpark, it was very busy and there were hardly any spaces. She stopped the car behind some parked cars and prepared herself for the conversation but then noticed one of the cars was ready to pull out. In a fluff she reversed her car at an awkward angle and allowed the car to retreat. Then she attempted to park in the space while continuing the conversation with the nurse.

'What exactly happened? Where is he now? What has he hurt?'

'So… have you parked the car yet?'

She lost her shit. 'I am trying but … oh… for god's sake.' She reversed and tried again. This time there was a guy in a sky-blue SUV giving her the death stare. She tried again. He was too close behind her and she didn't have space to manoeuvre. This time he blasted his horn and she nearly jumped out of her skin. It was the last thing she needed. She attempted the third time and the guy behind her started screaming profanities at her and swerved around her, she noticed a child seat in the back seat but no child and thought to herself. The poor child that has that man as a father.

'I want to know the truth. Just tell me.'

'Mrs Bolton, Tom has gone to hospital in an ambulance with suspected spinal injuries. The other nurse is currently on the phone with your husband, and he said to stay where you are and he will pick you up. Mrs Bolton…'

The woman just let out a cry that only a mother would know, like a rite of passage when something that is the most precious part of you is totally out of your control. She was staring straight at the uncaring man in the blue car and everything seemed surreal, even the look of that man, he seemed very odd. He gave her the finger; his finger was a distinct yellow colour, so very odd. Nothing made sense anymore.

Having manoeuvred past the most stupid woman on wheels, he expertly reverse parked into a car park marked for small cars only. He marvelled at himself for his driving and chuffed that only men really knew how to reverse park this well. Then he realised what a tight fit the space was.

It fits. Where is the rule book for what dictates a small car! He smiled to himself and felt very clever, despite the fact he had to hold his stomach in and only half open the car door to get out. He looked back and did feel the nose of the car was slightly poking out.

'Well sue me!' he thought and walked off with that cocky walk of his and it always looked as if his pants were just a little too short in the crotch. He had one last look and then re-assured himself if someone hit him it would be their fault. There were enough security cameras around here and he would be able to identify them. On he marched.

Arriving at the office of the herbal supplement supplier he was expecting his usual gushing from the receptionist but when she looked up her eyes widened a little and she seemed to look distracted when she greeted him. She was staring at him. He knew he often had this effect on women, they were always a little clunky around him at product launches, usually trying to hide their baby fat in oversized clothing and their tired circles under longer fringes. There was something akin to movie star status he felt when he was surrounded by his online followers.

But the look this woman was giving him was different, she looked a little concerned.

Maybe it is just that time of the month. Women are so hormonal! He knew all the signs. He seemed to be surrounded by hormonal women. He sat down in the relaxing waiting area surrounded by magazines preaching fitness and health, of course all supported by a good supply of herbal supplements.

An aroma diffuser was bubbling away on the receptionist's desk and the fragrance was a divine mix of sandalwood, geranium, vetiver, and a hint of citrus. It reminded him it was time to book in for a facial, it had been three weeks, and he was due. He would get Maddy to set up the appointment and then she could write a post for him about the visit. He was feeling very stressed, and this would be something to look forward to. Maybe tomorrow?

He really did like this waiting room, maybe it was time to get Maddy to re-organise his office to be a little more Zen like. He messaged her with a list of instructions including directions to prepare a new secret folder on Pinterest of "Zen office ideas" for him to discuss with her.

He could feel eyes burning into him from the others waiting in the sitting area. It was always that awkward moment when he wanted to say, 'Yes, it is me, Orpheus. People are always too shy to ask.' But just before he went to say anything to the others who were awkwardly staring at him, the director walked out in his usual warm and welcoming manner.

'Orpheus how are…' he was holding out his hand and then rather dramatically started slowing his pace in what was usually a very warm welcome.

'Wowa mate? What the hell has been… Oh… Oh okay, look quick come on into the office.' He quickly switched his hand away from the handshake option and placed a gentle but guiding hand on Orpheus' shoulder and whisked him away from the prying eyes of the others in the waiting room.

As soon as the door shut, the two men had a rather awkward moment where the director was just staring at Orpheus, looking between his face and his hands. Then he said rather oddly. 'Have you noticed it happening on your feet as well?'

Aware that leprosy was rare and pretty much eradicated in Australia, he didn't need to be too worried, but that is how he felt. He looked down at his hands and caught his reflection in the glass on a framed print on the wall. There were no large welts or missing digits.

'I give up!' He laughed. 'What is the gig? I don't get the charade!'

Discreetly removing himself from being too close to Orpheus, the director sat behind his desk and resisted putting his hand to his mouth. 'Orpheus it must be the tanning pills. Have you been following the directions on the bottle? What else have you been taking?'

Orpheus still hadn't said a word, he was confused, and he really didn't know what all the fuss was about. Yes, he had been taking the tablets, he had also decided it might work a little faster if he doubled the dose. Well, they were just natural ingredients found in our food after all he had convinced himself.

The director placed his hand out on the desk, palm up. 'Put your hand next to mine.'

Awkwardly Orpheus followed the instruction and cautiously offered his hand up for inspection. The difference was instantly blatantly obvious. His hand was a definite tinge of orange. It looked as if he had been peeling carrots all day.

He flinched. 'How on God's earth have I not noticed this? Holy shit! What the hell have these things done to me?' He pulled out his phone and looked at himself with the camera in reverse. He couldn't see it, but he knew if he stood next to the director it would be obvious.

The director repeated himself. 'How many pills did you take? Did you follow the recommended dose?'

Orpheus was flustered and embarrassed, he felt like a fool. How could he go to all the events lined up in his diary looking like this? Makeup, gloves, oh God he would be the next Michael Jackson. His world was spinning.

'You have taken more than we agreed, haven't you?'

Admit nothing thought Orpheus. Admit nothing, blame it on them, a couple of tweets and I will take them down. These arseholes can't laugh at me. He was getting frantic.

Attempting to calm him down and recognising the look of vanity terrorised before him, 'It's okay mate. It will just take a little while to get out of your system. Don't stress, everything will be fine.' Bloody damage control. Jeezzus… of all people this little start up prick. For fuck's sake calm him down.

'A simple solution. I will organise daily massages and you can start a cleansing regime immediately. I will get a formula prepared for you; this will flush your system. In fact, you will never have felt better.'

The director stood up from the desk and walked around to Orpheus, placing a hand on his shoulder, on the same spot as before. Like it was the safe, non-sexual, non-tan-contaminated place. He was doing it in a blokey reassuring way that a mate would at the pub. However, Orpheus had only ever seen it done in movies as he didn't really go to pubs that much.

'You see the product has a carotene-based colour additive, the same thing that gives food an orange tint such as carrots and pumpkins. Unfortunately, it does the same to people, especially when you take more than the recommended dose. It is going to take three to four weeks for your skin to return to normal.' He felt Orpheus stiffen up.

'Mate, I think it is probably best we give this whole thing a rest. You know… like the blogging thing you do with us. You know… just until you' and then he laughed at his own joke before he delivered it. 'Get your colour back.'

Orpheus felt as if he was getting a cease-and-desist order. How could they not want him? It was like an awkward teenage romance gone wrong. "It's not you, It's us." No client had ever left him before. He couldn't see what all the fuss was about. He was determined to see the tanning tablets through the full course. He wanted to be the face of the product and he desperately wanted a tanned face at that.

'But first I think we'll send you for a blood test, mate.'

Chapter Twenty-Two

BLOODLINE

TO BERNADETTE, MATHIEU WAS the open book she had already read and discarded. If only he would just piss off, always hovering about. No wonder half of the staff at the embassy were ready to throw him under the bus. How they despise him. She only had to tolerate him for a couple of hours today and then hopefully only a couple more after that for the rest of her life. There were some people you simply didn't want to waste your oxygen on.

As a courtesy Solange arrived at the embassy entrance to quickly exchange pleasantries with the Ambassador. He was an agreeable man who had good taste in clothing and wives. His current wife was a delight. She was so busy playing bridge and socialising with her bevy of diplomatic friends that she was more than happy to leave the decisions about the interior design with Solange. As a courtesy Solange ensured she had a token input. Something that could be written up in a media article at a later stage. And for Her Excellency Madame Durand that was all the involvement she wanted. She really did believe in leaving work like this to the experts which was indeed a relief to Solange.

Ambassador Durand offered tea and refreshments; the maids ready with the tea service set up in the private kitchenette beside his office waiting for the bell to chime. But there was no need. Solange politely declined as she was due to meet with Bernadette and Monsieur Arnaud shortly. This was simply a courtesy visit to update the progress of the project.

She had nothing to worry about as Ambassador Durand believed she was more than capable of seeing the refurbishment through without his interference. He made a slight comical reference to the fact he was sure Monsieur Arnaud would be capable of overseeing the project on his behalf. He was delighted at the fabric and paint samples and absolutely thrilled to hear about her artwork. It would truly make a statement on the parlour wall and would be a perfect conversation piece. He loved the story and the connection of a French artist. He also loved that the Smithsonian Institution refer to it as one of the world's most mysterious birds. Yes, he did like that concept, and it would be charming to talk about this topic during social occasions. Quite endearing.

Their meeting was short, and they were both pleased with the outcome. They were on the same page. Excellent. The Ambassador called for his driver to escort Madame Lanquetin on the short walk to the residence as his next appointment had arrived. The driver was a tall older gentleman, immaculately dressed in a suit with shoes that shone so she could see the reflection of the clouds in them when they walked outside. They exited the rear of the embassy building and it felt like they were going on a secret treasure hunt.

The gardens were exquisite and manicured to within an inch of their lives. The group of gardeners were dressed in well-maintained uniforms of identical green overalls and matching broad brimmed hats were removed as they greeted the driver and his guest in a most pleasant manner. Solange really did feel that by stepping through those embassy gates, she had stepped through a portal into a place of aristocracy she was allowed to be part of even if for a short time.

The garden was fragrant with the scent of gardenias and the heavy blooms of wisteria were trailing across an arbour along the garden trail. There was certainly no water restriction in this sanctuary. While she had noted the rest of Canberra was a dry dust bowl with scorched earth and gum trees that seemed to be about to explode into flame under the hot summer sun, in direct contrast this was like a real-life Monet Garden.

The entrance to the residence was a combination of terracotta coloured pea gravel with sandstone pavers highlighted by a series of planter boxes sat either side of the beautiful antique double doors. The cream colour of these doors had seen better days and was about to undergo a transformation, along with the wooden shutters Solange had ordered to frame the four double doors opening onto the gravel. The two-story house was a mixture of architectural styles and had originally been constructed in the late fifties. Solange had worked closely with the appointed architects who would ensure the building retained the authenticity of the original architect's plans but would be uplifted by a few additions to enhance the aesthetics and the practical logistic considerations for deliveries and food storage.

She could hear the diggers at work at the rear of the building for the newly approved swimming pool and tennis courts in order to appease the Ambassador. She had assisted in designing the courtyard terrace to ensure it flowed with the internal design concepts. There was no doubt it would truly be magnificent when completed and she was thrilled to be part of this project.

The front door was slightly ajar. As a courtesy the driver knocked to signal their arrival. However, Solange said she was fine from here. She had been to the residence many times now and was convinced the escort to the residence was simply a diplomatic formality. Security requirements ensured visitors were not able to stroll around the grounds unattended. The driver had been around long enough and felt comfortable enough to leave the lovely Solange to find the others by herself. After all she now knew this worksite better than he did.

The removalists were almost finished packing up the personal belongings of the family. They had moved into serviced apartments for the period of the refurbishment. There were still a few final things for them to attend to. They wore white gloves and treated the place as if it were a crime scene. Their shoes were covered with fabric booties a surgeon would wear even though the rugs had all been removed and the carpets all replaced. It was a nice touch though and showed a great respect for another's possessions and home. She appreciated the gesture.

Solange walked past the tapestry-lined hallway. These items were still to be removed for storage. It stung at her memory as she stared at the delicate work and marvelled at the craftsmanship it takes to create such an object of beauty. For Solange knew a lot about tapestries, having studied them in detail during her degree. She had studied at the Gobelins tapestry workshop in Paris. From the notes that had been handed down to her from her family history, she knew her great grandparents had been master tapestry artisans at the factory and her grandmother had started to work there but only for a short while before the war.

It had always been a great disappointment to her to learn the tapestries in her heirloom trunk were nothing but cheap imitations. Similarly, it had always baffled her why they would have kept them. They were very simple, in fact quite dull visions of the four seasons, the frames were ordinary and the thread of low quality. How she had wished they were originals with glimmering gold threads and luminous qualities. Certainly not for the monetary value but for the sentimental value and pride in her heritage. Since learning they were nothing of quality, she had always felt a little cheated by them. She was still appreciative of the connection they brought, knowing they had been possessions of her great grandparents. However, it was a little like being given a piece of glass in a ring instead of a diamond. Why would her family even have had them?

She was in a world of her own when she heard Bernadette call out her name. She turned to see the striking woman walking towards her with a large smile and her arms outstretched. They warmly hugged and kissed each cheek like lifelong acquaintances much to Mathieu's distaste. He instead greeted her with a soft handshake that she could easily have done without. He was of course pleased with her as not only had she delivered on her promise of a complete design package exactly to brief, but she had also excelled in the other area of their - as he described it "agreement".

She had managed to arrange the personal delivery of two paintings initially purchased at a supposedly deceased estate auction in a small sleepy French village which just happened to include two small and obscure paintings by none other than the French master Paul Bermond. The precious works were cleverly slotted in amongst a dozen other non-descript works forming part of the art consignment.

Solange had been under instruction from Mathieu to purchase that particular lot no matter the final bidding price, he had groomed her in the way she should bid, like a poker player not showing their interest too early. Luckily for Solange it had been pouring with rain in the days leading up to the auction and on the day, there had been further storm warnings. There were only a handful of people in attendance, and she was able to secure the purchase without drawing any attention to herself. She simply gave her shipping details to the clerk and completed the required customs paperwork for Australia, then began the nervous wait until a few months later her heavily packaged delivery arrived. As instructed, she carefully removed the two paintings from their frames, placed the painted canvas between thick cardboard and slipped them into a large, unmarked envelope.

To the auctioneers it was just a pile of old junk. Items from several deceased estates. To Solange they were two things; antiques that would be revived and given new life and appreciation in her upcoming projects and the other outright stolen property worth a small fortune exchanging hands in plain sight with receipts to prove the sale. She had already on-sold them to Mathieu for the princely sum of twenty-seven euro each noting on the invoice they were in simply, "Still life: pear and fig" and "Watercolour of a woman and child". Even the act of re-naming such fine works sickened her. It was the ultimate betrayal to an artist. She was no better than a common thief.

He didn't let on at all they had had any side dealings and instead remained completely detached. He had been thrilled at the sight of the envelope when Solange had presented it to him in the carpark of a café earlier in the day. He had briefly studied the works in his car before brazenly walking the envelope straight into the embassy and slipping it into a diplomatic bag addressed to his partner in France. Smiling at this clever ruse, he could only begin to imagine the smile on his lover's face as he opened the satchel to see the beauty it contained. The private collection they had already begun to amass would soon be complete with a few more of these gems.

Bernadette was far too focused on Solange to notice any unease. They naturally walked to the main parlour which was now devoid of all furniture, fixtures and fittings. This was more the blank canvas Solange enjoyed, it signalled the start of something very special. A new beginning.

She pulled out her phone and went to take a photograph when Mathieu prevented her. 'Ah Madame. This is on the grounds of an Embassy. You do not have permission to take photographs on the property. The signage at the front clearly displays the…'

'Oh, don't be so stupid Mathieu. She is a designer. It is what they do. She needs it for her records.'

He was incensed. 'Madame did you mean to be so rude or is it perhaps you were not thinking when you said the word.' And he paused for effect. 'Stupid!'

'Yes, I meant what I said. Plus, the Ambassador will enjoy seeing the before and after photos. I would also like to have copies for my records.' Bernadette continued without hesitation.

Mathieu was truly enraged by this behaviour. This woman really was extraordinary. She knew no bounds. He had had enough and excused himself to go and speak to the Ambassador about her immediately.

'Well thank God that bothersome man is gone. Show me your plans I am eager to see the fabric swatches now they have arrived.' Bernadette had already signed off on the actual plans for the refurbishment, the plumbing and changing out of two internal walls. She approved of the new cornices and adored the carpet and wallpaper selection. While the carpets were a fine wool, they had to be hard wearing in the high traffic areas plus the handloomed rugs would assist in keeping the floors looking immaculate.

The wallpapers were designed by Solange in conjunction with a French design house. The look was a modern take on an eighteenth-century floral design. The colour palate, muted greens and soft yellows for the parlour and a pale blue and cream for the dining room was superb. Each bedroom was a unique grouping and would be given inspirational reference names to match. For everyone simply loves a name that brings with it the romance of a story.

When Solange opened the giant presentation folders of fabrics, Bernadette caught her breath. She was full of admiration for this young woman. This to her was confirmation she was, absolutely without doubt the descendant of artisans, this woman had it in her blood, and it was the bloodline that had led Bernadette to her in the first place.

'So very talented Solange. Yes, you can be taught design but for some it just comes naturally. Were your parents artistic? I imagine your family home was full of colour and beautiful art.' She already knew the answer. Just seeing this folder confirmed Solange was exactly who she thought she was, and she would have the knowledge she was seeking.

'I don't really know. Sadly, my parents died in an accident when I was very young. We were only living in a rented house in Adelaide while my father was working at a vineyard. Honestly, I think I got my skills from learning design at university.' Solange continued to flick the fabrics back and forth creating a kaleidoscope of colours. She was taking a moment to compose herself. There was a vibe in the air and either Bernadette knew about her arrangement with Mathieu and wanted in, or she wanted to report her, or she was just being nice. But that was hardly likely as lately no one seemed to be genuinely nice to her, they all wanted something. Everyone was having a go at her no matter how hard she tried to please or how neatly she presented her posts online. There was always someone writing a nasty or threatening comment.

Bernadette took the hint and knew not to press any further, instead asking more about the course. It was like putting blinkers on a scared horse. She needed to calm her down because she knew she was the one. She just knew it and was rarely wrong. This was the woman who was going to lead her to the missing art. Whether Solange knew it or not, she was going to assist, and they would liberate these prisoners from a time when the world was a very different place. They needed to be returned to their rightful home and into the hands of those who knew how to care for them. Bernadette imagined a trail of sales dockets and ledgers that would take her to the end of her days to track down, but she was prepared to re-home as many as she could.

On the other hand, Solange's grandparents may well have been co-conspirators and somehow ingeniously redirected the art to another château but with a sign Bernadette resigned herself to the fact it really does only happen in the movies. The only fact she was aware of was that this young woman may not be aware of it, but she would in some way know the story of the missing art. Bernadette was duty bound to carefully get the information out of her. She had spent her life being patient to get her results and now would be no different.

Chapter Twenty-Three

THE KEEPER OF SECRETS

JEAN-FRANÇOIS HAD THREE BEST FRIENDS also called Jean-François and it was not by mistake. He knew exactly why – it was the deep respect people in the village had for his family; a type of offering tinged with awe. His grandfather and father also shared the same name, as in fact in some form did most of the male population of the village. Although, the tradition was a little watered down by his generation; there were names like Jean-Pierre, Jean-Marc and Jean-Luc all still partly in honour of a man who knew so much about everyone and yet shared so little.

The tradition of honouring with names was usually reserved to credit saints and was once restricted by law at the end of the 18th century. Then in 1966 a new law permitted a limited number of regional or foreign names, substantives, diminutives, and alternative spellings. Only in 1993 were French parents given the freedom to name their child without any constraint whatsoever – well, within reason one would imagine.

His father had been affectionately referred to as Monsieur Dubois le grand homme – the grand man. His grandfather had earned a title bestowed upon another war hero of the time Charles de Gaulle who was often described as both tall and grand, so he was fittingly known as Monsieur Dubois le grand et grand homme. The men in this family were indeed held in high esteem and for very good reason.

In recent times in the cobblestone streets of Caunes-Minervois men would step aside for Monsieur Dubois le grand homme and bow their head slightly while the women conducted a discreet reverent curtsy. Until his last days he had dressed as if going to the office and yet his main daily tasks had involved going to Le Petit Bistro for a café au lait and an almond croissant. Life as a widower had been very routine. Even the young children in the village thought of him as a hero, yet he wore no medals and there would never be a statue in his honour.

It was rare he had ever paid for a coffee or a beer in the local cafes as there was always someone giving a knowing wink to the waiter and paying before he had a chance. While appreciative of these gestures it had been difficult as he was always concerned this could be mistaken as a bribe or inducement.

While his days of influence were certainly over, he was known as a man of honour, someone trusted by the community… for he had known that secret. In all his seventy-two years he had only ever discussed the matter with two other people, his "tall and grand" father, and his son, also named Jean-François Dubois the current Notaire of Caunes-Minervois. Extremely relieved he had not received a nickname and despising the American style of adding the title Junior when sharing a name with your father, he was simply Jean-François Dubois.

As a civil-law notary, he was a specialised lawyer in the family private practice. Once completing his undergraduate law degree and one-year master's degree in law, Jean-François had chosen to do a two year in office traineeship at his father's practice, supplemented with four semester long practice courses and capped by a master's thesis. By the time he completed all this his father had passed away and handed the practice to him. Eager to expand the business, he was knowledgeable in specialisations such as European Union law, company law, intellectual property, farm tenancy and agri-business. His legal activities varied from real estate matters, domestic affairs such as adoptions, marital agreements and sadly divorces. Yes, he knew everything about everyone in the little village and they were all very aware of it. But just like his father and grandfather, he deeply respected their privacy.

He always walked with a spring in his step as the device on his wrist was constantly reminding him to meet his step quota. His eyes had the fine lines that start to come with age and wisdom, his hair a little more salt and pepper each year. Always conscious of maintaining a perfect weight he ensured Friday morning was weigh in day, followed by coffee and pastry with his good friend Pierre Guichard the Maire of the village, followed by a few Pastis after work together as well. Jean-François was Godfather to half of the village children. He was very much a big part of the village; this village was his family. He also guarded "the secret", a curious file had been handed down through the generations under strict instructions that required a code to be presented prior to accessing it.

However, Pierre did his best to find out what was going on. He had heard rumours of mysterious benefactors, sealed files and dark secrets from clerks who had worked for the Dubois, and he was always trying to get to the bottom of it. If something was happening in his village, he needed to know. Proud that funds had been injected into his village to support the refurbishment of a historic trust restoration project – a château that was severely damaged by fire during the Second World War. Pierre had been keen to work closely with the project manager a bossy woman named Bernadette from Paris. He desperately wanted a tin box back that had been found in the château. It would be perfect to add to the museum collection. He would put a call in to her later, but for now, he was going through his to do list before his meeting with the fire brigade to discuss the wild weather and anticipated flooding. They were predicting the l'Argent Double: the main river flowing from the mountains was overdue for a centennial flood. The storm event looked severe enough to deliver the prophesy. Evacuation shelters were being prepared and shelves were being emptied of tinned foods.

Chapter Twenty-Four

FINAL FINESSING

LOOKING BACK ON ALL THE MONTHS of hard work and the additional stress of Mathieu watching her every move and pressuring her to do the unimaginable, this was the moment she had been looking forward to. The planning of the soirée, the time of celebration and festivities, when the Ambassador would proudly show off his new residence to an adoring if not a little envious audience. The guest list was filled with all the other jealous Ambassadors and their spouses along with diplomats, various government representatives and corporate identities. It would be an evening of beautiful music and fine champagne.

The Embassy had sent one of their official cars to collect Solange and she was certainly appreciative as they drove past the long line of people lined up for the taxis which seemed to snake around at a slow pace leaving freezing passengers shivering in the tunnel of wind blowing past them. The driver, as to be expected was well groomed and polite, he opened her door, and she shuffled in gliding across the smooth leather seats. He also knew when to engage in conversation and when to simply drive. They started off with the usual polite chat and she enjoyed speaking in French with him, but then she excused herself to check her messages and scrolled through the twenty odd messages that had come in while she was on the flight. One of them was from Ivy who she was aware had just returned from one of her exciting trips. Curious, Solange clicked the message open but caught her breath as she read on.

I know a very big secret about you, and I can't believe you have been holding onto this for all of your life. Of all people I would never have suspected you and to tell you the truth I was a little surprised. Very sly Solange! I must go, and I will see you face to face to talk more at the soirée at the Embassy. I will try to catch up with you before everyone arrives.

The shock made Solange turn noticeably pale. She stayed silent and stared out of the window putting her phone away into her bag. Oh God she knows about the stolen art. She knows I am a thief. I can't text her to explain. I need to see her in person. Who else knows? The driver was very perceptive and knew something was not right, but it wasn't his place to say anything. She concentrated on slowing down her breathing.

Once her laptop and handbag had been scanned by security at the embassy she was greeted again by her driver. He really was such a gentleman. She appreciated the fact it was him escorting her and not Mathieu for he had been delayed. They walked through the front doors of the embassy to the muffled sound of voices talking on phones and printers expelling documents of everything from visa applications to media statements. Suddenly conscious of the sound of her footsteps, she walked a little more gently on the glossy wooden floorboards and was relieved to reach one of the beautiful silk carpets that softened the sound of her footfall. And then she noticed the sound of another's shoes, and it was unmistakably Mathieu, the sound as if he was doing it on purpose. He was such an annoying ponce. She got the vibe she wasn't the only one who felt that way about him.

Ambassador Durand took the meeting in the main board room and kept the attendees to a simple list of Mathieu of course, Bernadette via Skype, the delightful Solange along with his social secretary.

At the start of the meeting Ambassador Durand invited Bernadette and Solange to be guests at the residence for the gala event in the coming months. He would have his secretary explain the requirement for the maids to ensure all their personal belongings were out of view for the "open home" during the viewing period so he apologised for any inconvenience this may cause them. He usually didn't get involved in the minutia of details such as this.

The guest list was presented to them and was in order of precedence. Solange slowly exhaled imagining the work that went into finding out all the diplomat's rankings. This was a whole other world to her. She was delighted to see the names of Sonja and the other social media influencers from her agency as it would be a treat to be able to see them socially and show them her work in action. She scanned the list for any other familiar names and recognised the media outlets and some reporters and journalists.

The dress code would be cocktail. And as Solange was soon to discover this would mean she would be free to wear a dress with an above the knee hem or as modern fashion now dictated even an evening pantsuit. She had to work out something that would be stunning as this really was an evening she was looking forward to.

Bernadette had a selection of outfits from remarkable couturiers she could easily select from so this was the least of her concerns. She was most interested in finding a way to spend more time with Solange to try to probe her for any more information on her relatives and their knowledge of the missing art. All she needed was the next clue. Just a few words would set her on the next path to possible discovery. She had thought of setting up a meeting before the event but knew that would be of no use as the poor young woman would be a bundle of nerves ensuring everything was perfect for the event.

The secretary had everything under control and issued everyone with a draft run sheet for the event schedule. There was a separate copy for the Ambassador which included details for his appointment with his masseuse and barber. She had also prepared the draft speech the Ambassador would deliver and handed it out for comment. The copy Bernadette received via email was watermarked with "draft – not for distribution". The secretary would collect all copies at the end of the meeting and Bernadette had agreed to delete her emailed copy. This woman ran such a tight ship not even Mathieu interrupted her. He didn't need to as she was so efficient and had thought of everything, to the point there was very little need for the meeting. It was more of a briefing as they were being informed what the secretary wanted them to do, say and wear. Somehow none of them except for Mathieu (on the pretext he didn't like being given instructions by anyone other than the Ambassador) took offence to this as they were impressed at how well coordinated the event was.

The event was to be a highlight of her social calendar and Solange could not wait. As she headed to the airport, she started to google different styles of dresses… or jumpsuits she might like to wear. She already had an idea of the shoes as she had been sent several pairs from a new start up brand and they were… well she couldn't think of a better word – delicious! She knew she would make front page of a number of fashion and design blogs.

Shortly after the meeting on her way back to the airport Solange picked up her phone to re-read the message from Ivy. How could she possibly know? The phone was still on silent from the meeting, and she could see a call from Bernadette coming through. She answered immediately. Bernadette simply wanted to meet with her after the event, so they planned to catch up for lunch at a restaurant in Manuka a few suburbs away from the Embassy… and away from the prying eyes of Mathieu. It was to discuss another possible project, something very close to Bernadette's heart.

Solange tried to sound delighted but could not disguise the apprehension, concerned there may be something a little darker going on. She knows!

Chapter Twenty-Five

PREDATORS

BERNADETTE LAID THE CONTENTS OF THE blackened tin box before her, carefully presented as if ready for a forensic examination. Her computer screen showed details of the owner and his obituary. Emotionless, a stock photo of the face of the young man stared back at her, his military uniform handsomely presented. Wilhelm Fünten, killed in action in 1942, Caunes-Minervois, France. Her dogged and determined research would ultimately lead her to the truth, she knew there would be a reward if only she could decipher the contents and work out what had happened at the château and despite the fire there was no real evidence of the artwork in the rubble. She knew there had to be more to the story.

*

1942 CAUNES-MINERVOIS, FRANCE

FOR WILHELM, WAR WAS THE MOST MAGICAL TIME time he could imagine. Never in his life had he pictured himself living in a castle, despite the fact it was now devoid of any inhabitants or food. Deserted châteaux were a part of war, but this château housed something far more precious, a rumour known only to a handful of people, and Wilhelm was privy to this secret. It was filled with the treasures he had dedicated his life's study to - art. A collection of over two hundred precious artworks hidden away ironically from exactly the person he was. A Nazi art hunter.

Later that evening while lying still in the wet mud, he held his breath to stop himself shaking and then ever so gently squeezed the trigger. His aim was impressive. In just under an hour, he was able to bag eight rabbits. However remarkable that was, the act of skinning the rabbits impressed his colleagues the most. For Wilhelm though it was quite cathartic, the closest thing he would find to meditation during a war. The way the soft velvety fur peeled back with a flick to reveal glistening flesh and sinew did not offend him. Instead, the act made him feel closer to his Maker in a most comforting way.

'Sir there really aren't many fresh vegetables left. It is still so early in the season. We have collected some turnips that have seen better days and only a handful of undersized carrots.' The youngest of the soldiers, a pale boy who looked to be straight out of school laid out his pitiful offering. The kitchen was predictably enormous and was able to cater for around one hundred guests in its day. But today was not that day.

The burly gunnery officer was now taking on the task of cook. Despite the shelves being lined with mason jars filled with pickled delights and stewed fruits decorating the shelves, the cook who had more skill in shooting than cooking didn't have the creativity to incorporate these items into his rather dull rabbit-based menu plan. Now, staring at the beautiful cursive writing on the labels it was the only time he wished he could read French to help identify the rows of dried herbs lined up in the smaller mason jars. He remarked, 'They were certainly keen on cooking in this place, the herb stash is full. Just wish it was the same for the cellar.'

Wilhelm was secretly very pleased the wine cellar was empty as he could not imagine orchestrating his plan with a troop of solders suffering hangovers. He had been planning this operation for far too long and could not afford to put a step wrong.

'There will be plenty of time to drink and celebrate shortly.' A murmur of acknowledgement supported his theory. 'What are you creating here chef? Rabbit soup?' he flicked the cook on the back of the ear as he walked past him looking into the large industrial sized saucepan.   The contents of the pot reminded him of a part of the river where he grew up, when after a storm the debris would wash itself away from the hillsides and form into an impasse that threatened to block the stream.

'This, Sir, is my version of the Bayrischer Goulash... with rabbit. It will make you feel like you are at home.' He waved his arms wide and bowed in a humorous gesture. The others all laughed. It felt good to laugh and good to be inside a warm kitchen.

Wilhelm responded wittily, 'My home... was not the retirement home.' The banter would continue well into the night while the soldiers took shifts to go on watch and others prepared the sleeping areas. This was indeed a change of scene for them all – a grand château hidden away in an obscure part of Southern France. The secrets this place could tell. But Wilhelm already knew them all.

Before the war, for hundreds of summers, young school children in France enjoyed weeks on end of education on the finer things life offered. Music lessons were taken in the shade

of the enormous plane trees, their massive branches crying out
to be tamed of the kilos of leaves that weighed them down. The
cooking lessons were directed by skilled master chefs teaching
their young apprentices the difference between a ragout and a
fricassee, all the while tasting the delights of the season. They
would learn how to set the table for an eight-course meal and
understand the importance of order of service. But for the
children the lesson they enjoyed most was the art class, where
they could make pinch pots with wet clay in the morning and
then paint during the sunny afternoons using all the colours of
the rainbow. They would learn the history of the great masters
who had created works of art that spoke of life and hardships,
of love and suffering. These classes were also taken out in the
open under the great guarding plane trees shielding them with
dappled light.

When the leaves started to turn brown it was nature's
way of warning it would soon be time for the children to return
to their usual lives in the villages or cities, back to books of
algebra and science experiments. For the carers and teachers, it
was a sign that soon they would close off most of the building,
in a ceremony where shutters were gently closed and locked,
like little eyes shutting one by one. Next the dust covers would
be delivered to each room, and gradually they would take their
places and guard everything, keeping watch until the next
summer.

But now ironically, it was Wilhelm's turn to briefly
guard the Château du Créapsy and her precious inhabitants. He
knew the artworks were there somewhere, secretly tucked away
in the many cavities and hollows, in attics and behind false
walls that only gave up a hint of their location due to the
obvious rushed plaster work or freshly painted façade. It was

obvious they were not original residents of the château but instead temporary lodgers harbouring from an adversary.

He wanted to talk them out of their hiding places and let them know he would keep them safe. He wished he could whisper, I'm not who you think I am. Looks can be deceiving. However, it still wasn't time to get them to show themselves – better they stay mute and out of harm's way. There were still those amongst them that hadn't yet been vetted. He still had to complete some final tests.

Wilhelm had handpicked his troop for this assignment, and he himself was selected by the Führer on high recommendation from various galleries and universities. If the Linz art gallery was to become one of the greatest cultural centres in Europe, it had to feature specifically selected iconic artwork and it would take an expert in this field to ensure the initial vetting. It was an honour Wilhelm wished had not been bestowed upon him, but he knew the other option would not only bring dishonour to his family but would ensure their fall from grace, certain imprisonment and without any doubt, eventual death. One simply did not reject such an order from the great leader.

In addition to having studied art history in detail, he had always taken a particular interest in the conservation and preservation of art. The clever and attentive young man quickly worked his way through a career path as a well-respected museum curator, usually a position reserved for those with connections. Wilhelm was able to create a reputation for being the best. A kind of art detective in curator clothing. He had a photographic memory for details, dates, names and techniques and he was the perfect person for a mission such as this.

The assignment quite simply was to seek out and confiscate the art reserves stored throughout France. German intelligence was able to intercept allied air force maps that specifically indicated areas to avoid during planned bombing raids. It was obvious there would be something valuable stored in these locations. All indications were that it would be precious art. There were some pieces in particular that were being scouted for and the accolades for presenting these items would ensure glory.

The process for selecting his team was extremely simple. He had created such solid rapport with many of his past colleagues and some college contacts that they all eagerly agreed to form up as part of his mission, with one exception. One thirty-year-old Sergeant who was assigned to their unit, he was always incensed and rubbed the others up the wrong way from the start. Despite all the other members of the team having received their military training, they were fairly passive when it came to handling weapons and certainly none of them had ever killed another man. The Sergeant despised being part of this group and ensured they were all aware he resented every moment of it. He wasn't in the war to protect a group of posh art types swanning around the countryside. He joined to kill as many of the enemy as he could. Now the only thing to kill was rabbits.

Wilhelm gathered the men together while they were having their meal. He announced after an inspection he did believe there was precious art hidden within the building. The following day they were to commence knocking out the false walls without damaging the art. They would then create a detailed itemised list of all the art and regroup them into a safe space inside the château that would later be the final staging place before they were moved into the vans. It was too risky to move the items straight into the van as the weather was changing with storm clouds forming and the rain constant since their arrival. Without correctly wrapping the art to protect it from the weather they would be simply wasting their time. All of this plan depended of course on the actual art being behind the false walls, but he was certain it would be. The tell-tale signs were all there. He just knew the château was hiding something very precious.

He sent the Sergeant out to do a patrol of the grounds which he did begrudgingly for there really was no need as the place was silent. There were no houses nearby and the locals were simply terrified of the soldiers and could hardly even look them in the eye as they passed through the village earlier that day. Nothing but frightened old women hushing small children into tiny houses. Once the Sergeant had left the front entrance and could hear the old door squeaking on his hinges as it closed, he immediately changed his demeanour. He knew he could trust his team, the Sergeant however presented as a problem. It was quickly agreed there was only one way they would be able to achieve their new goal and ensure their own safety. He had to be dispensed with.

The first part of the plan was quite simple. In the morning, he would set the team in action to demolish the wall, retrieve the art and create the list. They already had a fair idea of the contents as they were rumoured to be items missing from the Louvre and he was sure there would be a few pieces known to be national cultural treasures. To take these paintings out of France was a crime in itself, but to risk some of them being labelled "degenerate art" where they would be publicly burned and forever lost was a tragedy he could not live with.

The second part of the plan was a little tricky. Wilhelm still believed there were good men in this dark sad world. He believed there would be someone in the village that he would be able to find and trust, but who? He would have to find this man himself, to shake his hand and look him in the eye. He needed to be reassured he could request his assistance to save the art and this request would be fulfilled.

The third part of the plan was simply deadly. The Sergeant had to be eliminated from the group, but in a way that would not be suspicious or bring ill will to the locals in the village. And he would not ask such a thing of his men. This task of saving the art was his own risk. The fact the other men were prepared to assist was a miracle, but he would not ask them to kill for him. That was a task he would have to see through himself.

At first light Wilhelm and the gunnery officer drove into the village. As expected, they didn't encounter anyone, but they were aware they were being observed. Terrified eyes followed them as they got out of their truck. They walked from door to door until finally one opened and in very broken French Wilhelm asked the elderly woman who opened the door if there were any men in the village. It was no surprise that no one was willing to offer up any information. There was simply no way and he had to admit he totally understood their reservations. Over the years he was sure that in situations like this they had never seen their men return.

He then asked. 'Je veux voir un notaire s'il vous plait.' The woman shook her head as if she could not understand and he persisted repeating the sentence again to her asking simply if he could see a notary. He looked closely at her and imagined her fear, but she was silent and would not meet his eyes. He pleaded with her a moment longer and then realised he must try another.

He persisted a few doors up, imploring that he needed assistance. Once again there were many eyes watching his every move. Children were hushed and the only sound he could hear were some cranky chickens clearly agitated. Again, he persisted and to his surprise a young girl walked to the door holding the hand of an elderly gentleman. His hair was snowy white, he was extremely tall and held his head high showing intelligence and bravery. Upon seeing the German officers at his front door, it seemed he was presenting himself for his last moments on earth.

'Monsieur êtes-vous un Notaire?' He asked questionably, imagining the poor old man was not actually a notary but just being presented to him as a live offering.

'Oui, je suis un Notaire monsieur.' The old man, acknowledging he was the public official they were seeking, straightened down his jacket with his weathered hands and awaited his instructions. He was baffled when Wilhelm let out a shout of joy and quickly reached to shake his hand. The gunnery officer slapped Wilhelm on the back and they both spoke excitedly in German very quickly to each other.

'Je suis Jean-François Dubois.' Introducing himself to these two young men he felt there was something different about them compared with other German officers he had seen. They were still full of the joys of life and seemed to see through the dark days with eyes of hope. He was cautious, but he was prepared to be civil to these men. Now he was curious. What did they want from him?

Wilhelm had reached the limit of his schoolboy French and without a common language to share, he used his notebook to try to draw some pictures, but quickly realised this was simply folly and would serve them no purpose. He then asked. 'Anglais? Do you speak English?'

'Non.' Jean-François shrugged his shoulders. Curiosity was leading him down a dangerous path. He knew he should not involve anyone else. It was better to keep this simple. The more they struggled to communicate the more he knew he needed to find a woman by the name of Adeline Lanquetin as she had lived in Paris most of her life and knew some words of English through her work at the Gobelins tapestry workshop in Paris. But to involve an innocent young woman could be disastrous. He had always been a good judge of character and he felt he could trust his instincts.

'Pardon. Un instant.' He politely asked for a moment as he called out a name at the top of his voice. The two officers wanted to laugh at the strength this old man had in his voice as they hadn't picked it. He spoke with such authority. He was a grand and dignified man indeed. Shortly after a small girl aged about eight presented herself to him. He passed her instructions that seemed to express the urgency and moments later a young woman appeared at this door. She was calm and clearly only there because of the trust she had in the old man. Jean-François asked the woman if she would be able to assist to translate for the officers in English. Although she agreed, this proved difficult at moments, but it was the best option they all had.

Wilhelm's plan soon became evident, and it was also made very clear the risk they were all about to take. He was able to express that he was an art curator before the war, and he could no longer continue to steal the cultural heritage from France. He was aware that half of the art they were about to recover would be burned and the remainder sold off with only a few to ever be put on display. The thought he was enabling this was more than he could bear.

His recovery plan was already in action back at the château, but he needed assistance to ensure the safety of the art once it was removed. He asked Jean-François to assist him to find another place for the art to be hidden. He would then burn down part of the château and complete his report that the art had been lost in the fire. And this was why he needed a notary, a public official with a solid reputation of trust, someone who had built their life on this role. Immediately, he knew Jean-François was exactly that person. He hadn't planned on including Adeline in this, but she was necessary for the communications. He felt she understood the importance of art considering her chosen career as a tapestry artist had been cut short because of the war.

He needed to find a way to hide the art until the war was over, and he felt that would be soon. Despite all the positive propaganda, he knew the clock was ticking, and the Germans could not continue their strong hold. In earnest, he planned to come back after the war as a penance for his crimes and assist with the re-building of art collections throughout France. But in the shorter term he was committed to doing whatever he could to prevent further destruction.

Adeline could feel her heart racing, she felt this situation was most unusual and perhaps a feint for them to give up valuable information. However, the more they spoke and planned, the more she realised the two Germans sitting before her were the ones in most jeopardy, for if their plan was discovered they would surely be killed instantly.

The plan was that Jean-François would be the keeper of the list, hidden deep within a sealed file and Adeline assisted to provide a perfect solution. She would be able to disguise four of the paintings behind simple tapestries that would remain on the wall of her house. Within each tapestry would be a postcard of the village with part of an encrypted message detailing the location of the storage facility. At the end of the war all four tapestries would be presented to Jean-François' office. The list and location of the art would be revealed, and the art could then be returned to its rightful owners.

Jean-François knew the perfect place for the art to be stored. It was simple and would not raise any suspicion within the village. He had promised not to breathe another word of this location, the secret to remain sealed in the file. The precious collection would be hidden in plain sight within the walls of an ancient salt market that had been closed up for hundreds of years. Adeline ensured that four of the key pieces of art were hidden behind plain tapestries, their postcards stitched into the backing. Wilhelm insisted on using the red thread from his small art tin box he carried with him to discretely tie a section onto the end of the wires on the back of the painting. This was his mark, a visual cue to recognise they were part of the same collection when identifying the art.

Days later when all of the art had been wrapped and stacked into the trucks ready for removal, he ordered the Sergeant to burn down the château. A request that delighted the soldier as he rushed to gather his supplies and it wasn't long before he was splashing gasoline onto soft furnishings. The act of striking the match would be the last thing he would do, as a fatal bullet wound would ensure he would now be consumed by the fire as it quickly raged around him. Wilhelm knew it was necessary for him to have committed this murderous act, a casualty of war that still shocked him. It was so simple to take another person's life. Just far too simple but also extremely crucial, for there was no way the Sergeant would have participated in the plan to save the art from certain destruction at the hands of a dictator that knew the power of cultural property during war. Now all evidence of murder and the missing art would be burned to the ground.

Chapter Twenty-Six

DEATHLY DECISION

JUGGLING CLIENTS WAS A SKILL. Keep them close, keep them closer, but never ever lose them. Sonja was smiling through her conversation with Sabby the creative genius behind the fashion label Culture Constructions. She liked the woman but felt like a ten-year-old calling her by her nickname. Sonja wanted to be frank and say something to the effect of. For God's sake your name is Sabrina. So, use it. But she would never let her ego be exposed. She thought Sabrina was a really nice name, so the woman should just use it. After all her own name was Sonja, she didn't insist people call her Sonny. Then she laughed as that was the name of Amanda's dog, the female oodle, doodle or whatever fancy name they had. Didn't the Clintons have one? Or was it Theresa May? She had plenty of time to let her mind wander as Sabby was harping on about colours, textures, models, catwalks, launches and then she started paying attention when she heard a key word... "influencers".

It was assumed Amanda would wear the crown again, after all she was the lifestyle and fashion influencer, plus the current brand ambassador for Sabby's clothing range. Sabby was extremely precious when it came to who she would allow to wear her clothes. Amanda had always been her darling, they drank espresso martinis like they were water and were like "twinnies" except for the hair colour. They photographed well together and complimented each other. Tonight, Amanda was wearing the latest release from the current season, a bright flowing silk dress in a daffodil yellow and cinched at the waist with an extraordinary belt made from the same fabric in a purple colourway, her shoes were ridiculously high in a plush velvet. Fans were lining up to be photographed with Amanda against the photo wall backdrop made of roses dyed in every colour of the new range ensuring the photographs were "Insta-worthy" and would feature well in feeds.

Sabby had recently been accused in a controversial social media shaming event because she didn't make her garments in sizes larger than a twelve. Even then, Sabby felt her clothes should be nothing larger than a ten. She herself was a perfect petite eight, oh so wishing to be a six but no amount of dieting and pilates could co-operate in making that happen. It was rumoured in the industry she had the size six label sewn into her own clothing; the other rumour was she had been seen eating tissues before her last fashion launch.

Each launch was bigger than the last, and the last had been whopping! The current launch featured a troop of the most highly skilled ice skaters she had somehow managed to arrange onboard a luxury cruise liner that was having a one-day break for maintenance between cruises. They allowed Sabby to use the ice-skating rink for the parade. The light show, and music were simply out of this world. It was the skaters and the way they modelled the fashions that made it truly unique. During the final change, the lights were turned completely off, the only light was the faint green of the exit signs. And then with the most dramatic of strobing and four direct spotlights the lead skater was seen performing a pirouette within a large hoop suspended from the rigging. Some of the women remarked how it reminded them of their music boxes from when they were children, and the beautiful ballerina would spin to the music.

They were mesmerised, she was truly spectacular, and they had never seen anything like it. Almost every buyer in the audience had that image burnt into their retinas and were visualising it in the window next season. Sabby was a genius.

It was by the pool deck for cocktails when Sonja finally got to talk with Sabby. The glamourous skaters had changed footwear to the highest of heels much to their coach and the entertainment director's trepidation as they came sashaying past to great applause. Even Sonja was impressed, and she had certainly seen everything, well almost everything in her time. This range was aptly named the "Ikebana Collection" - fusing Japanese style prints and bright fabrics incorporated into a modern take on a traditional kimono. A type of cape that could be belted and worn as a dress. It was extremely ornate and guaranteed to get coverage on front pages of glossy magazines and fashion influencers. But Sabby was insisting she would only release a select twenty of the kimono cape dress into production and she would allow only two of them to be given to influencers on the proviso they be auctioned off for charity at a later date.

As Amanda was the primary brand ambassador for Sabby's fashion label it was a safe bet one of these darlings would be heading her way. Sonja would make sure of it. She could already see Amanda and her beautiful red locks draping from an emerald green or perhaps a deep ocean blue. Yes, she would see to that, and her work here was done.

She had four other social engagements on the following day and Sonja felt she really didn't need another drink as she was having trouble fitting into some of her clothes lately and it wasn't because they were shrinking. Sonja looked around at the success of the event and felt joy she was associated with the achievement. She had certainly given Sabby a helping hand with promotion in her earlier days. Now it was time to sit back and let her rewards flow in.

'Ah… Sonja, are you going so soon?' Sabby was using a baby voice which annoyed the shit out of Sonja. She wanted to answer in a patronising voice herself but resisted.

'Everything is so wonderful darling. The night has been such a success. Just marvellous. You must be so happy.' She tried to play down her quick exit strategy.

'It is just… there is something I wanted to discuss with you and my day is booked out tomorrow. And you know what it is like one thing leads to another and then the week is gone. I need to talk to you about Amanda.' Sabby jolted her chin up and met Sonja eye to eye sensing this was not going to end well.

'I don't want her as ambassador for this range. I really don't know how else to say it but there has just been something about her lately that… well has been rubbing me up the wrong way. She seems a little distracted. I don't know what it is, but I have this intuition and I just don't think she is right anymore.' At that moment Sabby had a tap on the shoulder and it was one of her retailers asking for a photograph. The woman had the lead skater in a handgrip and was desperate to get a photo of the three of them. The skater was smiling like a film star, always on show despite the loss of blood to her left hand and the fact she hadn't felt her toes in almost a decade. Sabby obliged and the woman talked on and on about the range and how it was truly remarkable. Sabby was a true fashion icon. This is what Sabby lived for and she was delighted to lap it up.

Meanwhile Sonja was still frozen in position, her eyes glazed over. Having Amanda in the key piece of the collection was the money shot she was expecting out of this deal. She certainly hadn't seen this coming. In fact, she had only seen Sabby days earlier and there was not even a hint of anything like this. What on earth had Amanda been up to? What vibe was she giving off? It was all news to Sonja.

Once the retailer had finally finished lavishing Sabby with praise Sonja made her move. She didn't strike like a viper but acted nonchalant. 'I understand, it is the pinnacle of your career. The most important range to date. This is your call. Once again, an absolutely fabulous evening, truly spectacular. You are going to be written up so well for this launch. Well done, Sabby.' It actually sounded like she meant it. Well, she did mean the fabulous and spectacular part but what she really wanted to do was bitch slap the stupid millennial and remind her that loyalty in this industry was one's best method of defence against ruin. And boy oh boy could she ensure someone's reputation suffered if she wanted to – she had the means and now the motive!

Sonja made a direct line for Amanda and informed her they were both leaving. Without any questions Amanda knew something was up and just like the French at a cocktail party, they just discretely disappeared. No fanfare and no fuss. Except for Amanda throwing up in the carpark when she was informed, she had lost her best contract on a whim.

Two days later Sonja arrived at Sabby's design warehouse, sidestepping all the accoutrements of the white witch. Dream catchers were hung throughout the room, their delicate feathers spinning with the stream of cool air coming from the air conditioner. The pink salt lamp was glowing in the corner and on the table beside them was a menacing set of tarot cards laid out and then untouched. Sonja sidestepped the charms and spells as she was balancing a large bunch of white oriental lilies. There were so many in the bunch they were rather hard to carry without shaking. The women air kissed both sides trying to imitate the European style, Sonja wanting to simply put her hand on the skinny bitch's chest and push her to the floor, but she played along.

'You know the tarot cards were not positive on the day of the parade. I mean no harm to anyone, but there was something that appeared, and it made me very unnerved, it was a warning. I use my powers for good. I am not punishing her behaviour but protecting her.'

'Ahh… who are you talking about?'

'Amanda.'

'What do you mean Amanda? What has she done?'

'Oh, she hasn't done it yet. But this may assist in protecting her from instigating these actions.'

'Sabby. Have you actually talked to Amanda?'

'No.' Sabby tilted her head indicating that was a ridiculous question.

'Has someone told you something about Amanda?' Sonja insisted.

'The cards. They told me what she is planning to do. They are the sign something is not right. I will not be able to sustain the negative energy from her.'

All this white witch mumbo jumbo didn't sit well with the straight-talking Sonja, but she knew her limits. The contract could still be saved. She persisted.

'I can see your concern. Yes, those cards.' She stared at the cards. One one-thousand, two one-thousand, three one thousand. Right long enough staring. Fuck me sideways this woman is a complete and utter nutter. She counted to herself to ensure a lengthy enough observation. 'I can see your energy flow is a lot better today.' Sonja glanced at the staff scurrying around busily packing orders.

'Yes, the orders are flowing in, and it is beyond our expectations. Now, I hope there are no hard feelings about Amanda. I went looking for her, but she must have left early. Have you told her yet?'

Sonja smiled and thought to herself how she would really love to reply. What do you think silly bitch? That I run a charity? Of course, I have told Australia's number one fashion influencer she is not required for your latest range. Despite being the ambassador for your range for the last five years, you have unceremoniously dumped her. You, however, still have a contract with my agency. But you wouldn't have a fricken clue if your arse was on fire. So... I will educate you my delicate little petal.

Instead, she replied. 'Oh, Sabby she was very sensitive to your wishes and totally understood that perhaps this range was not what you had in mind for her and that possibly in the future...'

Sabby looked at Sonja in a way a child would at a broken kitten. 'No, I just don't think Amanda is what I am looking for anymore.' With that she walked off in some type of dream state towards the cutting room. Sonja wondered what she was on, her behaviour was very odd.

Sonja followed. 'The kimono dress... cape... was exceptional, and I really do want to have some involvement with the range.'

'They have already been allocated and I am shipping them out shortly, I think they will leave in the next hour or so.'

Sonja had to work quickly. She was going to have one of those kimono dresses on one of her girls. People didn't say no to Sonja, and this drugged out little upstart was certainly not going to. It was time to play her joker. She leaned in closely and whispered a short statement that was a long-held dark secret between the two of them. It did the trick, Sabby turned even paler.

'Luke darling.' Sabby was trying to sound casual but really sounded like she had been kidnapped and was making the ransom call. 'Lukie can you please get the kimono dress we were sending to Emily. Now… before the courier arrives. Now Lukie.' Luke was looking very confused as to why he would give the dress to Sonja when this was heading for her opposition agency.

'Ahh erm Sabby do you really mean Emily from…' He leaned over and whispered the name of the agency into her ear. Sabby swished her hand at him like he was a fly.

'Go. Go. Just go and get the dammn dress. Don't question me.' Now she was sounding a little hysterical and all the patternmakers and cutters stopped their work enjoying the show. 'Sonja let's go out to the reception room I want to show you some other items from the collection a little closer.'

Sonja enjoyed the terror in the woman and relished in her power. She had worked hard to achieve it and she always needed to keep a joker up her sleeve for moments just like this. 'I know it is a compromise, but a contract is a deal and if we don't keep our promises. Well, where would we be?' Sabby looked at her with those little girl eyes that seemed to be rolling back in her head. Sonja thought they might need to call an ambulance, maybe she had overdosed.

Luke waltzed in with the dress in a large, zipped garment bag and handed it over to Sonja as if it is was a child given over in a custody battle. He sighed dramatically and lovingly patted the bag. Sonja rolled her eyes at the theatrics.

'Look, Amanda will get over it, I will find something else for her. She is popular with more of the mall style retailers, so I will push her down that direction. But I can assure you the gown is in safe hands with your new ambassador. Although not known for being a fashion icon, I promise she will be striking in this gown and will bring with her a whole new audience. I have never let you down before.' And with that Sonja got out of the place before she might need to conduct CPR on this frail little sparrow.

Chapter Twenty-Seven

OPHELIA

DESPITE HER FAMILIAR SURROUNDINGS, Solange had found it difficult to sleep. There had been a wolf pack baying at her door. She had tossed and turned all night, at one stage forcing herself to get up and prepare a camomile tea. But even the soothing fragrance of the tea could not help to calm her thoughts. She had no need for apprehension, for the day ahead was simply a sequence of events mapped out for her and was well and truly out of her hands. She was merely to be on show and lauded for her work on the residence. Besides, she had attended hundreds of gallery launches, product unveilings and countless open homes, this was merely another event.

She was very uneasy about Sonja's decision a few weeks earlier. It had come as quite a surprise, and she was uncomfortable about the way Sonja had manipulated her into agreeing to comply. She felt like a puppet and for the first time actually considered leaving the agency. After all she really did not need the additional clients the agency had sent her way. She was already far too overworked and spreading herself too thinly across her regular client base. Some of the new clients did not really fit that well with the ethical stance on sustainable products. But Sonja was the master of convincing her to comply. Solange felt truly ugly for not remaining herself, for not being able to stand up for what she believed in… and sadly she felt she had gone too far and there was no turning back.

In the same way that Winston Churchill had described his constant companion of the black dog, Solange had begun to feel the same shadow. Now, at times she fed on misery, despair, and melancholy. She did give herself credit for her ability to perform on cue and morph into a chameleon of delight when required. No one would have ever known. No one suspected, and she felt that no one would want to believe even if she had the courage to share her dark secret.

In the preceding months, Solange did have the courage for one thing. She privately sought professional help and was indeed diagnosed with severe depression and anxiety. Her cure came from a script pad, but the patronising face of pharmacy assistants at randomly selected malls told her what they thought about the pills they were dispensing. Solange was terrified of someone recognising her and had found it necessary to seek the advice of a psychiatrist as her world was gradually starting to crumble around her.

She had become obsessed with completing the work at the residence to the highest standard, higher than any project she had ever completed before. The obsession was distracting her from all other projects. She had stopped providing her administrators with content and direction and this in turn had them missing deadlines and her online posting regime had become so mismanaged she was losing followers. She didn't concentrate on eating well enough and was looking pale and frail. People were starting to comment.

But it was the sleep. For there really was none. Solange could not put her head on the pillow without worrying about the smallest of things and in the dark of night these things grew tentacles and became larger and more foreboding. Everything was taking over; everything was momentous and impossible. The medication and therapy sessions were a start, they were definitely a step in the right direction to get her anxiety and depression under control. She had been the master of disguises when it came to hiding her emotions and the effect it was having on her life. But now she had made a change. She was, however, very conscientious and would never let any of her colleagues or followers be aware she needed help. This she believed would reflect negatively on her reputation and in this game your reputation was worth more than gold.

At first, she had only taken half of the medication she had been prescribed as she was concerned the Doctor might have been a little heavy handed on the script. She had also consulted Google and it recommended lower doses, so she carefully paced out collecting her prescription to the timings as if she were taking the full doses. This also allowed her to keep drinking alcohol. She did feel a little guilty about that, but she had so many public events to attend - it was part of the job description.

Whenever she attended a session with the Psychiatrist, she would always complete a patient status survey on their iPad. Each question answered with careful consideration, aware she might implicate herself if she wasn't careful, cautiously always selecting at least one option on the more positive side. Always careful to tick she had reduced her alcohol intake; acknowledge she was taking her allocated medications and state her sleep was improving. One of the questions that always made her stop and think was. "In the last week have you had occasion where you have felt so out of control you may embarrass yourself publicly." This question did indeed terrify her as her public profile was her life. But while it frightened her, she was always aware of the importance of this little check box in her life.

As the weeks went by so did the lack of sleep and this fuelled the anxiety and paranoia. Was someone following her to her car at night? Had someone been in her house? She was sure there were some things missing. She always felt like there was someone watching her. But it was the online abuse that she didn't know how to deal with. Why were so many people being this cruel and nasty, well at times vulgar and obscene? She could not un-see some of those words and hateful comments. These people worked very hard to achieve this outcome. Nasty, hurtful and very threatening.

She was overthinking everything. Over-planning, overscheduling and quite simply over everyone. But she still couldn't bring herself to be truthful in the survey. She was just too used to being the person everyone wanted her to be – even to her therapist. The gaslighting effect was taking its toll, the fallout was too great.

It seemed such a simple option. She went doctor shopping to get sleeping pills so her own GP wouldn't be involved, and then when that pill didn't work, she sought another. In the week leading up to the soiree for the official launch of the residence she was so overwhelmed with work and so exhausted from lack of sleep she started to self-medicate with her own cocktail she believed would "take the edge off". And to her relief it did. She slept the sleep of the dead. Waking up was the hard part, but she always did and managed to get herself together and set off for her next busy day ahead, devices pinging and chiming, constant reminders she needed to be somewhere or have something done.

Solange had been taking screenshots of the messages and saving them to a dedicated album on her phone. That way she could torment herself repeatedly looking through them, just wondering why so many people hated her when she hadn't even met them. Some of the comments were so personal.

She was dreading seeing Amanda that day for very good reason. She knew how hurt Amanda would be over the recent decision and Solange felt she was just the pawn in the money-making game of Sonja and Sabby, but Amanda wouldn't see it that way. She had seemed so withdrawn of late and was quite short with her on a recent phone conference for the agency... and that was before "the" decision.

She knew she would be in Ivy's bad books as well; she hadn't been returning her calls. Especially when she found out how Ivy had visited the village of her relatives in France. Solange nearly fainted when she heard that. What did Ivy find out while she was there? What did she know? Would she write about it on her blog? She just couldn't face all of that right now, so ignorance was her choice of action.

Orpheus – she could always rely on Orpheus. He had her back; he would always be there for her. He was so kind and thoughtful, so funny and witty. She felt a genuine closeness to this man who she could trust with her soul.

The anxiety attack that followed was not what she would have expected. Of late she had taken to have her heart racing, her mind flashing with options, her computer open generating to do lists. But this was different. A calmness washed over her, and she felt so in control and had the answer. She poured herself a decent serve of straight brandy, no ice or mixers and then slowly and rhythmically drank it. Knowing the effects would calm her even further and help her get through the day. She could feel the numbing sensation as it went through her limbs, and she actually liked it. She questioned herself whether she had taken her medication and in her forgetful state took her second dose for the day. Then she sat in the gilded upholstered chair facing the garden to meditate. The alarm on her phone alerted her it was time to get dressed for the event and clear her possessions from the room.

Solange looked in the mirror and touched up her makeup. A light spritz of hairspray and she dabbed on her favourite fragrance. She felt as if she was gliding as she walked. Everything felt so right and calm.

Hardly able to lift the heavy lined silk quilted cape onto her bird like frame on her own, she took her time. Perhaps she should take another pain killer before she left the room. Her ankles were already starting to ache in the killer heels the designer had selected for her to wear with the outfit. Putting the jacket on was like stabbing Amanda in the back. She could not believe she had agreed to be the ambassador for the new range. She took a moment to admire the fabric. The oriental print was mesmerising and for a moment she was lost within its intricate pattern. The long-dropped bell sleeves were very dramatic, quite theatrical as she admired the view from the mirror. She slowly buttoned up the false front of the jacket and tied the sash haphazardly off to the side in a jaunty half bow. Not exactly how Sabby had asked but she felt she was entitled to a little poetic licence after all.

The butterflies in her stomach fled when a sharp knock wrapped directly on her bedroom door. Her response was a little subdued and without even asking who it was she simply opened the door. It was Mathieu standing there and for a moment he just stared at this beautiful petite creature in this glorious couture creation.

'Bonjour Madame. I have come to escort you over to the event, the guests are arriving in the main reception area.' He was sharp with his greeting as he looked around the room, disappointed at the state of it. He knew that Solange was aware the room would need to be on show within the next few hours and yet she disobeyed his request. His anger was evident, and he spoke to her like a disobedient teenager.

'This room is in no state to be on show. What were you thinking? What are you… Are you drunk? Are you on a substance?' His mind ticked over quickly as he was thinking of ways to micro-manage the situation. The Ambassador could simply say in his speech she had been delayed at the airport. No one needed to know she had already arrived. He would have the driver take her to a nearby hotel, confiscate her phone and computer and then stay with her. None of this was to get out. Damage control was his speciality.

'For all of this time I have given you the courtesy you have deserved as a contractor to the embassy. I have treated you with respect due to your connections with the art industry. But now I see that I need to treat you differently. You have lost my respect; you are weak and not worthy. You cannot be trusted. Do not ever take me for granted for in me you will find a formidable enemy. I will change your path. I will make your world very different. Can't you see this Solange?' He was pacing now; his eyes were menacing, then he walked up to her and was standing far too close. She attempted to back away and he gripped her arm so tightly it terrified her causing her to let out a screech. He was furious and now knowing she would not need to be on show he slapped her so hard with the back of his hand that the outline of his large oval ring clearly left its mark on her cheekbone. She was thrown across the room onto the floor and sat up seeing stars.

Her reaction was delayed, and she didn't even cry. In fact, she felt nothing. She was numb. A feeling came over her like a warm cosiness, she suddenly felt strangely relieved. Like nothing could ever really hurt her again. She didn't feel scared of the angry short man who was yelling abuse at her. He was so irate; spittle was forming in the sides of his mouth and she watched with the curious innocence of a child. Mathieu yanked her roughly to standing position by grabbing her by the hands and was tempted to hit her again when he remembered their conversation was being recorded. He needed to manage his own damage control immediately.

'Madame. Stay here. Do not leave the room. I will send the driver for you.' He looked at her, but she was having trouble focusing on him. 'Do you understand me?'

'Oh yes loud and clear.' She acknowledged wanting to mock salute him, but her arm didn't really have the energy to raise that high.

Mathieu turned around cursing under his breath. This woman was a liability to the Ambassador's party, to the reputation of the embassy, and most of all to him and his private art acquisitions. She was going to need to be dealt with harshly. But first to delete the recording of their conversation for fear it picked up the slap. He picked up her phone, laptop and took her keys to the bedroom door and used them to lock the door behind him. He marched off down the hallway cursing how she was not getting away and embarrassing him like this.

Everything she had worked for was now jeopardised. It made sense now all those cruel messages, all of those menacing insults, this man's power and influence did truly extend past the embassy gates. She had nowhere to hide. The shame of her past would never stop shadowing her and this man was now holding the torch. Solange calmly sat back down in the chair holding her cheek that had bruised up in a large welt. She could feel the sting of it, but emotionally she was in the calmest state she had ever experienced. Nothing could harm her. She was at peace, albeit a little claustrophobic in her imprisoned suite.

Wide eyed she innocently stared out the window with a pout, then without any thought simply opened the unlocked double French doors out onto the patio. A blast of frosty air confronted her, but she was already numb to its chill. In a daze, Solange walked towards the rose garden where a few blooms were still gripping on to their last days. She was distracted by the glistening blue water of the new swimming pool, it was mesmerising. In her hypnotic state she opened the glass gate and welcomed the icy cold water as she stepped onto the shallow ledge. She was longing to feel the weightless freedom it offered, beckoning her deeper she slowly made her way into the aquatic wonderland. The water seeped into the quilted jacket, edging its way further and further until the weight seemed to free her of all that had been haunting her. She had never felt so content.

Chapter Twenty-Eight

WHAT HAPPENED THAT NIGHT

IT IS SAID THAT EVEN IF AN EMBASSY WAS AN INFERNO, the fire brigade would have to watch it burn down unless given permission to enter by the head of mission. On the day Solange died, the police felt the same way. They had received plenty of phone calls about a famous woman that had died in the swimming pool at the Embassy of France, most callers insisting they remain anonymous. However, as an ambulance had been called the Ambassador permitted police onto the grounds, and shortly after the coroner was able to remove the body.

Later through social media, the police would see the actual events unfold as they were posted online or sold to media agencies. The police and news helicopters provided additional footage. Nothing like this really happens in the nation's capital. Exclusive footage of police chasing a car to the airport provided opportunity for a live break in telecasts. As a result, Mathieu was prevented from boarding a flight at the airport by the Federal Police.

'I know my rights as a diplomat, I am to be afforded the privileges of my office.' Despite how highly he thought of himself, the reality of the situation dawned on him when he made eye contact with the Ambassador who was flanked by police. Despite his claims of bluff while shouting about diplomatic immunity, his position was considered a considerably lower rank which restricted searches only on diplomatic premises. Canberra airport didn't count. The security team had already sent the recording of the incident in Solange's room to the Ambassador's phone. This of course would not be disclosed during Mathieu's brief interview with the police, it would wait until he returned to France to face his reprimand.

Upon return to the embassy, Ambassador Durand and a select team met with Mathieu in the conference room, a place that was once so familiar to him and now so foreign. Looking dishevelled and confused, his world was falling around him. He pleaded with the Ambassador. 'She was drunk and clearly a drug addict. I did it to protect you from the embarrassment. Can't you see how it would have ruined your event?'

The Ambassador was calm when he spoke. He was dignified and in damage control. 'Mathieu, we have the recording of you assaulting Solange immediately before she was found dead. This doesn't look good for you.'

Before the Ambassador could finish talking Mathieu interjected. 'You should be thanking me. She was stupid, she would have talked. She would have given us a bad name.'

'Mathieu let me be clear. In this situation there is no "us".'

For a man usually immaculately presented, he was offended at the smell of his own body odour. Sweat mixed with foul breath from the numerous cigarettes he had smoked was making him feel ill. His mouth was dry, and his head ached. He looked around at the other people in the room and obviously knew the Minister Counsellor or "number two", they had clashed many times before when Mathieu would step on his toes relating to matters of security or administrative decisions beyond his authority. The other man he couldn't place. He was obviously French but non-descript, someone that could easily hide in plain sight.

'Let me introduce Marcel a member of the security team from the Ministry of the Interior who has been monitoring your behaviour over the last four months.' Ambassador Durand looked toward the quiet man dressed in a simple navy suit who merely nodded towards Mathieu, not even offering a verbal greeting. 'It has been brought to my attention you have been operating an illegal art supply business through the designer Madame Lanquetin. Albeit a forced and hostile agreement we would believe.' Mathieu went to speak but swallowed his words as Ambassador Durand continued. 'The Ministry has intercepted all seven of your diplomatic bags prior to allowing them to be collected by your partner. All details have been recorded and we have photographic evidence of all events. Your partner is currently being interviewed and you are to be sent back to France for further questioning and possible charges. That is all I have to say on the matter.'

The Ambassador left the room and the Minister Counsellor advised Mathieu of his rights and instructed he would be permitted to return to his house to pack for the trip. The rest of his possessions would be handled by a removal company and sent back to France. Marcel would accompany him on the flight and ensure he attend further proceedings.

Later in a debrief, the Ambassador and his "number two" shared their remorse for not acting sooner to expel Mathieu. They were also shocked and confused at the stupidity of his plan. Between them both they could not understand why he had made up such a convoluted plan to try to sidestep the authorities, when he could simply have purchased them through a decorator or second-hand dealer in France, avoiding the need to remove the artwork from their frames and have them travel around the world. For a clever man, the whole plan was simply mad and reeked of Mathieu and his dominating narcissistic ways.

Bernadette had been invited to attend the interview and would have loved to see the demise of the smirking assassin. She had been working closely with the Ministry as she had been advised of Mathieu attempting to purchase stolen art almost a year before the renovations had begun. Bernadette however had declined the meeting to sit with the others while they were waiting to give their statements at the police station. Her account would be brief, and she would only describe the scene she came across rather than admit her complete knowledge of the background events. Initially she had believed Mathieu had drowned Solange, but now it was evident there was more at play involving the unstable mental health of the fragile woman.

In times of shock and crisis behaviours can change, vulnerabilities can be exposed, and people talk. That is what Bernadette was anticipating... and baiting for. 'The poor young woman, so talented yet haunted. I had no idea what stress she must have been under.' She was genuinely saddened by the events and felt she could have done more.

The usually guarded Ivy was crying like a baby. 'I was so excited to see Solange today. I had some exciting news to tell her and now...' She started to sob, raw and uncontrollably. Amanda consoled her. She had a lot of practice consoling people lately and was hugging Ivy, rocking while staring wide eyed with exhaustion.

The tentacles of blame had wrapped around Amanda. 'She looked so beautiful in the Ikebana kimono. It was made for her; I was actually happy for her to be asked to wear it. I honestly felt it was right for her, but I didn't get a chance to tell her. She must have thought I hated her but…' Now it was Amanda's turn to cry.

Not the best at tactful repertoire, Bernadette pressed Ivy to tell her news.

'I am buying a house in the same village in France where Solange has hers. I hinted to her I had a surprise to tell her, almost teasing her. She wouldn't have had a clue what I was on about.'

The others looked at Ivy, confused. Sonja jumped in. 'Are you moving to France? Are you leaving?' Clearly, she was concerned and not because she would personally miss Ivy. She had already lost one of her star talents and now Ivy was delivering this bombshell. She may lose another.

'No, no… not moving. Just buying a holiday house. Somewhere to escape to for the European summers. I imagined writing my blogs from there and maybe expanding my horizons.' She waved her hand like swatting away flies. The whole idea of buying in the same village was so she could nurture her friendship with Solange. She wanted to become a real friend, and now the house would only be a reminder of what might have been.

Sonja showed a little cautious relief and then realised they were all staring at how callous her remark was. Without hesitation she blurted out. 'I know what I will do. I will start a foundation in her name, a charity. Yes, something to do with design, something, umm something that meant a lot to her… oh I know those birds she was always going on about. The one she had painted for the residence. The parrot that came back from the dead.' The others flinched at her choice of words. However, she hadn't noticed as her focus now was to control the situation from a public relations perspective. She was the master manipulator and could change the focus to a positive spin and it would have the bonus of being associated with her agency. Focus now switched to her mobile phone where she was adding notes about the plans for launches, events, and sponsors.

'Where is the village, Ivy?' Bernadette pushed to keep the conversation going.

'It is in the south. Oh, the little house is adorable. It is already furnished but I know the first thing I will hang on the wall is going to be the tapestry Solange gave me. It can take pride of place. That will be a special way to remember her.'

Amanda commented. 'I think Orpheus has been using his for dart practice. He told me he hated the dust collector. You should ask him for his. I must admit mine is in a spare room, but I might have to put it somewhere more prominent now.'

'I didn't get a tapestry.' Sonja looked up from her phone and when no one responded she got straight back to her task.

'Ivy, where exactly in France?

'I fly into the Toulouse airport and then…'

Bernadette almost snapped but she was desperate to find out. 'Ivy, what is the name of the village?'

With a face that expressed the look of "enough already" Ivy simply said. 'Caunes-Minervois.'

The puzzle was coming together. 'And so, you both have a tapestry from Solange, an old one?'

'Yes, and Orpheus has one… and Solange. I wonder how Orpheus is going? He is taking ages giving his statement. I bet he is playing up his heroics.'

Again, Bernadette continued her line of questioning. 'Four tapestries and you say she also has a house in Caunes-Minervois?' Bernadette was interrupted before she could ask any more questions as her name had been called by the police officer taking statements. 'If you aren't here when I get out, I will call you Ivy.' She quickly entered Ivy's number into her mobile.

Chapter Twenty-Nine

PAYBACK TIME

OH, WHAT HAVE I DONE? What have I done? Orpheus rocked back and forth quite literally like a madman in the interview room at the police station. In movies police lockups are always old concrete bunkers with blue painted bars. Or was that just in his imagination? Everything felt surreal. He looked around for hanging points. Not that he wanted to, but it was just a morbid curiosity, and he couldn't help himself. He also looked at the walls and wondered if there was someone watching him from behind a mirror. He neglected to notice the discrete security camera in the ceiling, he mistook it for a downlight. Clearly, he had seen too many cop movies and was more fixated on mirrors.

He wasn't hand cuffed and he had a decent flat white and a bottle of mineral water. He felt like a VIP witness. After his attempted rescue, the police asked half a dozen of the witnesses to come to the station and give a statement. He could hardly shower fast enough and get down there, this was pretty exciting. He was thinking of all the ways he could milk this on his blog in the coming weeks.

He couldn't wait to see some of the photos and video that people had taken of him during the heroic rescue. He was running ideas around in his head of how he could use those in his social media. He got his phone out and took a few selfies at the desk imitating shock and sadness. Then he did a few photos like a gangster pretending to blow the smoke off the end of his gun. And then the phone screen just turned darkly pixelated and froze, quickly turning itself off. He shoved it back in his pocket. Oh my God are the police monitoring my phone? He glanced around like a shoplifter and then he realised maybe water had got into it after all. He would go to the store after this to ask for a freebie replacement.

'Shit that is the last thing I need today.' He realised he had said it out loud and naively looked around again. Meanwhile, he kept himself mentally occupied going through the events of how he didn't hesitate to jump in the water despite still having his shoes on. He needed to think about how he could best describe the actual event to sound a little braver. He got out his phone to check for synonyms of brave, but it wasn't responding. He went to tap his smartwatch, but the water had already stuffed it. Perhaps the police could give him some type of statement he could use to claim them on insurance through the embassy. He was working on a mental list of things he wanted to get across in his statement and started to make an acronym out of them so he wouldn't forget. Phone. Watch. Shoes. Then he repeated it. Phone. Watch. Shoes. PWS. Then added suit. Phone. Watch. Shoes. Suit. PWSS.

He was working on adding to his acronym again when the door opened and in walked two of the friendliest looking people he had seen. He thought to himself. They must be the social workers to check on my well-being. How considerate.

'Hi Mr Butler, my name is Detective Glen Young, and this is my partner Detective Kate Scott. We appreciate that this afternoon was quite an ordeal for you.' The officers both shook hands with Orpheus and sat on the opposite side of the table from him.

'Well yes. I am still in shock. Thank you for the coffee and the mineral water. The service is great here who would have thought.' Attempting an awkward joke, Orpheus was instantly at ease with the two officers.

'Good to see you are comfortable. Is there anything else we can get for you?' Glen was a genuinely friendly guy. He had the type of face that made you feel like you knew him already. Tidy haircut and a neatly trimmed few days growth that was the look Orpheus was going for himself. Glen dressed very well, and it was clear he appreciated good quality clothing. His shirt cuffs were secured with fabric knotted cufflinks in contrasting colours. Orpheus liked the flair of this guy, and he was busting to see what colour shoes. Tan or black? He guessed a dark tan brogue, but he wasn't going to be obvious and take a look straight away.

Kate had some type of accent he couldn't quite place, she was smiling and radiated an upbeat energy. Orpheus really did have to admire these two they seemed to make a great team. Only good cop, good cop here. He smiled to himself.

'No, no. All good. Oh, actually a new phone and watch.' He laughed at his joke and then added when they looked a little confused. 'My phone and watch were damaged in the rescue, but I will get to the compensation request later. I've got a bit of a list going.'

'Sure, well we certainly aren't in any hurry. It is important we don't rush. You have had a big ordeal this afternoon.' In his time Glen had seen a lot of different reactions when people were dealing with the loss of a good friend, so he put it to the side. 'Take your time Mr Butler. Would you care to explain to us how you know Ms Solange Lanquetin?'

'Oh, so I thought you would know who we all are. I'm Orpheus…You know who I am don't you?' Orpheus sounded a little prima donna like.

'Sure, sure, but it would be good if you tell us all those things.' Glen was playing into the ego.

Orpheus launched into his life story while being gently guided through the express version by Kate. Suddenly Orpheus thought he might have misjudged Kate, she was being bad cop. She shouldn't rush him. This was interesting stuff; his life was interesting. Eventually he got to talking about Solange and the first time they had met. It was through Sonja, and it was at one of her monthly meetings. She rarely brought anyone new into the agency. She had selected her current stock of influencers so well they didn't leave. They were all shocked to meet Solange. She didn't really fit the bill of what it takes to be a social media influencer.

Glen stopped him there. 'And what exactly is that?'

'Simply it is a genuine burning desire to be the best of the best. To win all the contracts. To have the most hits, the highest stats. That type of thing. Solange just seemed to float around she wasn't in the game like the others. It baffled me as to how she got to be so famous. Honestly, sometimes she was just hopeless at keeping her social content updated. She could go days, sometimes even a week. A whole week without posting a thing. But when she did the place would go crazy. She had the "X" factor. Everyone was curious about her. She was mysterious. There were so many questions I always wanted answers to but… well she just wasn't the type you would corner in the bar and get her drunk, so she would talk.' Orpheus laughed. 'Gosh now I've got verbal diarrhea, blabbing away like this.'

'That's okay. We understand it has been a tough day. Can you tell us about the function today and when you first saw Ms Lanquetin?'

'The Embassy was hosting a reception to celebrate the opening of the new residence for the Ambassador. Solange had been working on the refurbishment. You know like the interior designer, plus she did some painting of a bird. Apparently, that was significant to her because it was rare or endangered or re-found – oh something like that. Anyway, she had been super stressed over the whole thing. I don't know maybe she had been running late on deadlines or something but lately she was as white as a ghost and seemed to be jumpy like she had just seen one as well.' He laughed again at his own joke.

'What time did you arrive at the function?' Glen kept pushing.

'Let me think. Well, it started at three o'clock, so I got there just a few minutes after. You know fashionably late!' Again, he laughed.

'Right so you got there just after three o'clock and where did you go?'

Jesus thought Orpheus this is getting tedious now. 'I got checked off the guest list at the entrance to the embassy and then followed the bunting flags along the side path to the residence which is only about fifty meters away.' He thought he had better continue or they would just keep pressing him. 'Then I looked for the nearest waiter with champagne and I grabbed a glass and couldn't resist sneaking a look at the swimming pool which was tucked to the side of the residence. It wasn't really out of bounds, but I did think if I didn't sneak a peek I might miss out once the Ambassador's security ramped up.' He paused for effect.

'That is when I saw a scarlet colour, no more crimson and at first, I thought my eyes were playing a trick. The shape was all distorted and I found myself screaming like a banshee.

I just threw my champagne onto the lawn. Opened the glass pool gate and jumped in. Honestly, I could have broken both of my legs as I didn't know how deep the pool was.'

Glen's voice sounded genuinely concerned for Orpheus. 'Right mate. Yeah, pretty dangerous, you wouldn't have known.' He paused for a moment as if he were imagining the danger. 'So, when you went to the pool was there anyone else there?'

'No. No, it was just me. And well Solange, but you know she was already in the water. She was already dead. But like I didn't know that. I just jumped in.' Orpheus was starting to feel the strain of the day take over, like an involuntary jet lag. The lights in the room weren't the best and he thought one of them was strobing slightly adding to his headache.

He took a moment to reconsider what he had just said and rephrased it slightly. 'Well, when I say it was just Solange and I… I mean there were about two hundred others, but they were all preoccupied talking and weren't really in the line of sight to look into the pool like I had.' He couldn't resist adding. 'You know these diplomatic events, well everyone who is everyone must be invited. It was like the cast from the United Nations plus partners.' His poor attempt at humour didn't gain any response but he continued. 'And all the socialites who just want to get their faces in the social pages. Ivy, Amanda, and I were there along with Sonja representing the agency showing support for Solange and her work.' He paused, rubbed his forehead, and whined. 'Any chance I can get a Panadol? It has been a really big day.'

Glen seemed genuinely to acknowledge the request. 'Sure, I will see what we can organise. But first can I just clarify when was the last time you spoke to Solange?'

'Oh, well ahh. Probably a few days, no maybe a week ago.' He rubbed his index finger across his chin mimicking Rodin's statue of the Thinker.

'So more like a week ago?'

'Yup, yes. That would be right. We talked on the phone.'

'Did she give off any indication she wasn't her usual self?'

'No. No. Nah. No, actually she seemed fine. I really don't know why anyone would kill her. You know she was extremely popular she had tens of thousands of followers. I am sure a lot of people were really jealous of her but to do that - wow that is really next level.' All the sudden he felt a real rush of heat all over his body and he put his hands under his thighs. They were starting to shake a little bit and he didn't want to give off any misleading messages.

Kate had worked with Glen for a few years, and it was very clear that Glen had a job to do and he had done it many times before. It was a job for which he had the skill and the gravitas. It was also very clear he was so much smarter than Orpheus and was just waiting for the perfect moment before he went in for the strike. He would give him as much time as he wanted to continue grandstanding, there was certainly something very shady about this guy and Glen was just shaping his space.

At that moment the door opened bringing with it a blast of fresh air from the over air-conditioned corridor and a uniformed police office. 'Sorry to interrupt. Detectives Young and Scott, the desk officer has asked to see you.' Glen apologised, and all three officers left the room, leaving Orpheus to contemplate drinking his cold coffee but he just couldn't do it to himself.

In the corridor Glen turned to Kate and they exchanged the glance that said we will talk about some of those comments in a lot more detail, but they knew better than to say anything that close to the interview room. The interrupting officer spoke in a hushed voice apologising again for the interruption. He assured them they really did need to see what was waiting for them in another room. A computer was set up with a live feed to another station, the officer waiting to speak with them. He introduced himself and explained that he was from a suburban station in Sydney. However, it was the woman he had with him that was of most interest to them.

At first it was easy to assume she was either the very young wife of Orpheus or the much older daughter. They didn't show their surprise when she introduced herself as Maddy, the much maligned, over worked, underpaid and very underappreciated personal assistant slash babysitter of Orpheus Butler. She had a clear plastic storage tub sitting on the chair beside her and a very satisfied look on her face. They asked for Maddy's consent to record the filming of the conversation and Maddy was more than happy to assist.

Very used to discretion, she couldn't give a rat's arse anymore. Maddy felt like Judas revealing the true identity of Orpheus as she continued. It was payback time, and she knew Orpheus had been up to something, but murdering that beautiful talented woman was beyond what she thought even he was capable of. She had been watching the events of the last year and it was like watching a slow television event except instead of a train ride across the Nullarbor Plain, she had been watching Orpheus destroy the life of Solange. Slow and steady, enough to send you to sleep and then every now and again a little something would pop up. She kept notes of all of these times she was hoping to one day use it against him if he didn't give her a pay rise or as insurance in case God forbid he ever tried one on her.

'How long have you been employed by Mr Butler?' Glen was ticking the boxes in order of his usual path of enquiries.

'Look I don't mean to be rude but can that all just wait? I want to show you what I have on him. He isn't the person you think he is alright.'

'What do you…'

'Hey, I am sorry if I am sounding rude, but I am sure you can only hold him for a short time, and I am not wasting a second of it.'

They weren't actually holding him, he had just come in of his own free will to make a statement, but they didn't need to explain. They got the message loud and clear, shut up and let the lady dish up.

The first box contained a pair of snowshoes and both officers felt their excitement diminish until Maddy tipped the right boot up onto the table and about seventeen USB flash drives fell out. All had tags and labelling with some type of code along with dates. She didn't give them time to ask.

'Drone footage of Solange. Weird hey? Solange walking to her car. Solange at a café and creepiest of all - looking in at Solange while she is in her bedroom. Well like she is dressed and everything she just seems to be walking around looking for things.'

'How do you know what is on them all?' Kate was curious about the real connection between these two.

'I know everything about the man. I even think like him. I am him.'

Glen and Kate had to resist looking at each other and sharing the crazy person eyes.

'What I mean is that, like all his writing. You know all the online stuff? You do know who he is right?' They both nodded as Orpheus had given them a verbal sales pitch moments earlier. 'Honestly how do people think he does all of that? It is me. I write his blogs and newsletters. I set up all the live Facebook events. I put sticky notes all over the sides of his computer screen, so he has topics to talk about. I prompt him, and it is all scripted.' She doubted she was getting through to them. It was as if they were one hundred years old, they weren't keeping up with her.

'What I am saying is that I use his computer all the time. I can see everything he has been up to. I had to laugh as I was the one he sent to buy all of the USB flash drives, so of course I was curious as to what he was doing with them. It took me two days to find out where he was stashing them. Well, it was certainly a place his wife wouldn't look. I'll give him that!'

Maddy was all fired up and could hardly contain herself. This was her time to shine. She held the left boot in her hand as if waiting for a drum roll. 'And you are not going to believe what he was hiding in this shoe.'

With that Glen and Kate both shouted out to her to wait up. The smile froze of Maddy's face as she was confused and then she nodded as she saw them get out the plastic gloves... just like in the movies.

'Actually Maddy, if you don't mind, I might just ask the officer to glove up, take that off you and tip it up. Have you already touched whatever is inside?'

'Yeah, but you know the finger prints from me are only because I wanted to know what it was right? Like there isn't any way you think I would have killed her right? Jesus. Should I get a lawyer?' The smile had gone.

'Let's just have a look, shall we?' The curiosity had gotten to Glen, and he didn't answer her properly. The officer tipped the boot up and out fell a hairbrush. A tortoise shell handled soft bristle brush, and yes there was a fair amount of long black hair caught up in those bristles. On closer inspection there was a slightly faded gilded label in cursive font – Galeries Lafayette. Glen asked Maddy not to touch anything on the table again as they would need to put everything into evidence bags.

Maddy nodded and smiled. Evidence bags. Cool.

There was obviously another item in the plastic tub because it was too large for the tub. It looked like an old picture from a charity store, the frame had obviously taken a beating when it had fallen off the wall or been thrown into a bin. On closer inspection Kate called it. 'Is it a tapestry with some type of art underneath? The tapestry is perished, and the painting seems a bit scratched but what is the significance of this Maddy?' Kate was leaning into the computer monitor. She instructed the officer to have a closer look. 'Can you gently pull the tapestry away from the painting a bit and look down towards the frame? What is it?' The officer complied, decades of dust and fibres fell onto the desk, the smell was slightly offensive. He held the painting closer to the camera on the monitor. Kate could see something and asked him to pull the tapestry back even further.

Maddy couldn't help herself and she reached in and pulled out the small piece of card jutting out. 'It is some kind of note. In French.' The officers gloved hand snatched it out of hers. 'You know Solange gave it to him? She gave one to him, one to Amanda another blogger and one to Ivy the travel writer.'

Kate inspected the item on her screen. It was a sepia post card from a French village. The writing on the back didn't seem to be written like it was from someone on holiday but seemed to be more part of an address written in large font and only including part of the content. It didn't take a rocket scientist to work out that the rest of the address must surely be contained within the other two tapestries given to Amanda and Ivy, along with the one Solange had retained for herself.

There was another strange feature of faded red thread sewn onto the card in a simple cross, it matched thread tied onto the wire at the back of the painting. Now Kate asked to take a closer look at the art which was difficult without damaging the tapestry any further, so she thought best to leave that alone for the time being. However, something caught her eye on the back of the frame. There was a very official ink stamp with three rows of German writing on the right side and another stamp of three green circles no larger than a pen lid. This was a little beyond her pay grade, they had specialists able to advise on this. And whether it really had anything to do with the case or not had piqued her curiosity. Regardless she would push for it to be investigated further, and quickly.

'Maddy considering this evidence you have presented us with I would really appreciate it if you wouldn't mind sticking around so we can get a statement from you. You have certainly done the right thing bringing this to us.' They settled Maddy in and got one of the volunteers to get her some refreshments until they were able to get her statement.

Shit just got real! Glen and Kate discussed their plan of action and stepped up the procedure. Getting search warrants for Orpheus' house and car, along with confiscating his computer, phone, and watch.

Interesting how one look can make everything change. Glen gave Orpheus the look. It was launch time, the space was shaped. 'Orpheus, in light of evidence that has been presented to us I must inform you that you are now a suspect in the death of Ms Solange Lanquetin. You are being arrested under suspicion...'

His mind was running over time with what to say next. Do I call a lawyer? Or is that like an instant admission of guilt? Do I just explain it is all a big mistake and I... well I don't really understand why I am here? I certainly didn't kill Solange. There were plenty of witnesses who saw me try to rescue her. I hadn't held her head under, she felt pretty dead to me when I first touched her in the water.

He flinched at the thought of having touched a dead person. It was as if death was contagious, and he instantly thought of his own mortality. He still had deadlines to meet and invoices to file. He couldn't die yet; he had a book to write and now Solange was dead he could make a fortune out of it. All the research on her would pay off, all of those messages he had sent to her using pseudonyms to poke her and see her response. He had so much material.

He stood up and then he sucked in his breath as if he had seen a ghost and slapped his hand over his mouth as he let out a little involuntary noise. Shit, shit, oh shit, shit, shit. All that trolling of her online. Oh, fuck the drone footage. He had plenty of it, but the police would never find it. He hid it well enough they would never find it. Fuck, would they know I changed her settings in her phone, so I knew where she was through

Snapchat? Trying to get her hair for an ancestry test. Oh, fuck that is going to look really bad.

Orpheus snapped. 'Can we all just calm the fuck down?' he slammed his fists on the table. In his entire life he had never fainted before. The police officer's voice sounded like a radio playing in another room and then he felt hot like the gates of hell had just opened and invited him in. The fucking hairbrush. Holy fuck! He dropped like a stone.

There now that's my boy. That has confirmed it. You are a complete nut bag! Kate had picked him from the start. Now to tidy things up and get this crazy narcissist arrested.

Chapter Thirty

THE POLICE REPORT

AMANDA'S INTERVIEW WAS VERY SHORT in comparison to the others. Her statement was brief as she really had only arrived on the scene after Solange had been removed from the water – in that cape. She had openly explained how others may have perceived a jealousy that did not actually exist between the two women. Amanda was much better than that, she had other things on her mind. Much more important things. Like the fact she had been unable to assist her mother to kill herself in time.

Again, she found herself in that place. The place that removed all gloss and excitement from her life. The place that sucked the life out of her. Eleanor's house. Well, it is what they had all called it, after all it was the only place her mum could live now, and it was like a house, in that it had functioning kitchens, toilets, living rooms, and bedrooms. However, in this facility they were all called commercial kitchens and were out of bounds for patients, the toilets were a hand-held bedpan made from a high-grade cardboard, living rooms were sad waiting rooms and bedrooms were wards where they were offered no privacy at all.

Despite Eleanor having private health insurance she was not concerned about sharing her room with others in the hospice, it provided some type of company rather than a private room where she would just stare at the walls. She wasn't one for television and now her eyesight had all but diminished she was happier just to feel the presence of others.

Amanda sat down and then quickly stood up to rearrange Eleanor's side table. The information booklets were starting to pile up. Even she couldn't make an amputation brochure seem more appealing. She almost slapped herself for thinking it. Sitting down quietly she thought she would just have to wait out the time until they brought Eleanor back, but she couldn't. Without even willing her limbs to move she seemed possessed and just started walking without a plan or destination. There was absolutely nowhere to go that was of any interest to her in this place. It was just death's waiting room. It creeped her out.

Walking down one of the faceless corridors she was snapped out of her trance by a tap on the shoulder by one of the doctors. 'Mrs Starr? I'm Doctor Madden.' He stared at her for acknowledgement and then she awkwardly held out her hand to shake his. She acted as if she did recognise him – but she didn't. Amanda had been so deep in her thoughts she had almost forgotten where she was. Dr Madden glanced into the small glass panel of a treatment room next to where they were standing and opened the door. 'Can I have a word with you Mrs Starr? About your mother?'

Without any hesitation, Amanda just walked in and then felt immediately very uncomfortable and unfamiliar in this room. There were no chairs in the room, just a skinny single bed covered in thick vinyl. The room smelt of disinfectant, more than the rest of the place. She didn't like the feel of this room at all.

In a very low but friendly tone, he gestured to the bed and patted the end of it. 'Why don't you sit here? This room isn't really designed for meetings, but it is the best we can do at short notice.'

Amanda complied and sat down not wanting her hands to touch any surfaces in the room. Her mind had gone into overdrive wondering what treatments people had done in here. Hospitals and hospices were such a foreign place and she wished she could keep it at bay. Of course, she knew who Dr Madden was as she had spoken to him about half a dozen times, but it felt like she had been woken from a deep sleep and didn't know where she was. This place had a strange effect on her.

'Amanda.' She just said her name in a quiet and reserved voice but had meant to say it in a way that indicated for him to use her first name and to stop calling her Mrs Starr for it wasn't even her married name. She was so tired of having that battle with everyone and needing to explain it time and time again how she didn't take her husband's name. Anyone would think that it was the 1950's the way that…

'There is no other way to talk about this, but we need to discuss Eleanor's options at the moment. I know we spoke a few days ago but her condition has changed. Mrs Starr is there someone else you would like to have with you while we have this discussion?'

'Amanda.' She did it again. Is he even listening to me? She thought to herself. This is not how these conversations are meant to be done. They are usually in movies with snow falling outside the window and fairy lights twinkling back, with the support of your loving husband and a box of tissues. And a big comfy sofa, not a hard vinyl operating bed! She felt a little lightheaded.

Dr Madden moved closer and spoke in a soft but firm voice. He had done this so many times, it really was something that came naturally to him now. Delivering bad news to relatives, while it didn't really get any easier, he had a formula and was using it now. 'Amanda, as you know, Eleanor's condition has been deteriorating rapidly since she was transferred to the hospice, since the amputation of her right foot. As you are aware, we have managed to keep the wound clean and it is healing as well as can be expected.'

Amanda just stared back at him. Feeling like a child with her hand clasped in her lap and her legs swinging loosely above the ground. She didn't like the fact her handbag sat next to her on the vinyl bed, so she moved it to her lap to avoid the germs and subconsciously hugged it.

'I have just done a check up on Eleanor, we had to keep her on the ward for longer than planned for observation and I am about to have her moved to a private room.'

One step closer to the end thought Amanda. God's waiting room is what it really should be called.

'Although not a standard room as such.'

She stared right through him. She did not comprehend.

'Amanda your mother is being moved right now into a high needs ward and I feel it is the best course of action to put her into an induced coma.' He then continued to describe in detail more medical terms than Amanda could cope with, so her mind started to numb. 'We will keep her in this state and with constant monitoring, but I have to tell you we are not sure she will regain consciousness again on her own.' And with that he just stopped talking.

Amanda continued to stare and felt she was in a state of disbelief. She knew she couldn't get up off the end of the bed herself. She would just sit. She was kicking herself she hadn't acted on her previous plan to go to enact their promise to each other. Well before this time they would have taken the trip to Switzerland and finished off Eleanor's life in a dignified way at a time of her choosing. This had been the plan, but Amanda had allowed herself to get too caught up with her work, her dogs, her fighting with her husband and daughter, the terrible embarrassment of being removed as ambassador for Sabby's clothing line and the jealousy when she found out it had been given to Solange, but being a true professional she just let it ride for there would be something else on offer around the corner no matter how much it had hurt. She just stared at the whiteness of the room and asked herself how did it all come to this?

'Take your time to absorb what I have told you. Have you got any questions?'

They both just sat there. This was also part of the formula. The sitting.

'I thought this was a fairly standard procedure. I know we were warned of complications, but I was not expecting this. I am not blaming. I am just shocked.'

'Would you like me to find one of the nurses to come and sit with you for a while?' Another part of the formula.

'Yes, I think I need to have someone help me comprehend what this really means.'

'I can assure you the staff will continue to look after your mother and her needs. They are very well trained and experienced. She is in good hands.'

Amanda wanted to lash out with all sorts of questions like, What sort of life is that though? What would you do if that was your mother? There were so many questions she wanted to ask but they weren't really questions, perhaps more like statements.

Dr Madden used the phone on the wall. In doctor talk he was clearly asking for a support nurse to assist Amanda. 'A nurse is on the way. These staff are very experienced in these conditions and will be able to explain the situation to you in more detail and help you to find resources to assist.'

They both sat there in silence for there was nothing more to be said, but Dr Madden wasn't going to leave Amanda alone. He was worried she might fall off the end of the bed as she looked a little unsteady. He still had two more families to update with bad news, but he patiently sat and waited to handover to the nurse.

The stale air locked in the room was disturbed by a friendly face carrying a box of tissues and a bottle of water. An anonymous shoulder to cry on was exactly what she needed. Everything had just fallen apart, and it was foreign territory indeed.

Chapter Thirty-One

A NEW BEGINNING

DURING HER INTERVIEW WITH THE POLICE, Ivy had a few questions that needed to be answered. The police had Solange's phone and had seen the message from Ivy but were unsure if it was threatening. What secret did she know she was holding back from Solange? And then they started on why she had changed her name from Lourdes to Ivy. This was a secret she thought she had left behind many years ago. She subconsciously rubbed at her unseen micro tattoo – never ever forget. All those years ago, she had been assured that when she legally changed her name it wouldn't come back to haunt her. But here it was, the memory…fresh as the day it had happened. It was time to explain.

*

2009 SOMEWHERE OVER THE ARABIAN SEA

THOUSANDS OF FEET IN THE AIR, the ever paranoid twenty-year-old Lourdes was applying all the skills she had developed in the years following her mother's murder. After witnessing the horrific event, she carried these memories close and was always jumping at shadows. She vowed it was time to take control and enrolled herself in self-defence classes especially designed for women. She was disappointed when she found herself in an old dusty hall with an overweight man who appeared he may need saving himself. He was cumbersome, unfit, and uninterested.

Next, she hired a personal trainer who was an ex-police officer. He knew lots of tricks and his training schedule was gruelling. He would give her a thirty second head start and chase her through busy streets. He threatened to tread on her heels and cause her to fall on her face as an incentive to run faster. He got taken out in a giant rugby style tackle by a hotel security guard on his way to work who thought this guy looked like trouble. So now her personal trainer was in a moon boot recovering from a fractured ankle. While this type of training got her adrenaline flowing, she didn't want the flight response... she wanted to fight.

The skill she most valued was observation, her trainer had taught her to be perceptive and always aware of her situation and circumstances. It had now become second nature, especially when flying. She would always board as early as possible to observe other passengers and their behaviours as they entered the plane, earmarking the troublemakers. Sure enough, they were the ones first to complain to the flight attendants how everything was too hot, too cold, or not enough vegan options. It was her superpower, and she was right every time.

Lourdes always selected the aisle seat. Always. She preferred to be at the rear of the plane. That way she always had the best observation point. Likewise, she never sat in a room with her back to the door. She was always alert and forever watching for trouble.

It started out with the sound of a light tinkle, like a glass had broken on carpet. Not something most others had even noticed as the lights were dimmed and most were lulled into the restless sleep a long-haul flight brings. Bunched up under the airline blankets, shoes kicked off with abandonment, and cheap eye masks barely covering their eyes, they were oblivious to the events unfolding.

She froze and stilled herself, listening carefully in the direction the noise had come from. She noticed some shadowy movement and then steadied herself in case it was simply exhaustion playing tricks with her. She could hear blood pulsing through her ears, the sound she had experienced the night of her mother's murder - unmistakably the sound of death. She felt like the scared little ten-year-old girl all those years ago, hiding behind a thin concertina shutter. She wanted to run; her mind willing her to lock herself in the toilet where she would be safe. But her body was telling her something else.

There was clearly something going on. Muffled voices of a man and a woman. The man's voice deep and controlled, the woman trying to stay calm but clearly terrified. She could see the spiral cord from the intercom phone on the bulkhead stretched into the food preparation zone. Only part of the woman's profile was exposed but Lourdes could see from her body language she was being threatened. Then the woman seemed to step back into the zone sharply, it was an unnatural movement like she had been pulled back. There was definitely something happening and this time she wasn't going to hide; she was going to act.

Lourdes gently unbuckled her sash belt and slid out of her seat. She walked backwards towards the toilets and the rear food preparation area, away from the altercation. Keeping her body low and moving slowly she planned to alert the crew. She was surprised to see there were no flight attendants at the rear galley area, clearly it was their rest break time, and they would be tucked away in one of the many hiding places giant aircraft harbour. With every step she gathered her thoughts for what was occurring behind the hidden panel toward the front of the cabin. It could quite easily be an argument between staff but in all her travels she had never seen a cross word passed between staff. They were like characters on a Disney parade, always smiling and waving no matter the situation.

She scanned the seats and noticed the empty seat in the emergency row belonged to one of the men she had earmarked as a possible troublemaker. There was something about him and the way he just didn't seem at ease when he entered the plane. He was a little agitated and expressionless while surrounded by holiday makers excited with talk of the spring weather of Europe. He wasn't dressed appropriately and looked uncomfortable in an ill-fitting checked jacket and suit pants. His hair needed a cut, and he had unkempt facial hair. All these things had her on edge from the moment she saw him.

Planning for a worst-case scenario she needed to be prepared. But the thorough scanning process at the airport had always made her feel defenceless as she had to pack her oversized Swiss army knife in her checked in luggage. With stealthy movements she edged her way forward and lowered herself to the floor collecting a woman's spiked heel from the floor as she passed. As she drew closer, she could hear the altercation and it confirmed to her a situation was unfolding. She crawled closer she trying to glance at reflections from the shiny plastic on the signage on the walls, but this provided no assistance. Even closer now and she was able to confirm her worst fears, she could hear the man threatening the flight attendant and despite the woman trying her best to speak calmly she was now crying as she spoke, and her voice had turned into a guttural pleading for him to remain calm and to stop holding her.

Without any delay, Lourdes jumped to her feet and into the food area. With the adrenaline she felt her body was twice its size and she had no fear at all as she grabbed the man by the head and started stabbing at his throat with the spiked heel. The man was overwhelmed with surprise and fumbled, lashing about with his arms and a piece of metal he had managed to detach from one of the food trollies in his hands.

The flight attendant was screaming now as the phone cord had been pulled tightly around her throat choking her and then during the altercation with Lourdes, he had hit her hard on the bridge of her nose with his elbow as he was fending her off. Now, the sharp metal was stabbing at Lourdes and slashed through her jeans and down her thigh, but she kept stabbing at the man's face and neck with the sharp point of the heel. She was unsure if the sticky blood was from the woman or the man, but she kept stabbing.

Her head hit the side of the metal food locker and she could feel her own blood stinging her eyes. Like a woman possessed, there was nothing that could stop her from stabbing. Until she heard a pop, like a pen going through a plastic cover, but it wasn't plastic, it was his throat. The action changed as the man desperately covered his throat with his bloodied hands, trying to keep the hole sealed and not let the gurgling blood fill his throat. He was confused and dazed and flayed about into the aisle falling into people who were scratching at their heads with their eye masks on their foreheads and their hair teased out in a frightening display.

Lourdes chased after him, her attack was frenzied and relentless. The man was now on the ground and kicking at her. She received a kick to the face and heard her nose snap, the shock sent her reeling backwards. In the panic, other passengers began responding in the tightly confined space they were all attempting to subdue the man and hold Lourdes back. Eventually they restrained him with a necktie and began administering first aid to the unconscious man.

The police report stated Lourdes had stabbed the man forty-seven times to the face, neck, and torso. He had died from asphyxiation due to blocked airways from the puncture, along with severe blood loss. Both the flight attendant and Lourdes had broken noses and serious cuts. The airline had insisted they both be attended to by a leading plastic surgeon. Lourdes along with other passengers and crew received extensive psychological treatment, she had trouble talking about the event.

Lourdes who was named after the city of healing and miracles did speak again but she found her voice as Ivy. For ivy is the strongest of plants that can grow in the harshest of environments as it is evergreen, always growing and developing. No longer did she want to be associated with this event or the witnessing of her mother's death. It was time to turn over a new leaf. Life wasn't all about being on guard, life could be about enjoying yourself and seeing all the beautiful things and places it had to offer. After the tragedy of this event, it was time for Ivy to re-discover herself all over again.

Chapter Thirty-Two

FINDER OF SECRETS

IT WAS THREE MONTHS SINCE Solange was discovered in the swimming pool at the residence, and in that period, soul searching had been done and new friendships forged. It was Bernadette who bravely reached out to Ivy following the initial police investigation. In Bernadette's world there were only a handful of people who knew who she truly was. She was due to retire within the next year from her civil service position but could never retire from her hunt to find orphan paintings.

It was time to be brave and take a chance, and she was pleased she had. For in Ivy she found a worthy ally, once she had heard about the genuine honesty with which Ivy delivered her statement to the police. She had also told of Solange's concerns about trolls, bullies and aggressors who were quite frankly terrorising the gentle, lovely woman. Ivy also mentioned that she had stayed at Solange's family home in France, this was indeed news to Bernadette. She was not aware such a place existed. At first Bernadette had assumed perhaps all the art that filled the walls was of the missing collection but as it transpired, it was a collection genuinely and legally purchased by Solange at auctions, through markets and from deceased estates. Bernadette had studied photos of the house online and from the images that Ivy had sent her from her own time in the house. But Bernadette knew the house had more information to give up and believed it was worth a visit.

Ivy was due back in the village to finalise the purchase of her new holiday house. She had kept this news as a surprise from Solange and was going to let her know after the party at the embassy. The poor woman was so stressed and didn't have a minute to spare. This was fun news that needed to be celebrated over a long lunch with a well selected champagne. But the moment would no longer present itself and Ivy vowed to do something special in the village in honour of Solange. She would talk to the Maire, a very agreeable man who seemed to always have an eye for an opportunity or a chance to promote his beautiful village. Of course, she would also talk with the notary during their appointment.

The two women met at Toulouse airport and shared a hire car for the drive to the village. It poured with rain for the whole drive, but it didn't dampen their spirits as they were both full of excitement about the ensuing adventure. Chatting with ease they spoke highly of Solange and how they had no idea how bad the state of her mental health was. She seemed so calm other than the one time at lunch with Ivy, but then afterwards, it was as if she had taken Ivy's advice and shaken off the negative energies of the keyboard warriors. Neither of them could have anticipated the added stress caused by Orpheus and his unusual obsession. They had always picked him as a weirdo, but he surpassed even their worst thoughts.

Driving into the village, it seemed like the car was on auto drive as Bernadette navigated the narrow streets heading for the Abbey car park. But Ivy called out to stop when driving around one of the corners as she spotted the restauranteur, she had met on her previous stay setting up his tables in a brief moment of sunshine. She had been practising her French.

'Bonjour Monsieur. Ça va? Ahhh umm deux cafés s'il vous plait.'

He burst into a smile and sung out in his best English. 'Oh darrrlink. You are back. Yes, yes two coffees on their way.' He tossed his tea towel over his shoulder and ran towards them, insisting they park illegally at the front of his café. 'The Maire will understand. He likes you.' And he cupped his hands and shouted the coffee order to his wife through the giant double doors of the café.

Bernadette and Ivy laughed like teenagers. They were sure the whole village just heard their coffee order as he shouted so loudly. As did a certain Maire who was walking around the corner. He gave a joking evil eye to the owner of the restaurant and greeted the two women with a welcoming double kiss. He had met them both on previous occasions under very different circumstances. Then he politely asked for the keys, so he could re-park the car.

'Such service Monsieur. This village really knows how to welcome people. Merci beaucoup!' Ivy smiled at the kind man. The two women had barely sat down before the Maire returned to join with their gossip. They chatted in a mixture of French and English. But it didn't take long at all for Bernadette to get down to business. She had really decided the time had come to stop withholding information and to share the situation before it was all too late and the last of her chances would be gone. They were most intrigued as this was the most exciting thing they had heard in a long time.

The Maire was dumbfounded. 'You are telling me that from the small tin box containing scraps of memories from the château you were able to work all of this out?'

'Yes Monsieur Maire. I had known for a long time the château had been used to store the art, I knew it had been intercepted by the Germans and I was also aware the château had been in a disastrous fire. The German Officer's small notebook contained a single name, that of Adeline Lanquetin which led me in turn to Solange. With her family history it was clearly her. She was the only living person that had any knowledge of what happened to the art. But as it happens the poor child really didn't know. In fact, I believe she suspected her grandparents were involved with the theft and this brought her great distress. I blame myself for not being more open with her, but I thought I might frighten her away if I told her I thought she knew anything. As it turns out, her grandparents were true to their word in not sharing the information with anyone until the war ended. But unfortunately for them they did not actually see out the end of the war due to illness and the clues were thankfully handed down to the next generation and then the next.'

'The clues, what do you mean? What clues?' The Maire asked.

'There were four tapestries that had been hanging on the family wall. They were not from any famous tapestry house; they were simply decorative items with no value. Unless of course you were aware the whole time they were covering four of the pieces from the Green Circle Collection. A collection of over two hundred missing art works from the Louvre during the Second World War. Not only did they protect these paintings, but they also contained postcards that when joined together provide a password or code leading to the next step. And that is why Ivy and I are visiting. We need to ask if these postcards are of significance to any of you?' She held out the postcards to the Maire and he was able to identify the locations and commented how one of the photographs was taken just near where they were sitting, but that is all he was able to work out.

Then with a start he exclaimed. 'I think I know what to do with them.'

Bernadette froze and stared at the Maire. 'What Monsieur? What do you think it means?'

'As you can see, when you arrange the cards in a certain order, the handwriting seems to match up as if it is running across in a line. But the words don't make any sense, it is as you say some type of code… and I happen to know a man that knows all of the secrets of this village. In fact, he has the title "custodian of secrets" bestowed upon him for a very good reason.'

Bernadette smiled at the irony that the "finder of secrets" was indeed about to meet her match. It was like a movie script. 'Who is your mystery man?' she gasped, attempting to contain the excitement.

The Maire addressed her directly. 'Jean-François Dubois.'

'The Notary?' Ivy tilted her head. 'I am seeing him this morning to finalise the sale of my house.' She urged the Maire and Bernadette to join her at the appointment, so they could ask him about the postcards.

It was settled. They finished their coffees just as the rain began to patter around them and then went to check into a bed and breakfast nearby. They were not able to stay at Solange's beautiful quaint village house as it was taken off the booking platforms until her estate had settled. Ivy was beyond excited as she too would soon own a house in this delightful medieval village, and she took a moment to reflect with sadness that she would not spend any time there with Solange.

Chapter Thirty-Three

GREEN CIRCLE COLLECTION

USUALLY, THE SECRETARY WOULD PHONE his office to announce the arrival of the next appointment. But when the posse arrived including Pierre the Maire, she thought it best to personally announce them in case he wanted her to do something, like call the police! They all looked agitated and worked up.

He had just been expecting the lovely Australian woman Ivy, so had worn his best tie and hoped he hadn't overdone it with the aftershave. He also had bad news for her as her house purchase had fallen through the afternoon before and as he knew she was on a long-haul flight thought better than to break the news by email. He would do it in person and explain the technicalities of what had happened. The arrival of Ivy along with an older woman and Pierre, seemingly in his official capacity as the Maire had him a little anxious. Was this woman her lawyer? … and what was Pierre doing sticking his nose in on business like this?

He went out to the waiting room and greeted them with a warm welcome and then herded them into his office. There weren't enough chairs, so Pierre simply sat on the corner of his friend's desk. If it were anyone else Jean-François would have asked him to move.

'Thank you for all coming in today, but can I ask why you are all here? Ivy our meeting was to discuss the proposed purchase of a house. Am I correct?'

'Yes Jean-François you are correct, but something else has arisen. In fact, only in the last few hours, and I am afraid I have hijacked our meeting to discuss it.'

English was his second language, and he was confused with the use of the word hijack as he had seen it in American movies, and it usually involved balaclavas. 'I see, please continue.' He hesitated as he didn't have a clue.

At this point Bernadette stood up to introduce herself in French and explain her two roles in life. He was taken aback for a moment, thinking back to the little house Ivy had wanted to purchase and wondering if it was worth all the fuss that the French government would send a senior representative to discuss such matters. He still had no idea, until Bernadette lay the four postcards on his table so the words matched up. Collection Circle Vert.

And there were the three words he had kept secret from his staff… and the secret kept by his father and his father before him. Those three words had never been spoken in his presence other than by those men, and now here it was. The code to release the file. Overwhelmed he stood up, covered his mouth with his hand and genuinely took a moment.

'Je comprend. I understand this code.' Their eyes were anxiously awaiting his next reaction. 'Can I ask though? How is it you came into the possession of these cards?'

Bernadette swiftly explained the whole story in French as there was no time for anything to be lost in translation. Her heart was beating faster but she had learned from previous experiences that until she had the paintings in her hands there was still a great chance of disappointment.

'I have waited for this moment my whole life. But I did not believe it would ever happen while I was alive,' he genuinely exclaimed with his hand across his mouth.

A bit dramatic and typically French! Ivy thought wryly to herself. She still didn't really understand the whole picture.

"The words on the postcard. They are the name of a file which has been kept in a safety deposit box at this firm for the last eighty years. My grandfather and father had passed down the instructions to me that I was never to open them until I had been given the name of the file in four pieces. Even I did not understand what that meant. The four pieces are clearly the four postcards. This is unbelievable. I am amazed this is happening.'

Jean-François excused himself to get the folder from a safety deposit box within an ancient safe at the firm. He was the only one to hold the key and had remained true to his promise to not even glance into the folder. He returned almost ten minutes later with the safety box in his hands. He sat the box on the table as Pierre stood up to watch the reveal. The key was old fashioned, and a little difficult to turn, but he opened it and yes there was a booklet inside, some type of ledger with handwritten entries and codes running across the pages.

He handed the book to Bernadette assuming she had seniority over the matter, and she did not hesitate to receive it. She gently placed it on the table, and he moved the lamp over closer for her to see all of the detail. This was the moment she had indeed waited for. She could see the names and details of what was undeniable, it was the Green Circle Collection. She could feel her breathing become shallow.

'This document confirms the list I had been searching for. But what happened to them? Is there anything else in the box? Is that it? Is that all we have?' She was sounding frantic and rightly so as she had been hoping there would be some indicator of the listings of the private sales the officers had profited from. For that is what she had believed had happened to them all along. She would have used such information to trace them back and find them. But there was nothing.

It was at that moment the ever-calm Jean-François simply said, 'If I may Madame.' And he took the booklet in his hands and closed it and then handed it back to her smiling. Puzzled she looked at the cover and it was very clearly marked. "Paintings stored inside the disused 16th Century salt market, corner of Rue du Plo de la Sal and Rue Notre Dame in Caunes-Minervois." Jean-François and Pierre knew the facility very well.

It had always been there, just a part of the village. It was an oddly shaped dome about one story high and had a set of stairs to the side, picnic table and seating had been permanently placed on the top. It had a trellis with ivy growing across it and at the entrance a sturdy round grinding disc from a millhouse fixed as tourist display. No one paid any attention to the old salt market building other than to battle for a car park around it at the end of the working day.

'Take me there. I must go there now!' Bernadette was already standing with her handbag on her shoulder and umbrella in hand.

'But what are the chances of anything surviving, being stored in that space even if they were in there? We have had the recent flooding, hardly a building was spared in the village either from water flooding from below or rain through rooftops. Who knows what has been happening in there?' The comments from the ever-practical Pierre were totally ignored as the group were already walking out the door. Jean-François called out to his assistant to cancel his appointments for the day. She signalled back did he want her to call the police after all? He laughed and assured her all was well, and he would phone her shortly to explain.

Pierre was a handy man to have on their side. Within an hour a group of labourers were called back from a roadworks job to meet him at the salt market. Next, all the cars had to be removed and a stray dog contained. The roadworks foreman decided to knock through a small part of a side wall where he could see the brickwork was slightly different, maybe indicating where the facility was last closed off.

They pretty much held their breath while the digger moved forward to dislodge the area and then the workmen moved in with their drills and sledgehammers. Bernadette shouting out to be gentle and Pierre shouting out to go faster. It was a circus. Eventually one of the workers broke through but they wouldn't let anyone near the structure until they had cleared some of the rubble out of the way and put in a bracing to support the structure. This time Bernadette was definitely taking a hard hat and she leaned in covering her mouth with her scarf as the air was swirling with concrete dust. She used the torch from her phone and couldn't quite see. She put her phone on video, stuck her hand inside as far as she could go and slowly moved the camera about. When she pulled her arm out it was grey with dust. She wiped her phone clear and pressed play. To her absolute amazement she could see the shapes of what had to be the paintings, wrapped in heavy canvas lined up from one wall to the other sitting on crates.

In the shock of what she had seen she wandered back a few meters and just sat on the hard ground and cried. She had been searching for this her whole life. To think these treasures had been sitting here in the street for all this time. Hiding safely in plain sight. She cried, everyone just staring at her, no one knowing what to say.

Her next words were very stern yet delivered with a smile. 'Pierre, we need to clear the area. I will organise a specialist team. They will be here by the end of the day. Jean-François, please record the events of today and Ivy, you simply need to buy champagne. Tonight, we celebrate!'

Bernadette certainly had a dedicated team ready to jump when she called. They were on the afternoon flight and brought with them a small truckload of equipment. The local police had never seen a crowd this size gather in their little village, it was much bigger than the year the Tour de France had passed through. Pierre was in heaven imaging how an event like this would ensure publicity. The whole world would soon find out how this tiny village had been protecting precious art for all this time.

The specialist team set up tents and closed off streets. They had giant spotlights and many large vans. The discovery had made history, save for a few paintings that had rain-water damage due to leaks in the storage facility. The others had all been carefully covered and protected off the ground. The storage location was a perfect choice, on top of a hill and immune to flooding. While mostly airtight, the space still had a notable moisture in the environment, but this could be dealt with by the clever scientists back at the Louvre. Bernadette watched in awe as each artwork was identified and checked from the list. They worked through the night, and she was thankful for the delivery of a delicious meal by the restauranteur and the champagne by Ivy. They all shared a glass.

In the early hours of the following morning Jean-François finally remembered he really did need to advise Ivy the sale had fallen through on her house, and he had thought of another plan.

He was aware that Solange's house would soon be put on the market once her estate was finalised, which was common knowledge. He recommended he didn't represent her for the sale as he wanted to ask if she would be interested in joining him for dinner the following night... well that night in fact. They both laughed, and Ivy agreed she would love nothing more than to buy Solange's house and keep it running as part of her legacy to her. She had also requested to keep the cover of her tapestry and once released from the police she wanted to have it framed. She would talk to Pierre about creating some type of memorial to Solange and her family's efforts for assisting to protect the cultural treasures.

Ivy also thought she would continue Solange's work and support Sonja in fundraising for the Night Parrot. She was sure the world would be a better place now that both the artwork and the Night Parrot had come back from extinction. Solange had been one special lady, and this would indeed be a fitting way for the world to remember her.

Jean-François reached out to hold Ivy's hand. He didn't know what had come over him, he was so caught up in the moment. She held his hand back and didn't let go.

'Ha now if we are to get serious... there are probably a few things you need to know about me.' They both laughed, but she knew she would find a time to tell him about her alter-ego... but just not... right now!

Chapter Thirty-Four

ANONYMITY OVER ACOLADES

THE LOBBY OF UNESCO HOUSE IN PARIS was filled with large posters of famous artworks. They were clustered under titles in both French and English indicating the various recovery operation code names. The event was in recognition of work accomplished by the Office Central de lute contre le traffic des Biens Culturels (OCBC)/Central Office for the Fight against Trafficking of Cultural Property. As the mission was global, the task force had received assistance from UNESCO and Interpol.

'Your Royal Highness, Excellencies, distinguished guests, ladies, and gentlemen. Welcome to the fortieth international convention on combating trafficking in cultural property. I will be your Master of Ceremonies for this evening's gala event. Tonight, let me introduce our keynote speaker Monsieur Robert du Lac who is no stranger to dealing with the theft of artwork. He has first-hand experience, as a number of his descendants had entire art collections stolen during the Second World War. As you are only too aware this story is also true for many thousands of European families.

The battle to return lost art continues. I am aware you are acquainted with our guest speaker as his reputation for art recovery is second to none. His brave adventures have inspired many to uphold what is right and just, ensuring the provenance of art is respected and defended. Please join me in welcoming Monsieur Robert du Lac.' It was clear the audience was eagerly awaiting the speech as it was the highlight of the event. He walked onto the stage to an eruption of applause.

'Bonsoir and good evening distinguished guests, ladies, and gentlemen. I am honoured to be invited as guest speaker this evening. Yes, only one day retired from my day job and here I am on stage. I just can't keep away from it.' The audience laughed, they all knew he would never really just vanish, for this world was his lifeblood. They had a lot to thank him for.

'I know you are all impatient to hear about the most recent discovery, but I must insist you settle in for a little history lesson first.' Several guests laughed as the majority of the audience were either professors of history, antiquity authorities or experts and known entities in their fields.

'As an operative for the OCBC, I was not undercover as some are... but that doesn't mean my adventures weren't perilous and dramatic.' Robert cleared his throat for a little humour. 'I have certainly been in odd situations when conducting my work - even a car chase! Most however are as boring as the service station cheese sandwiches and coffees I had to endure during my time. As a French man you can imagine my pain!

The story most of you want to hear is the case best known in the media as Operation Code Breaker. Then I promise to tell you maybe one story about a car chase... seriously.' He was playing the audience and they loved him for it. He was their idol in the art world, the man who had found homes for more displaced art than any other agent.

'Across the globe, stolen art decorates the walls of galleries... and sadly their storerooms. It is hidden away in the safes of banks and corporations or attics of people who perhaps may not even know the true value. These works of art used to have loving families and hold pride of place. Then in times of conflict they were thieved from walls, leaving only a shadow of the frame. And now… in a lot of cases only photographs and lists remain, housed with recovery agencies, consultants, galleries, police forces and libraries.' He took a long pause as he visualised the many times he had come across such sights.

'With my other hat on as a curator, I was often invited to see clients with private collections to request loans for exhibitions. This was exciting, entering the world of a serious art buyer, or often just someone with too much money! I loved seeing the places they displayed the art. Some would hide them to reduce their insurance premium. Others featured the work behind their desk connected with security alarms, like a hunter displaying antlers.

The most intriguing of all my visits seeking art for upcoming exhibitions was at the office of a tech firm in the United States. Security was tight. They were in the process of creating computer-based code for colossal machines that today fit in the palm of our hand. Yes, for those of you who are wondering…I am that old.' He walked away from the podium and across the stage. It felt so formal standing behind the lectern, like he was back at university. The spotlight followed him, and the lapel microphone enabled him to walk freely. All eyes were glued as they knew the story, but this was "the" Robert du Lac telling it.

'I had been instructed to use the main entrance, the one with glossy gold letters emblazoned across the top of the revolving door. However, something drew me to the other side entrance, where there seemed to be a buzz of people coming and going. They all had the same look about them, uniformed office attire and all men. They moment the outgoing crew walked into the sunlight they instinctively shielded their eyes; it reminded me of vampires shrinking away from the light. Then they snapped off their identification badges and headed off without talking. The incoming stream of staff all secured passes to their coats, keyed in a four-digit code and entered through the doorway – no emotions.' He charaded the robotic movements.

'I had to know what they were doing. I was captivated by this building and its android occupants. Up closer all the windows were covered with shutters. I actually asked a couple of the staff what they were working on, and they simply ignored me. Curiosity got the better of me, I had to know what they were working on. I went to a newsagency and bought a simple brown clipboard and a cup of coffee. I followed a group of men as they walked towards the door. Instinctively they held the door open while I hugged the clipboard to my chest and juggled my coffee apologetically. They didn't even blink an eye; I had just managed to smuggle myself into this highly secure building. It was as if I was invisible and the clipboard my camouflage.

I marvelled at this rather odd workplace, with row upon row of men at keyboards typing away. They looked like ants all performing a task in a trance. They were not typing letters like a secretary but formatting codes into computers. This was a foreign world to me, and I wanted to stay and marvel at the oddity of it. No one made eye contact with me or challenged my presence, they just stared into their glowing screens.

My eyes broke away and I was mesmerised again, not by the computers but rather the art, it lined the walls and staircase. My curiosity piqued and while slowly climbing the stairs I was awe-struck to discover these were not copies but genuine originals. Instantly I recognised a number of them as part of the missing Sophie Villier Collection that had been on a watch list for decades. Standing on the staircase I could now see the enormity of what lay before me, over fifty pieces of art ranging from old masters to pieces thought destroyed during Operation Nero in the final days of the Second World War.

Surrounded by such beauty and history, I was entranced. Yet, the people sharing this space with them every day were none the wiser. It occurred to me then... what better way to hide your stolen art than in plain sight? And the rest as they say is history. The art was seized and returned to its rightful owners. Another successful mission.' The crowd couldn't resist clapping.

Over the cheering he shouted. 'Now do you want to hear about the car chase?' More clapping followed. He gently shushed them and continued. 'This was part of the recent closure of the long running Operation Circle Vert/Operation Green Circle. Now for a little bit of inside information. You may be interested to know that in Australia everything tends to get a nickname – even code names it seems! We ended up referring to this one simply in English as Operation Night Parrot.' Upon hearing the name, they clapped and cheered more. He really did know how to work this usually sombre crowd.

'Australia might seem like the other side of the world, well... let me tell you it is! That long-haul flight will make you want to sell your house to get an upgrade. I left France on a hot summer morning to wake up a day later in frosty cold Canberra. For those of you not acquainted with the Southern Hemisphere, that is the nation's capital and has more roundabouts than all of Paris. I did see koalas and kangaroos, along with four of the most beautiful paintings I have ever had the privilege to be in the presence of.' He clicked the remote in his hand and the screen came to life with photographs of the four pieces. The room started to glow with mobile phones as people could not resist texting the details to friends, family, media, whoever. This was big news in the art world.

'The research, patience and dedication of the task force assigned to this operation can never be fully appreciated. Sadly, the people responsible for all of the hard work should be up on stage with me, but in order to maintain their anonymity their identities remain concealed.

This mission was focused on finding hundreds of missing artworks from the Second World War. Each piece had been marked with three green circles to signify their importance. They were transferred from the Louvre to the safety of southern France and then believed stolen from Château de Créapsy. The German ERR division were tasked to acquire the art for the Führermuseum, as you well know the proposed Linz art museum intended to re-define cultural domination in Europe. However, it had been reported all art was destroyed by a fire at the château during preparations to move them.' He paused for effect.

'Settle in, you will be reading about this with your morning coffee as the story is just being released to the media. Thankfully these works were so precious they won the heart of their German captor who could not bear to see them possibly destroyed, as signs of the war ending were evident. He defied his senior officer's orders and with the assistance of the village notary, engaged the support of a young tapestry artisan Adeline Lanquetin. The young woman had escaped Paris at the start of the war and was extremely courageous. She had worked at the Gobelins tapestry mill and devised a ruse to assist in the protection of the art collection. She covered four of the artworks with non-descript tapestries and included a coded postcard behind each within the frame. The plan was agreed that at the end of the war, all four cards would be presented to the notary, this in turn would instruct him to release the file containing the concealed location of the artworks.

Adeline and her husband became the guardians of the work, hanging them on the wall of her simple stone house. But alas, the village was bombed within days. Adeline along with her husband and the German officer were killed. The notary remained true to his word and kept the file sealed and hidden away, unaware of the contents. As ordered, he waited for the code to be presented oblivious to the fact they were hidden in the tapestries. This instruction would be honoured through the generations of notaries.

After their death, the remains of Adeline and her husband's household were handed down to their young teenage son. He continued living in the village until he married, and the young couple had a daughter. Shortly after, they were lured to Australia to work in a vineyard. They travelled lightly with only a couple of trunks of memorabilia. And yes, the art, wrapped in its protected coat of tapestry took the long journey to the other side of the world.

Sadly, they died far too early. This time at the hand of the ocean instead of wartime aggressors. The paintings however, landed in the possession of France's representative for all things design – their daughter Madame Solange Lanquetin.'
It took a moment for the audience to absorb everything Robert had just said. He could see the look on their faces as they "clicked". The blogger found dead in the swimming pool at the Embassy of France was connected to the art. Half of the audience were already googling her name, eager for more information. A statement from the police presented them with the basic facts, while other news sites explained in more detail.

*

MEDIA REPORT – FOR IMMEDIATE RELEASE
AUSTRALIAN FEDERAL POLICE
20 August 2019

A 40-year-old Sydney woman was found unresponsive in the swimming pool at the Embassy of France in Canberra at 6:15pm (20 August 2019). She was unable to be resuscitated and was pronounced dead at the scene.

The woman was found to have high levels of prescription medication and alcohol in her system. Bulky clothing and the low temperature of the water were other factors in the drowning.

A male member of the embassy staff was later prevented from boarding an aircraft and was returned to his mission for further questioning, while another colleague of the deceased was held for questioning and has been charged with stalking, illegal use of a drone and other offences relating to the deceased.

Inquiries into the incident continue. Any witnesses or anyone with vision of the event are urged to contact police.

*

Monsieur du Lac continued. 'Madame Lanquetin was a kind and generous woman who was being stalked and blackmailed. She also had no idea of the treasures that lay beneath the tapestries and had in fact only recently gifted three of them to her closest friends.' He let the audience absorb this sad news.

'Fortunately for the art world, all four original art works have been safely returned. They provided the location details for the other two-hundred-and-ten masterpieces from the Green Circle Collection that have now been delivered to the Louvre for restoration.' Robert had hardly finished his sentence when the audience gave another round of applause and were on their feet cheering.

'The world works in mysterious ways indeed. Now... for that car chase.' The clapping stopped, and chairs were being shuffled back into place. All eyes were on the stage for the next instalment.

'... it was caught on camera by a news helicopter as I chased his limousine to the airport in my hire car. As he pulled into the airport drop off zone, the car was surrounded by police.' A photo showed Robert running towards Mathieu as he exited the car. 'Don't I look like I am in a Bond film?' He enjoyed delivering that line just as much as he enjoyed telling Mathieu the gig was up.

'Through the remarkable connections of an anonymous OCBC operative and the Australian Federal Police they were able to intercept an embassy official at the airport. Despite claiming diplomatic immunity, the Ambassador gave permission for him to be questioned in connection with the death along with his involvement in the acquisition of stolen art for his private collection. It was all happening in the nation's capital last week and what an outstanding result - returning these lost pieces back to the people of France!' Once again

Robert used the projector, this time to commence a presentation of images of recovered art from both the private stolen collection of Mathieu and the Green Circle Collection.

Now he changed pace. 'So now I simply plan to return to retirement. Hardly surprising, it has long been a dream of mine to become a volunteer at the museum. Showing the world of art to school children. Explaining different art movements… when the only movement they are really interested in usually is walking to the exit!' The audience laughed at him, and all rolled their eyes in mock sympathy. It would indeed be a lucky school child who would have the infamous Monsieur Robert du Lac as their tour guide. His smile was so wide and sincere. He was truly a living masterpiece himself. For the third time that evening the audience rose to their feet and the applause was something akin to that afforded to a rock star.

The Master of Ceremonies swept back onto the stage and thanked Monsieur du Lac on behalf of the people in the room and the citizens of the world. It was now time for the highly anticipated question time and hands were shooting up waving for the attention of the roving microphone. The first person to be given the privilege of asking a question was a woman in a glittering white and silver gown.

'Monsieur du Lac, on behalf of all the art lovers in the world thank you. Thank you for keeping our culture alive and for maintaining a vigilant watch over our precious identity.' Once again applause. 'I have one simple question. Why was the last mission re-named Operation Night Parrot? Is it a real bird?' She smoothed down her elegant gown and took her place at the table.

'Merci Madame for your kind compliments. Ahh the elusive Australian Night Parrot was thought to be extinct for over a hundred years. An intriguing little bird that hides in the spinifex grass in the Australia dessert. A simple green coloured bird, much like your grandmother would have kept in a cage, but it was so much more.

Considered to have vanished from the face of the earth. Researchers did not give up, they waited, watched, and they listened. Often misled by decoys of similar sounding or looking birds, then deceived with false sightings and tall tales. It only inspired them to remain as patient and as vigilant as ever. Many predators were to blame for the birds near demise; bushfires, drought, foxes and even bird watchers hoping to tick the creature off their list. The distinctive bird's call was protected for fear that it might give away its location, so it was concealed and hidden, never shared with anyone. Only after waiting patiently and giving the bird space and time would researchers be rewarded with the pleasure of a sighting. The world should take notice of this rare bird and the lessons it could teach us.

Ladies and gentlemen, Operation Night Parrot is about to enter its second phase. Much like the researchers who prohibited distribution recordings of the bird's call to prevent poachers. I too am prevented from providing further information on the next art recovery operation at this time. But what I can tell you is this. Like the distinctive cadence of the Night Parrot, the siren call of this elusive enigma is going to allure and intrigue us all once again. I promise you it will be worth the wait.'

Sitting comfortably in the throne-like antique chair in her Paris apartment, Bernadette turned to talk to the other two women. They were all watching the ceremony from a live feed, each with a glass of champagne to celebrate.

'Janine, the story you ran did indeed go straight to the hands of the person I had intended. You did a wonderful job on the article… in fact it was outstanding!' They clinked glasses. 'Plus, I simply could not have completed this mission without your insight into the crazy world of influencer marketing.' The young woman flicked back her ironed hair and thought about how nervous she had been conducting the interview in the same intimidating apartment a few years earlier. Despite knowing that it was a set up and all part of Bernadette's plan, the interview had wrecked her nerves but had shot her to great heights in the publishing industry.

She then turned to the other woman. With a giggle she asked. 'So, are you Sandrine or Sandi tonight? Whatever you choose, you are off duty – no maid outfits required! Tell me… who do you think was a hotter boss, the resort manager, or the Ambassador?' They all laughed at the success of their ruse. Then with great compassion raised their glasses to a woman they had misjudged and to the heritage she unknowingly saved.

Read on for an exclusive extract from The Kingmaker, an evocative mystery novel full of secrets and deception, from the author of Call of the Night Parrot, due for release soon.

The Kingmaker

Nothing is what it seems. A deadly designed lie millions want to believe.

They returned to their Kingmaker. Expectations high, it was time to re-energise the creative direction of their commercial empire.

Five artisans reunite at a French château where they met at a residency five years earlier. The number is important, it symbolises curiosity, freedom, and change, it also appears in the studio each time they disappear.

A tale of deception that will both whisper and scream into your imagination.

Chapter One

BLIND COURAGE

THE SOLITARY STATUE OF THE VIRGIN MARY gazed down over the tiny French village. It was rumoured she had kept the town safe from the ravages of the Great War. Generations later the current inhabitants naively believed she would protect them again. In the smothered daylight they ventured from the relative safety of their homes into the travelled lands and cobbled roads. On bended knee they bowed their heads in solemn prayer pleading they would not be the next to meet misfortune.

The residents of the château had an entirely different focus. A game of celebrity charades was in full swing. Much like the band on the rapidly sinking Titanic, they were in for the long haul and committed to making it a memorable ride. The ornately carved liquor cabinet was swiftly being drained while ensuing laughter increased. Anything to take their minds off the cold cellar below, where nestled alongside the dusty racks of sparkling wine that bares the region's name were the bodies of five artists, carefully wrapped in antique linen sheets.

About the Author

JANELLE VICTOR, an Australian writer enamoured with all things French, spent her earlier career as lead instructional designer for a Submarine training project. Drawn by the allure of life in the South of France, she now resides in the picturesque medieval village of Caunes-Minervois. "Call of the Night Parrot" is Janelle's debut novel.

Recipient of the prestigious Denis Diderot grant for writing, Janelle was also chosen as writer in residence at Château d'Orquevaux in France, where she further developed her next manuscript "The Kingmaker" due for release soon. When not immersed in writing you will likely find Janelle engrossed in a book under the comforting shade of a local olive tree.

www.janellevictorwriter.com.au

Instagram.com/janellevictorwriter

Facebook.com/janellevictorwriter